# Space Captain Smith

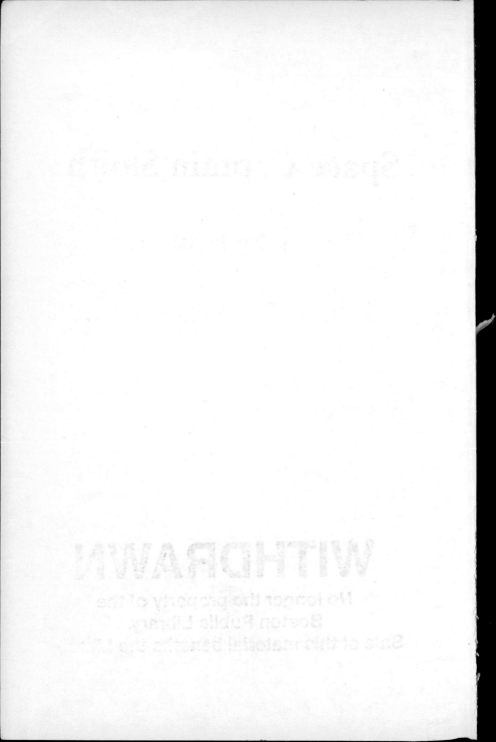

# Space Captain Smith

## Toby Frost

MYRMIDON

Myrmidon Books Ltd
Rotterdam House
116 Quayside
Newcastle upon Tyne
NE1 3DY

www.myrmidonbooks.com

Published by Myrmidon 2008

A catalogue record for this book is available from the British Library.

ISBN 978-1-905802-13-5

Set in11/14pt Sabon by Falcon Oast Graphic Arts Limited,
East Hoathly, East Sussex

Printed in the UK by CPI Mackays, Chatham, ME5 8TD

For Carole and Graham

# Contents

Chapter 1: Mission To Space!                          9

Chapter 2: Smith Meets Some Gentle People            38

Chapter 3: Smith Defeats the Space Ant Horde!        76

Chapter 4: One Night in Paradis                      96

Chapter 5: Taken Up the Bayou                        114

Chapter 6: Ho-Down of the Damned                     142

Chapter 7: Is Rhianna a Weirdie in Disguise?         171

Chapter 8: Cyber-gangsters in Martian Death Pact!    200

Chapter 9: Cultists Filched My Trousers              236

Chapter10: Pursuit                                   260

Chapter11: Gertie Takes a Pasting                    277

Chapter12: Back in the Empire                        294

# 1

# Mission To Space!

One dull Tuesday morning, the door opened behind Isambard Smith and Mr Khan entered the room. Smith stopped typing and looked round.

'I gather there's a problem, Smith,' said Khan. He was a big, slow-moving man whose mouth and chins all hung downwards, giving him a sad appearance. He looked like a walrus who had swapped his tusks for a desk job and was beginning to regret the deal.

'I understand you're not too happy.'

'No, Mr Khan, I'm not. I want to complain.'

Khan closed the door behind him.

'Sir, I've made six requests that I be given control of a starship and they've all been ignored. I've been with Valdane Shipping for nearly a year and all I've done is type data about asteroids into this computer. You know jolly well that I'd eat my own pants for a chance to get back into space, and yet here I am, still sitting here, wearing them.'

Khan nodded and leaned against the wall. 'Well, we are rather busy, what with the political situation and all, and it hasn't been easy to free up a ship—'

'But that's what I mean!' Smith cried. 'Sir, I want to do

something. The Ghasts are out there re-arming, and everyone knows they're coming for the British Empire sooner or later. It makes me cross that I'm stuck here, personalising this swivel chair with my arse while Gertie is plotting evil against Earth. By God, sir, if I had my way I'd jump into a fighter, zip over to their dirty homeworld, stick a laser under their radar, have a damn good mettle at the Ghast and show him my crack.' He paused, slightly out of breath. 'Except the other way around.'

Khan said, 'Well, then, I've got some good news for you. You're getting a ship.'

'A ship!' Smith sprang up. 'That's excellent! Will there be action, and danger?'

'There'll be hippies. Will that do?'

'Sir, I'll take the risk.'

'Good. You're to head to the New Francisco orbiter and collect a woman called Rhianna Mitchell. New Fran is a free colony: we protect it, but we don't own it, yet. It's a rum place, Smith, I warn you: full of hop-potting splifftokers and all sorts that the Empire still has to rescue from idleness and free love. You'll hate it. Takes a fellow with guts and a backbone to stomach a place like that. You know Midlight at all?'

'Spaceport on Kane's World, isn't it?'

'That's the one. You're to take her there as quickly as possible. You've got a ship and a pilot ready at the strip. Leave your car in the multi-storey. It's open this afternoon.'

Smith blinked, shocked. 'What, this afternoon today?'

'Of course. Not likely to still be this afternoon in three weeks' time, is it?'

Smith thought about it. 'Golly,' he said. Suddenly the empty tedium of the rest of the day had vanished, swept away in a whirl of rockets. He managed to put a thought together. 'Won't I need a crew?'

'Crew?' The walrus shook his head, and the chins followed. 'No. There's no crew, just an android pilot.

'Oh, the *John Pym*'s a fine ship, fine. Very quick, you'll find. You can take along a friend if you want, so long as he's not a foreigner or into funny stuff. I know what it's like on these long hauls. Fellow starts to forget that a handlebar moustache isn't for hanging on to.'

'May I take an alien?'

Khan grimaced. 'You don't mean that Morlock chap who runs round cutting people's heads off? They're savages, Smith.'

'He's a good sort, as it happens,' said Smith, a little irked.

'Very well then. I suppose it's best you're both in the same place.' Khan glanced at his watch. 'And you ought to think about leaving, if you're planning to pack some things.'

'Righto, sir!' Smith saluted. 'I'm on my way!'

Khan watched Smith go. He took his fob-phone out of his waistcoat pocket and dialled his superiors. 'Well, the trap's baited alright,' he told the voice on the other end of the line. 'There's one launched every minute,' he added under his breath.

Smith parked his car, collected the ticket and took his bag from the back. He wore his fleet uniform, the jacket open and his waistcoat fastened underneath. He was excited and slightly nervous at seeing his new ship, and had spent fifteen minutes in the toilet before setting out, waxing his moustache to a level of pertness carefully chosen to suggest to his men that he was both a waggish friend and someone whom they should never, ever cross.

The Valdane Shipping Company owned three space-craft on New London and part-owned eight more with the East Empire Company. As with most companies governed by Imperial Law, its members owned shares in the corporate property. Consequentially, Smith had always regarded the company vessels as his own, and smiled proudly at the thought of the shiny spacecraft waiting in the hangar, its brasswork polished and engines gleaming.

On his way down the slope that led into the hangar, Smith met Winston Parker, the master-engineer. Parker, a slight, dapper man, was a source of awe to Smith: not only did the engineer manage to *sound* like he knew a lot about spacecraft, he actually *did*, which was rare in the industry. He was the right person to get rather than his colleague, Bancroft, who was both very dour and bore a curious facial resemblance to a tree.

'Isambard Smith. And how are you today?'

'Fine, thank you. I'm just off. Have you seen the roster?'

Parker wiped his hands on a rag he wore in his belt like a badge of rank. 'Yep. Your android pilot's already on board – it's a woman this time. You've got a Sheffield light freighter.'

'I don't think I've seen one of those before. Do they fly well?'

'Not too bad. Of course, they can't read maps or reverse properly.'

'I meant the ship.'

'Well, they got it second hand. It's just come out of refit – new engines. Not exactly the company flagship, if you see what I mean.'

'I see. By the way, you haven't seen an alien around here, have you? About six foot eight with a face like a cross between a boar and an upturned crab. Probably carrying a spear and a bag full of severed heads.'

Parker shrugged. 'I dunno. It gets busy here.'

'He's got quite an unusual laugh.'

'Oh, that bloke? He's down the bottom of the ramp. You know him, then?'

'He's my friend,' Smith replied. 'I'll see you later then, shall I?'

'Much later, from the route you're taking. See you soon, Smith!'

As Smith approached the bottom of the slope, a figure hopped down from a stool, where it had been crouching. It was man-shaped – roughly – but stretched, taller and thinner than a human being. The creature loped towards Smith with the weight on the front of the feet and with a slow, lazy grace.

'Suruk,' said Smith.

A low, rattling sound came from the alien as he stepped into view. Smith saw the grey-green skin where it was not covered by his trousers, boots or armoured waistcoat, and he watched as Suruk the Slayer's tusks slid apart and his mouth opened up.

'Isambard Smith.' He spoke as if through porridge. Suruk straightened his fingers to show Smith his empty hands.

Smith pulled his sleeves back and displayed his palms as if about to pull a bunch of flowers from the air. 'Hail, Suruk, warrior of Clan Ametrin. I give you this much greeting.'

'Hail, Isambard Smith, who is called Mazuran in the speech of the M'Lak. I give you greeting too.'

There was a little pause. Smith smiled awkwardly. 'So,' he ventured, 'it's been a while.'

'Indeed. Moons have passed since last we met, battles fought and enemies fallen. At the bridge of Anrag I took fifteen heads. I overthrew the tyrant Dagrud War-Scythe and took his cattle as tribute to my skill. It was a glorious day.'

'Sounds pretty wild. I'm having a new patio put down. You and me both, eh?'

'Square slabs or crazy paving?'

'Square slabs.'

'The choice of a warrior.' Suruk picked up his pack, from which several short-handled spears protruded, and slung it over his shoulder. With his spare hand he picked up the bar stool. His physique meant that he was more comfortable squatting high up than sitting down. Smith had seen his friend sleep that way, like a nesting hawk.

They walked through the vast, shadowed hall, their voices echoing up to the concrete roof. There was something cathedral-like about the hangar, almost sepulchral. The ships were housed in massive bays that stretched off to the sides like transepts. Colossal arches closed over the bays, decorated with leafy swirls etched into the concrete in the New Gothic style of Britain and its colonies.

'So now. Do we go to bring battle to our enemies, Isambard Smith?'

Suruk tended to treat any expedition off-world as a cross between a cheap package tour and the Roman conquest of Gaul, with Smith in the role of red-coated compere to whatever bloody mayhem he decided to unleash. For the M'Lak, space travel was a ticket to sun, sand and severed heads, with the first two being highly optional. Smith decided to allay Suruk's hopes.

'Not precisely, no. We're actually going to collect someone from a space station inhabited by pacifists.'

'Fierce warrior pacifists?'

'No.'

'Edible pacifists?'

'I would advise against it.'

'Will we then deliver this coward into the sun?'

'No.'

'Is *anything* good going to happen on this holiday?'

'Not by your standards, I'm afraid. Still, our ship's apparently just been refitted, so we should be pretty safe. I should imagine it will have some decent weaponry to see off enemies.'

'Ah yes. Like the mighty dreadnoughts of your British Empire. Still, I would rather fight with my blades than use a gun.'

'Needs must, Suruk. We can't civilise the galaxy without dreadnoughts, you know. Sometimes we have to use force to teach our enemies to behave like proper people. Now, we should be here – oh.'

The nose-cone of the *John Pym* poked out from one of the alcoves in a slightly furtive manner, as if it had crept in to receive an accolade that it did not deserve. The front end of the ship reminded Smith of the snout of a rat that has been in many fights with larger, more vicious rats: battered, dented, discoloured and scarred. At one point, a great slab of steel had been riveted on, sealed around the edges with foam from a can. There was no gun in the nose.

'Interesting,' Suruk said. 'This vessel has clearly fought many battles. Is that camouflage on the upper part, or just mould?'

'My God,' said Smith, 'I thought they said it had been refitted! It looks terrible!'

'Maybe. But the orange warpaint will bring us luck.'

'I bloody doubt it: that lucky orange warpaint happens to be rust. The sooner we launch the better. Let's get going before the wings drop off.'

He walked around the side of the ship and down its length, reminding himself that this was a space vessel and not the chew-toy of some very large, enthusiastic dog. Even in this bad light it was clear how much of a beating the craft had taken. Extra armour was welded over blackened patches that could have been the result of dramatic space battles or drunken parking attempts. The few windows were scratched and had a dirty greenish tinge, as if viewed through pond-water. Smith had an image of the previous pilot, joystick in one hand, hip flask in the other, whooping like a redneck as he bounced from world to world in a state of crazed exuberance, frequently mistaking the nose-cone for a deceleration tool.

He climbed the steps and pressed the intercom button and it let out a tortured mechanical yowl. The noise stopped and a woman's voice said warily, 'Are you selling something?'

'I'm the captain. Could you open the door, please?'

'Er... yeah, alright. Can't see why not.'

Something moved heavily behind the door; bolts drawing back, he thought. 'It's open,' the woman said.

Smith turned the sunken handle and the door swung open easily.

The hinges had been greased recently; so too, from the smell of the place, had everything else. Smith ducked under the dangling cable of an intercom and stepped into the cramped hallway, tasting the air as much as smelling it. Suruk pulled the door closed behind him. 'I shall choose a room as my own.'

'Righto,' said Smith.

To the left was the cockpit. It had two proper seats and several which could be folded down in an emergency. One of the large seats – the pilot's – was currently occupied by a smallish woman of about thirty. There was a hamster cage on the other seat – the captain's – with the word *Gerald* taped to the front. As Smith entered, the woman took her boots off the main console, sat up and looked about for something to mark the page in the book she had been reading.

'Ah,' Smith said, consulting the roster sheet, 'you must be the crew. Miss Carveth, is it?'

She stood up. She was smallish and slightly-built, with a pretty, perky face that was at once unremarkable and difficult to dislike. Her blonde hair was pulled back into a ponytail, leaving a halo of brown roots around her forehead. It was a face that Smith had seen before: she was a simulant, and this was one of the standard facial models that the manufacturers used. She wore a white shirt and utility waistcoat. Her trousers had many pockets and were slightly too big, and had been turned up at the bottom.

'Polly Carveth at your service, within reason,' she said, looking him over. 'You're Captain Smith, right?' She had the demeanour of someone keen not to be volunteered for things.

'Indeed. Pleased to meet you. Do feel free to stand at ease.'

Nothing changed. She could not have got much more at ease without lying down. They shook hands.

'Nice to meet you,' Carveth said warily. 'I look forward to us working together,' she added, with the raw enthusiasm of one reading out a train timetable at gunpoint. She glanced over his shoulder and suddenly her face became more animated. 'Pissing heck, what the hell is that?'

'Ah,' said Smith. 'My friend, Suruk. He'll be joining us for the trip.'

Carveth had acquired an expression rarely seen outside Greek tragedy. She groped for words. 'Why?'

'Well, he's a friend of mine. It's useful for aliens to see the Empire. It helps them understand where all their hard work goes. Besides, he's quite comfortable with space travel. He's brought his own things for his cabin, and he's even decorated it with a stool.'

'Oh my God.'

'Stool as in chairs, not dung.'

She brightened slightly, but not much. 'But, he's *big*,'

Carveth observed. 'And he's got all those bones stuck to him!'

'He's my friend, Carveth,' Smith said coldly, tiring of this argument. 'He stays on.'

Her face came back to life. She considered the matter for a moment, which made her jaw move as if chewing the cud. 'He's got tusks and mandibles. It's pretty irregular, Captain.'

'Mr Khan said I could.'

A second passed in which it became obvious to Smith that she was resisting the temptation to repeat his last sentence back to him in a squeaky voice.

'Right,' he said, 'if it makes you feel any better, I will talk to Suruk myself. But I am the captain here, and we are taking off as I say.'

'Alright, Boss.'

Smith left the room. Carveth crept across the cockpit, to the open door, and listened.

'Pilots are like that,' Smith was saying. 'A lot of them think of their ships as belonging to them.'

'A lot of people think of their heads as belonging to them.'

'Don't start that. You're on the in-flight meals only for this trip. Alright?'

'Huh. As you wish.'

Smith returned to find Carveth in the pilot's seat. He placed the hamster cage on the floor, dropped into the captain's seat and said, 'Righto. We're all set. I've spoken to Suruk and he's agreed to treat you with kid gloves, as it were.'

'Good,' she said, and she gave him a wan, nervous smile. 'Let's go then, shall we?'

'In a minute. First, as captain I need to tour the facilities.'

'Second on the left. Don't flush until we're in orbit.'

Isambard Smith slowly wandered the inside of the ship, making sure that everything was alright. Everything certainly seemed present, but beyond that his knowledge thinned out somewhat. Behind the cockpit were the cabins and lavatory. To her credit, Carveth had resisted the common practice of putting a humorous sign on the toilet door about the Captain's log. Beyond that was an open area that served as a combination of galley and mess. On a longer voyage, capsules would be mounted here for suspended animation. The rear of the ship was taken up by the hold, largely empty, where an exploration vehicle could be stashed but was not. Behind it all were the engine and the various 'boiler rooms', which Smith intended to have as little to do with as possible.

As with every such tour he did, he had no idea what he was looking for beyond the strikingly obvious. A fire in his bed, or a man's feet hanging from the ceiling, would have given him reasonable suspicion that something was amiss; one blinking red light among whole rows of panels of red lights could have been any old thing. And besides, that was someone else's job. As captain, he could delegate to another crewmember. That was why ships had captains: to tell the crew what their responsibilities were. Unfortunately, discounting Suruk, an alien, and Gerald, a rodent, that left Carveth as the only possible delegate.

Finally, Suruk joined him. The alien pointed into the Secondary Air Cleansing Drum and said, 'This is the bladder of the ship, yes?' and Smith wondered who he was trying to impress. 'Absolutely,' he said, and he returned to the cockpit. 'Ready for takeoff,' he declared.

Carveth was reading the Haynes manual for a Sheffield Class Four light freighter. Smith noticed that by an odd coincidence this ship was also of that make. He felt mildly bothered, but could not quite put his finger on the source of the problem.

'Takeoff, takeoff,' Carveth muttered, running a finger down the page. 'One moment... set thrusters.'

The control panel, like much of the ship's inside, was squashed and complex. The levers, dials and spinning counters were separated by delicate brass scrollwork and Engineering Guild heraldry. Compared to the exterior, the inside of the ship was quite well kept.

A loud, indistinct hydraulic whine ran through the room as the great thrusters either side of the craft turned to fire downwards. Smith could hear the engines thrumming, shuddering with constrained power that ran through the floor and into the soles of his boots. On a hundred dials the needles quivered and stood up like hairs on the back of an understandably frightened neck. He leaned back and closed his eyes, feeling the craft come to life around him and tense itself to spring.

'We have permission to leave from control,' Carveth said.

'Thank them.'

'They say good luck. Cleared for takeoff.'

He opened his eyes. There was a row of junk across the windowsill, picked up from the myriad gift-shops of the Empire: a snow-storm paperweight of the Houses of Parliament, a red-coated toy soldier of the Colonial Army, a postcard showing a very fat woman on a trampoline with the caption 'Rotation of the Spheres on the Proxima Orbiter'. The left side of the ship lurched upward, and Parliament vanished in a blizzard. The postcard fell over. The right thrusters blasted and the ship levelled, rocking very slightly, nine feet off the ground.

'Feed power equally to the thrusters,' Carveth told herself, and the ship rose slowly.

A small and agitated figure had appeared on the outside viewscreen, seeming to perform a shamanistic dance. Parker's frequent upward gestures gave the impression that he sought to placate the sky god before the ship intruded into its realm. 'Whatever's he up to?' said Smith as the craft rose higher and the figure became increasingly smaller and more frantic.

Carveth clicked her fingers as if remembering something on a shopping list and picked up the microphone. 'Control? Could you open the overhead doors, please?'

The ship ascended. The top of the hangar sank down the windscreen, and suddenly they were surrounded by blue sky. Across the skyline, the thousand chimneys of New London stabbed upward like the mounds of a chain-smoking termite colony. Smith felt the ship tilt backwards, rising all the time, and hoped that Suruk had remembered to strap himself in.

'Here we go,' Carveth said, casually knocking half a dozen switches down with the side of her hand. 'Ready?'

'Ready.'

She fired the engine. With a great roar the ship tore upwards into the sky. In seconds the blue on the screen thinned and darkened into the black of space as they left New London far below. The simulant pulled a keyboard down on a metal arm, and her fingers raced across the keys.

She sat back. 'Co-ordinates are locked,' she said. 'We're on our way.'

'Journey will take about twelve hours,' Carveth said, scrutinising one of the screens. 'We're on a standard Imperial route, no danger of trouble from aliens or hostile powers. We'll dock at New Fran at about nine am, GMT. Once we're there, we'll have a few hours to do what we want and get ready for the next leg. The next stage is to double back into Imperial territory and work our way down towards Midlight. That should take a little longer – three days, possibly. So remember to stock up on mints at the duty-free.'

'Wise,' Suruk said, lounging against the wall. He had wandered in shortly after takeoff and was watching space with almost complete indifference.

Smith activated the navigation console and studied the route that had been programmed in at base, a confusing snail-trail across the border of the Empire. It struck him as just as likely to have been produced by a cat with an etch-a-sketch as a trained navigator. He decided to leave it alone, in case any attempt at reprogramming caused the Typing Assistant programme to appear on the screen and drive him mad with irritation as he tried to make it go away.

'Any foreseeable problems?' Smith inquired.

Carveth shrugged. 'Nothing obvious. The only thing I

would say is that New Fran is a Protected Territory, not a full British colony. The laws are different there.'

'Do they permit trophy killing?' Suruk said.

'I doubt it,' Smith replied. 'As far as I know, it's pretty liberal there – but not *that* liberal. Personal firearms are illegal, and your spears probably will be as well. No chance of bagging anything, I'm afraid. Shame, really, with these sissy free love types bothering everyone. I wouldn't stand for it, personally. If a chap tried to stick a flower down my barrel, I'd shoot off soon as blinking.'

'This is not my kind of a holiday,' Suruk said.

'Well, it certainly is mine,' Carveth said. She leaned back in the pilot's seat and sighed. 'Trip to New Fran? Yes please. People save up for that. I reckon it should be a good few hours we get to spend there. I don't get much chance to let my hair down. Have a few drinks, shake hands with Mr Bong... suits me.'

'I must say,' said Smith, 'what with you being a simulant and all, you don't seem much like a robot. Shouldn't you be counting rivets or something, not look-ing forward to getting squiffed?'

She looked around, frowning. 'I'm not a robot, as such. I am a person of synthetic heritage.'

'Does that mean your parents were robots, then? Did they hear the patter of tinny feet?'

'Most amusing,' Carveth said. 'I am a simulant. I would also accept "android", meaning one created rather than born. I am, however, almost entirely human tissue: I don't have wires or wallpaper paste inside me or anything like that, nor have I ever felt urges towards a pocket calculator. I'm altered to be able to interface directly with the ship, should it be necessary, except that this ship isn't actually fitted with a neural interface at all. That's about where it ends.'

'So someone designed you?'

'Yes,' she said, a little sadly. She brightened up. 'And you thought it was just a terrible mistake.'

'Well... I did wonder.'

Carveth turned to study the navigation screen. 'People get the wrong idea. I blame science-fiction writers, personally. It annoys me how they confuse the whole robot issue. I tell you, if I met that Asimov bloke, I'd harm him, or at least through inaction allow him to come to harm.'

'Does that mean you have a skull, then?' Suruk said.

'Not that you're having, frogboy.'

'Point made,' said Suruk. 'What is that on the scanner, fun-size woman?'

'Where?' The simulant leaned across and peered at the lidar dial. 'Probably just a rock... Wait a moment.'

'What's up?' said Smith.

'It's moving. Intercept course.'

'Can we get a closer image on the screen?'

'Certainly.' She reached to the seat pocket and came up with something black in her hand. 'Here. Binoculars.'

Smith stood up, pressed the binoculars to his eyes and turned the dial. 'Hard to see. It's all quite dark... Ah! I've got him. It looks like a great big sock with an engine at one end... and teeth at the other. It's a void shark.'

'Void sharks?' Carveth was on the controls in a second. 'I'll put out flares.'

'Is this a serious problem?' Suruk asked.

She glanced at him. 'Not unless you mind walking. They're interstellar animals. They feed on the metal in asteroids.'

'But we're not an asteroid,' Smith said.

'Not wishing to rob you of your Nobel Prize, Captain, but we are actually made of metal.'

'Ah. Right. Good thinking, crew. How long till they arrive?'

'Till they reach us? Two minutes, maybe.'

'Righto. This is war then, men. Carveth, hold our course and be prepared to move fast.'

'Yes sir.'

'How long till they close?'

'Minute thirty.'

'Ready the weapons system!'

'I can't reach. You're nearer, and you've got the key.'

'Key?'

She pointed across the cockpit. Smith followed her finger to a large locker standing against the opposite wall. 'What's that?'

'The weapons system.'

He stood up slowly, as if in a dream. 'You have got to be kidding.'

She shook her head. 'That's it. This isn't a dreadnought, you know.'

'I have noticed.' Smith took out the key and opened the locker. Inside there was a short-barrelled shotgun, a machine gun, a sword and some sort of service revolver. 'This is it?'

'Thirty-six seconds, Captain! Unless you want them

chewing through the hull, someone's going to have to go up top.'

'I'm a space captain, not a bloody roof-rack! Absolutely not!'

'Then we're walking home.'

'Don't we have anything that doesn't involve me getting on the roof?' He glanced at his companions and saw fear in one face, and an equally worrying enthusiasm on the other. Right!' Smith cried, exasperated. 'Suruk, fetch a spacesuit. Carveth, keep going. Try to delay contact until I can get out the hatch.' He reached into the locker and dragged out the machine gun. 'I'm going outside. I may be some time.'

In the armoured spacesuit Isambard Smith looked like a cross between a deep-sea diver and a medieval knight, with cricket pads. Suruk held the helmet while Smith clamped the gun harness to his side.

It was a big gun, a Maxim Cannon, designed to support infantry against aliens and light vehicles. Smith pushed a drum of ammunition into the side of the gun and watched the round counter spin up to 999. Suruk held out the helmet and Smith put it on and closed the seals.

There was a ladder leading up to the walkway that ran around the top of the hold, from which he could reach the airlock. Suruk closed the door behind him and Smith began to climb. He reached the top, sweating already, and pulled the lever. The hatch opened.

No weapons and full of rust, with a difficult robot for a pilot and a bunch of unfeasible sock-monsters trying to chew through the hull. And they had been in space less than three hours. Things were falling apart rapidly: at this rate, by day four he would have eaten Carveth and be dancing round a graven image of the sun.

As he climbed out of the hatch and onto the roof Smith tried to look on the bright side, and then tried to work out if there actually was a bright side. Yes: had he not had his handlebar moustache trimmed recently he would not have been able to fit his head into the space helmet at all. Not much, but something.

His boots locked onto the metal hull. He stood there, on the back of the ship, staring at the blackness around him, the tiny stars millions of miles away. Space had a kind of cruel, vacant beauty, a beauty that completely ignored mankind. Space would neither know nor care if he died out here. He could float for thousands of years, a skeleton in a suit, and never be found again, forever drifting in the silent gulf between the stars. That would be really crap. He pulled the gun down, ready.

'Are you out there?' Carveth called over the intercom.

'Yes, I'm here.' He kicked the hatch shut with a slow, heavy punt.

'Any sign?'

'I can't see anything. What does the lidar say?'

'Lidar says there's three of them, circling you. Should be visible soon.'

A lump of fear sat in his stomach like a rock. It had to be you or nobody, he told himself. Carveth was both the pilot, which meant that she was needed to steer the ship, and a woman, which meant that Smith had to protect her. Suruk wouldn't know how to use a gun, and would achieve nothing with a spear. Being afraid made no difference: Smith had to do this, because he was the only one who could.

He began to run down the length of the ship in great lazy bounds. Smith reached to his side and tugged the umbilical line from his backpack. He landed, pressed it to the hull and switched on the magnetic link.

'Smith?'

'Pilot.'

'I've got one coming in. Where are you?'

'On top of the ship, above the kitchen. Where's it coming from?'

'Can you see it?'

He looked around: his helmet restricted the edge of his vision, forcing him to turn on the spot to see. 'There's nothing here.'

'He's very near. I can't get a z-axis figure. I'm just comparing the lidar overlap. Hold on, it's coming through . . .'

Smith glanced around nervously. The damned helmet cut a third out of his view.

'Smith! Above you, now!'

His hands were faster than his neck: he jammed the gun upwards and let rip. The Maxim cannon bucked in his hands and Smith looked up to see a sky full of teeth. He saw the bullets hit the thing, tearing holes in its maw, and the void shark pulled away as gracefully as oil running through water, its long body slipping away from him and over the back of the ship. A cloud of purple dust streamed from a dozen points in the monster's side – its blood.

'Smith!'

'Got the bugger!' he cried. 'How many more?'

'Two. One's close, Smith.'

'How close?'

'I can't tell. It's following the side of the ship—'

Something moved at the edge of his vision. He leaped aside and the second void shark rushed past like a colossal eel, teeth champing on the vacuum where he would have been. Smith soared away from the hull, seeing the shark slide beneath him too fast for him to aim. The umbilical snapped taut, and he floated back towards the hull, boots stuck out ready to clamp down again. The void shark's tail flared and it slipped away from the ship. Smith opened fire. Violet bursts erupted down its flank and it whirled away from them, badly hurt.

'I got him,' Smith said. 'Where's the third?'

Something wriggled on the ship's flank. 'I see him,' said Smith.

He bounded to the edge of the ship. The last void shark was clamped to the side of the *John Pym* like a lamprey, trying to chew its way through the hull. Smith stood over it and lined the gun up with the point where its brain ought to be.

He fired. For three seconds he held the trigger down. Smith lifted the gun away and, motionless, the void shark drifted away from the hull.

He watched it go. 'Any more?' he asked.

'None. All signals moving away. What's the damage like out there?'

He checked. Where the void shark had been feeding, it looked as if a rock drill had been pressed lightly against the ship. Great scratches in the metal showed where its teeth had been. None had broken through: there were several inches of protection still left.

'It's not too bad,' he said. 'I can get a video camera out here if needs be.'

'No,' said Carveth, 'if you think it can hold we'll leave it until we get to New Fran. Then we can decide.'

'Righto. Could you open the hatch for me?'

'My pleasure,' she replied.


Paul Devrin could leave work whenever he wished: his father ran the company and the company ran several solar systems. In places, it served some of the Great Powers: France, Britain, China, the UFSA and even the Republic of Eden. In other places it worked for itself, controlled only by the distant whisper of international law.

'My apartment,' Devrin said, stepping into the lift. It began to rise. His face looked back at him from each of the four mirrored walls, clean and masculine, one step from a caricature of heroism. On occasion, Paul had wondered if his chin ought to be reduced. He worried a lot about his looks. Perhaps it made him look a little too rugged. Maybe it was that which repulsed women, not his exuberant use of cologne or his special bedroom needs. Tonight, however, whatever he did, no matter how bizarre, he would not be refused.

He turned to the lift guard. 'The delivery men come?' he demanded.

'Yes sir.'

'They made the delivery?'

'Yes sir. From the factory.'

'Alright.' He opened his wallet and took out a random handful of notes in New Yen, Freeland Dollars and Adjusted Sterling. 'You didn't see them come, alright?'

'Yes sir.'

'You take this and have a good night. You tell anyone, and you'll have a very bad morning. Got me?'

'Yes sir.'

The doors opened into the long, red corridor that ended with one door – his. In recesses along the way there were works of art that he felt reflected his personality: a statue of a bullfighter, the bust of a Roman emperor, a photograph of Henry Ford.

Two guards waited outside his door with the permanently startled expressions of people whose job gives them a substantial discount on plastic surgery.

'Good evening sir.'

'Hey,' Devrin said. 'Anything happening?'

'Nothing,' said the other guard.

'My package arrive?'

'Yes sir. The team from the labs left two hours ago. They left a message in your entrance hall. We scanned it for poison and explosives.'

'Excellent. You two take the night off, alright?'

They looked at one another, and although neither had a way of telling, for once their surprise was genuine.

Devrin watched them get into the lift. There were still several dozen men guarding the lower levels of the building. He was safe.

He swiped the door with his card, blew on a neural scanner and put his eye up to a lens. The door swung open, and his shoes clicked on marble as he walked in.

A big, heart-shaped box of chocolates sat on a plinth. He looked at the card on top of it. 'Your friend is in the guest bedroom. Have a good time! Best regards to you and your dad – the biolabs.'

Devrin shrugged and entered his own room. He took off his suit, undressed to his boxer shorts – new and silky – and his sock-suspenders, then strolled into the bathroom, thoughtfully sniffing his armpits as he went.

Of course, it did not matter how well he smelt, or how he looked. It would be a success no matter what. But he had his own personal pride to think about, and he put on some extra aftershave and a fresh dose of deodorant. He even used the bidet.

In his dressing gown, slippers and underwear, Paul Devrin left the bathroom rubbing his hands together. This was going to be good. He stopped in the hall to look in the mirror, checking his teeth for broccoli. 'Yeer!' he said to his reflection. 'We are gonna get it *awn*!'

He picked up the chocolates and put them under his arm. Straightening his lapels, he took hold of the door handles and threw the doors apart. 'Hey, sexy lady! We are—'

He stopped dead. There was the enormous bed, the bottle of champagne cooling in a silver bucket on the bedside table. But it was not right. A plate lay smashed on the ground, surrounded by raw, scattered oysters. More important, however, was the fact that the person on the bed was a middle-aged, portly man in a white scientist's coat and no trousers, gagged and bound. Someone at the delivery firm had got their wires very crossed about Devrin's special tastes.

The man was writhing and making moaning sounds. Paul realised that this was not for his benefit.

Devrin ducked down and took a gun from behind the nearest pot plant. He stalked over to the bed and pulled a stocking out of the man's mouth.

'Doc Petersen!'

'God dammit!' cried the man. 'Damn woman got free!'

'Got free? What?'

'She brained me with a plate and stole my keycard. And my pants.'

'What about the rest of the team?'

'They're in the wardrobe. She took their ID and passes too.'

Paul said, 'But, this isn't supposed to happen! She's supposed to obey my every wish! I told them to get me my dream date, not a fat naked scientist!'

'She must have realised, sir. She must have realised what we made her for, then planned her escape. I'm sorry, sir—'

'You will be! I'm calling my father! And Waldo!'

Devrin strode out the room, leaving Petersen prone behind him. He snatched an antique cellular phone from a plinth and switched it on.

'Security? Put out a coded message to my father on Cerberus Three. Tell him I'm going to need a bunch of men and a load more money, maybe even a ship. And get me Waldo, up here, now! Tell him to pull his best man off whatever job he's got and get him ready to do some serious work. Then I want this place gone over with a fine tooth-comb, atom by atom. Make that an atomic tooth-comb.'

A tiny, startled voice made its way up the line. 'Sir, um, alright, sir.'

'You are going to locate my ladybot right now, and you will either bring her back to me or shut her down! Nobody gets to keep my stuff! I want her found!'

'So, er, who is this bird, then?' Carveth said.

Smith had been dozing in the captain's chair. Having returned from the roof, he had promptly retired to his cabin and slept for several hours before wandering in to do the same at the helm. He had been dreaming about fighting off an enormous sock, and was quite relieved to be awake again. 'Sorry?'

'This Rhianna Mitchell. Who is she then?'

Smith rubbed his head. 'I'm not sure, actually.' He groped for the roster sheet, and Carveth put it into his hand. 'It says here that she helps run a health food shop and hydroponic garden centre. Apparently she's actively involved in meditation – is that possible? – and is secretary of the Society for Preservation of Endangered Alien Life. I wish I'd known about that before I shot three void sharks this morning. Are they endangered?'

'Not before this morning. She certainly sounds like a bucket of fun. Why're we transporting this lentil princess, anyway?'

'I don't really know. Perhaps she's put up the cash to charter a ship instead of waiting for a liner and buying passage like anybody else.'

'Very expensive, that. You don't make that kind of money selling mung beans. And she can hardly be running from the law – everything's legal on New Fran as it is. To be honest, I've been planning on adding Mary Jane to the crew roster myself.'

'Who's that? Sounds like an aunt.'

'More a soul-mate. Never mind.'

'Rhianna Mitchell may be a dissident. There's a lot of people coming to the Empire from the neutral states these days, what with the Ghasts re-arming and everything.'

'True.' She took a swig of her tea. 'Ugh! If you ask me, as soon as those spidery buggers have enough ships, they're coming straight for Earth.'

'They'd better not. If they make for London they'll find something special waiting for them, and it won't be a souvenir T-shirt, that's for damned sure. Bloody Ghasts. That's the trouble with aliens – they're all bloody foreign.'

Carveth shook up the paperweight, watching the snow swirl around Parliament. 'These neutral colonies are in serious trouble if it all kicks off,' she said. 'Still, I don't think we'll be in any danger with this Rhianna woman on board.'

'No?'

'Of course not. If they thought there would be trouble, they'd send something decent to pick her up, not this bucket of rust.'

'Good point. I thought it was supposed to have a refit before we left.'

Carveth shrugged. 'It has – of a sort. It's got a new supralux engine fitted – a big one. We go twice the speed in half the style. Shame they couldn't put a half-decent drinks machine in at the time.'

'That's odd.'

'Well, yes, it is. In layman's terms, this ship probably used to fly like a pig. Now it flies like a pig with a fire-work up its bum. I'm not sure which is better.'

Smith nodded. 'Well, it's all a bit strange, if you ask me. You don't know anything about this mission, and I'm the captain and I don't either. Doesn't that strike you as surprising?'

'Half of it certainly does. Still, I suppose we'll find out when we get there. Would you mind taking the controls while I ablute?'

'Not at all. We're on course, aren't we?'

'Oh yes. Just watch for trouble. Don't do anything I wouldn't do,' she added from the door. 'And don't crash the spaceship, either.'

# 2

# Smith Meets Some Gentle People

The needle dropped in the speedometer. In the civilised tones of a BBC announcer, the ship's computer said, 'We are now approaching the target destination. Deceleration has been commenced.'

Carveth returned. 'What's going on?'

'We're getting close. The retros are on.'

'Great.' She sat back down. 'You want me to say hello?'

'Please do.'

She unclipped the microphone. 'This is the *John Pym*, British Empire commercial light transport vessel 28 – dammit, they've put me in a queue.'

'Let me try. Put it on the speaker.'

Carveth flicked a switch. Light, insipid music filled the room. 'Bossa Nova,' Carveth said.

'At least it's not that bloody Strauss again. I suppose we have to wait.'

Suruk entered the control room. 'Ah, music,' he said thoughtfully. 'Am I interrupting a mating ritual?'

'No!' they replied.

'Is that our destination?'

'Yep,' the pilot said. In the windscreen they could make out the shape of the colony. It was the shape of a starfish trying to mate with a can of beans. Down each of the starfish's arms, little grey shapes were anchored to the station: spacecraft, many of them several hundred metres long. Smith squinted at the display as they drew closer. He could recognise many of them, representatives of the human Great Powers and the alien races of Known Space. Most would be refuelling, for New Fran made much of its money from providing services to ships and their crews. One of the arms of the starfish was reserved for repairs, and the ships there were dotted with white specs that were space-suited men.

'There's a Morlock ship there, Suruk,' Smith said.

The alien peered through the windscreen. 'Indeed. No doubt they are readying themselves for battle and warfare further on. I see no other reason why they would want to linger at this cowardly place, unless they are currently sacking it.'

The M'Lak ship was red, shaped like a huge cone with an engine at the rear. There was a screw thread running around the cone. As tended to be the case with Suruk's people, they had adapted human technology to fit their way of war: the cone was for ramming, the screw thread designed to help it tear deep into the guts of an enemy vessel. The nose of the ship would then drop off, allowing a horde of fighters to spill out and engage the crew in a boarding action before returning to their own craft, usually with a selection of heads in a bag.

'I look forward to speaking with them,' Suruk said.

The muzak stopped. 'Hi there! This is New Fran traffic control,' a woman's voice announced. She had the gentle American accent characteristic of the Franese. 'I'm

Summer, and I'll be your traffic controller today. Is that the *John Pym* I'm talking to?'

'Certainly is,' said Smith. 'We seek permission to dock, please.'

'Permission is granted. Your personal computer reference is being fed to your ship right now. Your ship will lock with our central computer and begin autodocking. Please stand by at the controls in the event of manual correction being necessary.'

'Do you have a gift shop?'

'We do indeed. You'll find shopping facilities in the central hub, above the residential drum. We would remind you that although marijuana is legal on New Fran, hassling people isn't, so take your fascist attitude problem somewhere else, okay? All major currency is accepted apart from M'Lak barter-trophies.'

'Thanks.'

'No problem. You have a good time, now, John Pym.'

'I'll try,' Smith began, but the radio was silent. He glanced at the pilot. 'Carveth? Engage the docking computer.'

'Docking computer engaged.'

'Bring us in, Miss Carveth.'

'Us brung in.'

The ship yawed slowly, and as New Fran came closer Smith saw the happy pictures painted onto its iron-grey sides. Lights flashed above a connecting tube on which were painted the words 'Peace – friendship – understanding'. This was going to be a tough place to stomach.

Carveth took the crew roster down from the wall and

tested a biro on the back of it. 'Right then, who wants what at Duty Free?'

They closed the ship door behind them and trooped down the connecting walkway in a group. 'I hope Gerald is alright in there,' Carveth said.

'The beast is well,' Suruk replied. Despite Smith's requests, he carried four knives in his belt and his sacred spear. 'It grows plump.'

'Captain, tell him he can't eat my hamster.'

'Crew, stop eating one another,' Smith said, not really listening. 'Now, I believe this fellow is coming to talk to us.'

A man waited at the end of the passage. He was short, in an open-necked, collarless shirt, with a neat little beard and curly blond hair long enough for Smith to regard him with suspicion.

'Hey there,' he announced. 'You must be Captain Smith, right?'

'That's right.'

'It's a pleasure, sir. My name is Chad. On behalf of the Free State of New Fran, I'd like to welcome you to the Free State of New Francisco.' He frowned, aware that he had got his standard greeting wrong, and said, 'Well, hi. If you'd come with me...'

The corridor opened out into a massive hall. Light, shapeless music wafted from speakers mounted in the roof. A frieze ran around the walls, showing children of the nations and species of the galaxy holding hands or, where appropriate, tentacles and claws. Soft-headed nonsense, Smith thought. There should be a picture of aliens building a railway and learning how to vote, with a dreadnought in the background to remind them to keep at it. It occurred to Smith that if it were it his son holding hands with a Ghast on one side and a Frenchy on the other, the boy would be getting a striped arse in no time at all. Luckily, and surprisingly (to his mind at least), he had neither wife nor son.

'I'm glad you like it, man,' Chad said at Smith's side. 'It shows like all the children of all the different races who have visited New Fran living in harmony, laid out in a like – what's the word, it starts with an M—'

'Menu?' Suruk said.

'Mural. Over there is the check-in desk. Now, is there anything you need?'

'Refuelling,' said Smith. 'It's to go on the Valdane Shipping Company standing order. I'm here looking for a friend of mine. Can I go through?'

'Of course. And you friend, and – whoa. Sir? Native lifeform? I'm afraid I'm going to have to ask you to leave your knives and spear behind.'

Carveth leaned in to Smith. 'Why the hell did he bring them?' she whispered. 'He knew there'd be trouble.'

'The M'Lak are a young and confident race,' Smith said. 'When they think there's hunting to be done, it's hard to curb their enthusiasm.'

'Touch not my weapons, fool,' Suruk said crossly. 'This spear contains my ancestors.'

Chad's manner became noticeably colder. 'Thin, are they?'

To their surprise, Suruk pulled the blades from his hips and boots, heaping them on Chad. Carveth peered at the mural, craning her neck to take in the dancing children.

'Children, eh?' Suruk said, passing Chad his last knife. 'I don't like them, but I could eat a whole one.'

Chad put the weapons in a locker and rejoined them. 'Now then,' he said, a little less certainly, 'how can I help everyone?'

'I'm fine,' Smith replied. 'Suruk, you're coming with me.'

'Yes. Let us hunt this woman together.'

'Carveth, it's up to you. You can come along or meet us back here in six hours' time.'

The simulant frowned. 'I'll have a look round on my own. I'll check the bars, in case she's hiding in some cheap booze.'

She watched them walk off: the upright space captain and his lanky, savage friend, each as alien to this place as the other. Carveth reached to the back of her head and unfastened her ponytail, then shook her head to loosen her hair. She turned to their guide.

'Hello Chad,' Carveth said. 'I am now officially off duty. Now that Thunderbird Two is safely docked and the muppets have departed, I think you can help me.'

He blinked. 'Uh . . . alright. What do you need?'

Carveth smiled, which made her look friendly, eager and conspiratorial. 'Well, Chad, I have a problem. By a curious technical error I have a spare rolling mat and a lighter which is rapidly gathering dust because there is nothing to roll or to light. And you look just the kind of man to assist. Can you point me to the duty free?'

Chad dumped his armful of knives on the desktop.

'Well, that's a relief,' Chad said. 'At least some of you English are sane.'

Carveth stood at the counter in the duty-free shop and started to unload her basket. 'I'll have these six bottles, this, these special biscuits and two packets of rolling paper, please.'

The attendant stared for a moment at the pile of goods in front of him. 'It's a long trip,' Carveth explained, patting her pockets for her card. 'Hell, it must've fallen out.'

'You looking for this, little lady?'

She turned. It was a big man who spoke. He wore the uniform of a fleet she didn't recognise, and even if he had been in civilian clothes he would have looked out of place: too solid, too muscular for the Franese. Not bad, she thought. Not bad at all, considering that this was Day One of the trip.

'Where'd you find that?' she asked.

'It fell out your pocket.' His mouth did not open very wide when he spoke, but he had fine features. 'You're not from round here, are you? British, right?'

'That's right.'

The man nodded. 'It's a nice place, Britain, apart from the god-hating apostates. That and that democracy thing.'

He seemed a little uptight to Carveth, but he was nice-looking. 'Oh, I agree,' she said. 'Apostates, eh? Running around, messing up the larder, eating cheese . . .'

'You don't know what an apostate is, do you?'

'No,' she said. 'Do you want to buy me dinner?'

'No,' said the man. 'I'm looking for a ship, the *John Pym*. You know if it's docked here?'

'Yes,' she replied, 'that's my ship, as it happens, with me in. And bunks.'

The man in uniform nodded. 'You know where the captain is?'

Carveth frowned. 'Hmm. I don't know if I should tell you that.'

He shrugged. 'Well, perhaps I can persuade you to tell me later, over a drink. Or maybe after that.'

'*Well*... in that case he's in the main hall, looking for Rhianna Mitchell. Hey, wait, don't go! There's loads more I could tell you!'

Smith paced away from the annoying dock officials, Suruk at his side. People moved out of his way. It seemed to Smith that he moved twice as fast as anybody else: the people of New Fran were like ghosts, wafting past as if carried on a gentle breeze. They were an insipid bunch, he thought, weak of spine and flaccid of upper lip.

To his left, a woman – possibly their equivalent of a schoolteacher – was telling a group of children how the colony was an important meeting point for the nations of space, a welcoming neutral ground where issues could be resolved without the need for violence.

'You are displeased,' Suruk said.

'Yes,' he replied, 'I am. I don't like this place.'

'I am surprised. I thought that humans longed for comfort.'

Smith frowned. 'It's not comfort, Suruk. It's more... I don't know. It's nonsense, all of it. Weedy nonsense. All this being one with the galaxy. Sissy stuff. You think the Ghasts believe that?'

'No.'

'Of course not. They'd annex this place in a second if it wasn't for our dreadnoughts. Everyone here would be slaves before they could blink – and the Ghasts give even less of a toss about their precious galactic harmony than I do.'

'I would not be a slave.'

'No, not you or I. We'd have a job to do. But there's too much faffing around in the world these days, not enough standing-up to alien aggression. The Ghasts need to be hit damn hard, and then hit again once they've got back up. And then some sort of long-term slapping programme needs to be introduced. Look at this,' he added, pausing by a group of small trees set into the floor. 'They've got bits of string on the branches. What's all that about? They're trees. They can't do anything, can they?'

'Excuse me?' a woman said.

Smith turned. She was middle-aged, with long hair and a white, shapeless dress. 'Yes, madam?'

'You mentioned the trees? We put the ribbons on the branches in recognition of Gaia, the universal spirit? We are interconnected to the trees, from whence we came.'

'Oh, I see now,' said Smith. 'Thank you, madam. I didn't realise that. I stand corrected.' They walked on. 'Utter pigswill,' he said to Suruk.

Smith did not hate nature: he just did not worship it. His devotion was instead directed towards Orsoc, the Imperial Code born out of the Revolution a hundred years ago. It stressed patriotism, social justice, democracy and

46

country walks. It had only two commandments: the first being 'Be decent' the second 'Carry on'.

'Perhaps you should be less sceptical, Mazuran. We of the M'Lak believe that all life is connected. Nature is everywhere.'

'Which is presumably why you like killing it so much.'

'Naturally.'

Ahead, the entrance hall opened into a shopping mall. This was not unusual: most colonies put their duty-free section as near to the arrival point as possible – but the decoration was very specific to New Fran. 'That's a lot of rainbows and dolphins,' said Smith, gazing around. He checked the roster sheet again. 'Now, we're looking for a shop somewhere around here. Just this way—'

Smith walked straight into a man in the uniform of the Republic of Eden Navy. He bounced back off the man's slablike chest, took a step backwards and had the chance to examine what had seemed like a blue, padded wall.

Edenites were bad news: they had the small minds and demented confidence that came with being religious fanatics. They worshipped something called God the Annihilator which, although their own invention, followed in Earth's long-established tradition of bearded, everything-hating gods. Luckily, the Edenites were confined to a few colonies that had banded together during the break-up of the Empire of Man.

This particular Edenite was of a type that Smith disliked intensely: solid, over-muscled, casually brutal and accustomed to looking over people's heads while speaking to them.

'Hey, dicksplat,' he said, looking over Smith's head. This meant that he was staring straight into Suruk's face, as the alien was standing behind Smith and was several inches taller than him. Suruk's tusks parted in his version of a smile. The sailor grimaced as though watching something putrefy, and looked down at Smith instead. 'Why don't you watch where you're walking?'

'Why don't *I* watch where *you're* walking, eh?' Smith retorted angrily. He was flustered and the pronouns seemed somehow wrong, but it was at least a quick response.

All three paused to reflect on the possible meaning of these words and then the Republic man said, 'Idiots. God-damned pagans and idiots.' He moved away.

Smith said, 'What's that supposed to mean, eh?' His voice sounded squeaky and weak to him, as it tended to sound in such situations.

The big man turned slowly, like a turret on a warship lining up its guns. 'You are an idiot. This place is full of pagans. Both you and the people here are damned by God, hence god-damned. Questions, comments, anyone?'

'Nothing springs instantly to mind,' said Smith. They watched the big man stride away, heavy and confident, and Smith said, 'Goodness! Some people, eh?'

'Isambard Smith! He dishonoured you and you allowed him to proceed! Had he insulted me, I would have cut off his head and coughed pellets down his neck.'

'We're unarmed, Suruk.'

'I still would have struck him. Let us see how he defends against the nine-fingers-fist of the Incongruent Lemur Style.'

'We can't just carve people up here. It's neutral territory. Now let's get on with this. I reckon Miss Mitchell should be very near.'

The Morlock sighed. 'Mazuran, I tire. This place holds no honour. I wish to seek out the crew of the M'Lak craft we saw as we arrived. Perhaps they will be more to my tastes than this empty hall.'

Smith frowned. 'Well, alright, then. I suppose you'd be better off on board a spaceship than wandering around here. But if I hear that you've murdered that man and chopped off his head, I will be *very very angry*, do you hear?'

'Oh, alright.'

'Good. I'll see you back at the ship in, let's see... four hours. Understand?'

'As you wish. Good hunting, Isambard Smith!'

Smith watched his old ally bound away and wondered if letting Suruk explore this place was wise. No doubt the Morlock would be safer with his own people, preferably on their own ship, than wandering around a shopping mall in the hope of finding something to attack. There was never any certainty that Suruk would not take umbrage at some alleged slight to his honour, lose his head and then cause passers-by to follow suit.

Still, no doubt finding this Mitchell woman would be much easier without Suruk's assistance. Smith walked on through the mall, feeling highly out of place. Above him, some sort of slow, hooting sound issued gently from loud-speakers. The place smelt of bath salts. He stopped to check the address.

*

The Edenite sailor reached the other side of the mall before he looked back. The greyskin had disappeared, and the scrawny captain was wandering about at the far end of the hall, consulting a bit of paper like a husband sent out to buy toiletries. The big man stepped behind a pillar and unhitched the walkie-talkie from his belt.

'Sir? I confirm personal audio-visual sighting of subject. Target located in vicinity of secondary target, apparently explorating the area. They're here.'

Isambard Smith found the right section of the mall and finally reached the place where Rhianna Mitchell should be. It was a brightly-coloured shop front, with large windows that displayed a number of products, none of which had any use Smith could be sure about. He peered through the glass and tried to work out what the weirdly-titled little tubs might be. Several had pictures of sea lions on them: he doubted that they actually contained essence of sea lion at all. Women's stuff, he decided, presumably expensive variants on Vaseline and carbolic soap.

A sign in the window said: 'Rediscover your spirituality and detach yourself from materialism. We accept all major credit cards.' Frowning, and deeply aware of how alien he looked, Smith ventured inside.

The floor was genuine-looking wood and his boots sounded loud on it. He looked around. The shelves were lined with tubs and bottles. Over the shop speakers, a confused-sounding man was mumbling a patchily coherent song about a tambourine, backed by tinkly sounds not unlike someone urinating onto a glockenspiel. The shop smelt of soap, talcum powder and foreign teabags. A poster on the wall advertised a poetry reading that Smith would have fed himself into a threshing machine to avoid. He picked up a tub of kelp exfoliant rub, turned it upside-down and, on spotting the price tag, put it back very quickly.

There was a woman behind the counter. Smith approached.

'*Namaste* and welcome to Bodyworks! Hi, my name's Rhianna,' she added, pointing with both hands to a plastic badge on her lapel. It said: *Hi, my name's Rhianna*. 'Are you looking for something today?'

'Hello,' he said.

'Can I help you?' she asked. Her voice had that lilting inflection common here. Without being actually hostile, her voice implied that she could not help him, because he was in the wrong shop and really ought to leave, now.

'Um, yes. I need to talk to you, I'm afraid. My name's Isambard Smith, captain of the *John Pym*.'

'Oh-*kay*.' There was a highly doubtful quality to her voice. She sounded as though she were gearing up to turn down an improper request with sad head-shakes and nearly-convincing regret, as if his perverted tastes were only just outside her repertoire. 'So how may I help you? Are you here to buy something for yourself—'

'I'm fine, thanks.'

'Shopping for a lady?'

'Certainly not! I don't know what you free love types get up to, but I can get a lady quite well without paying for – oh, I see what you mean. Um, no. Might I speak with you privately?'

'Mmn.' She nodded appreciatively, as if tasting

something. She had a long, elfin face with quite pro-
nounced cheekbones. It was the opposite kind of face to
Carveth's: Rhianna Mitchell was the sort of woman who
would look beautiful in the right circumstances, where at
best Carveth could look cute. Assuming she didn't say or
do anything, Smith added, recalling the negative influence
of Carveth's personality.

'Is this about a personal matter, Captain Smith?'

'Yes. It's quite urgent.'

Rhianna leaned in closer. 'Is it a spacesuit that's chafing
you?' she asked. 'We do a regenerative skin cream that
works very well. It would double as a useful starching
agent for your moustache.'

'No. It's personal because it relates to you. You are
Rhianna Mitchell, yes?'

'In this cycle, yes.'

'Right. I'm an agent of the Valdane Shipping Company.
I've been sent to transport you to Midlight via supralux
spacecraft.' He held out the roster, then turned it the other
way up when she started doing weird things with her
neck. 'See?'

'Oh, I see!' She laughed loudly, without inhibition. 'And
I thought you had a groin infection!' A young woman,
who had been looking at the products in the window,
moved rapidly to the next shop. 'Yes, that's me. When do
we go?'

'As soon as the ship's refuelled. That should be in about
four hours. You're ready, I take it?'

'Well... no. I didn't realise this. They didn't say. I'll
need to get my things together, and arrange cover for the
shop.'

Smith nodded. 'Can I help at all?'

'Sure. Could you have a look at the front? Of the shop, please?'

Suruk saw them in the garden. Two of his people stood in the main public park, in keen discussion. They were slim, tall, free of the podgy flesh and big stomachs of human beings. They stood with the weight on the balls of their feet, ready to run and fight.

No humans were nearby: the closest group sat twenty yards away. Suruk strode towards them, pleased to see his own type among these dull, peace-loving *Metchi'chuen*. They turned as he came near, tasting the change in the air as one of their own race approached.

'I greet you with honour, warriors,' Suruk said in his glutinous English, uncertain which M'Lak dialect they spoke. 'May your names be noble.'

'I greet you too, honoured one,' said the nearer of the two braves. He wore armour on his shoulders and long gloves reinforced with metal spines. Both had leather cuirasses as well as boots and trousers of human manufacture, restitched to suit their shape. 'Speak you Asur'ah?'

'Indeed, I speak it.' Suruk spoke many of the M'Lak dialects, which had their own specific uses depending on the circumstances. There was one used for archaic language, similar to Chaucerian English, and one used solely for confusing non-speakers, similar to Welsh. Asur'ah was used to communicate, rather than to annoy passers-by. 'Let us use that tongue.'

'I agree.' The brave sighed and slipped into Asur'ah.

'Whoa. That's a major relief. I totally hate talking in English. It's, like, really inexpressive, y'know?'

It took a long while for Ms Mitchell to get ready to depart and by the end of that time Smith was twitching with irritation. To him, Rhianna's personality combined a number of characteristics that were geared to delay their departure and wring the maximum possible quantity of annoyance from every minute he spent waiting for her. She was not only a woman, but a particularly vague variety of woman, who relied on a loose network of similar flimsy types to cover for her while she was away. This meant that she spent nearly an hour ringing round various people to deal with the shop. By the time that they were able to leave and head to her apartment to collect her things, Smith was ready to cosh her with the telephone and haul her back to the ship like one of the 'dinner things' Suruk was wont to drag on board any vessel that would have him as a passenger.

Smith sat on a bean bag in her messy flat while she put things in a big satchel. New Fran was linked into the BCBC network, and he watched a documentary about the planned construction of new frigates for the Imperial Navy, sipping a dung-coloured drink that Rhianna had found him in the fridge. It smelt of fruit, and tasted of mango, but seemed to contain both pips and mud.

The news came on. 'Will I need a formal dress?' Rhianna called.

'Probably not,' Smith replied. Footage appeared of the Ghast Empire: Ghast Number One was delivering a screaming denunciation of mankind, Britain, democracy,

Earth, Britain, the Council of Powers, and Britain in particular, his arms waving around like a semaphore machine in a hurricane. The endless ranks of Ghast troopers bellowed back at him on cue. Watching them, Smith felt angry at himself for sitting about, drinking some filthy herbal brew and acting as if the Apocalypse was not about to come. *I need a ship with guns*, he thought. *These aliens need to be taught a lesson, preferably one that they will be unable to learn from on account of being very dead at the end of it.*

'All set!' Rhianna declared, returning.

Smith stood up. 'Are you sure?' She wore a long green shirt and a pair of jeans that were wide and long enough to completely hide her feet. As she shifted position, Smith saw that she was wearing plastic sandals. Her bags were large and brightly-coloured. Surprisingly, the hilt of a wooden sword protruded from one. She was hardly dressed for life on board an industrial space vessel.

Well, she'd only be on board a few days. Besides, if any proper work was required she would probably be worse than useless anyway, proper clothes or not. 'Righto,' he said. 'I'll help you with your bags, shall I?'

'That's quite a ship,' Rhianna said. 'It must be extremely powerful.'

'You're looking out of the wrong window,' Smith replied. 'We're over there.'

He was sitting on his purchase from duty free: a large box of beer and two cases of teabags.

She peered through the glass. 'Well, that's pretty nice too. I mean, it's got all the right stuff on it – engine, doors, that kind of thing… it does have all the right stuff on it, doesn't it?'

'Oh, absolutely. Possibly in the wrong order – haha, just joking.' She looked at him uncertainly, and Smith stopped. 'It does. Honestly. Now, before we go on board, I would say that we do have a slightly unusual crew roster.'

'Really?'

'Yes. One of our crew is a Morlock – he's pretty much the ship's emergency mascot, the usual mascot being a hamster – and our pilot is a simulant. She's very skilful. Ah – and here she is.'

Carveth appeared at the far side of the hall, an expression of mild confusion on her face. As she walked she reached into a paper bag and took out a biscuit.

'Hey there, everybody,' Carveth said. 'Are you Rhianna?'

'Yes. Hello.'

'Just in case anyone's wondering, I smell of herbal tea,' Carveth said. 'I've spent my shore leave in a . . . um . . . a herbal tea shop. Now then, where's the big frog? I picked up his knives on the way here.'

'Should be here soon,' said Smith. 'I'll wait and put a message out if he doesn't show.'

'I'll get the ship ready in a minute. Can we go on yet?'

'I think so.'

'Right. Let me show you to your quarters,' Carveth said to Rhianna. She took the bags and wandered into the air-lock, Rhianna following.

At the far end of the hall, Suruk and his two new friends watched the Earthmen doing something unimportant at the airlock. 'Is it the guy sitting down, with the fur thing above his mouth?' asked Thadar Lorgan.

'That's him. He's Isambard Smith.'

'Whoa. He looks totally stupid.'

Suruk did his equivalent of shrugging. 'He's okay. Loyal and friendly, but he does tend to make a mess. Well, I'd best roll. Got a ship to catch.'

Thadar nodded. 'It's been great meeting you. We're waxing our blades and heading to the Eastern Rim tomorrow. Seriously man, if you're ever bored, stick out a signal on standard channel eighty-two and we'll tell you where to catch some seriously mean prey.'

'Thanks!' said Suruk. 'And if I get something good, you know I'll share.'

'Great. Catch you later, Suruk the Slayer!'

'Catch you later!'

'So,' said Smith as the alien arrived, 'were they nice chaps?'

'Their words were honourable. They provided hospitality worthy of a highlord. I give them respect.'

They strolled down the docking corridor to the airlock, Smith carrying his boxes of beer and tea. 'Carveth!' he called as Suruk closed the door, 'pull off and set course for Midlight, principal landing ground. Let's go.'

The *John Pym* pulled away from New Fran, giving a flash of its spotlights to say farewell. It swung round slowly, the huge thrusters pushing it a safe distance from the colony before the supralux engines kicked in. A glow appeared at the rear of the ship, swelling up from dull red to blinding white. The *Pym* shot into space, and in a second New Fran was fifty miles away.

Fifteen minutes passed.

A second ship detached itself from the colony. It was black, ray-shaped, without hard edges or welding-lines. It was also considerably larger than the *John Pym*. Its name, so far as it could be translated from a mere shriek of rage, was the *Systematic Destruction*.

Medium Attack-ship Captain Four Hundred And Sixty Two was sitting in his room, watching Number One conclude his speech. The television watched him back.

There were no doors on the ship, as privacy was seen as a breeding-ground for subversion. Instead of knocking, drone 86732-4 announced his arrival by stamping loudly on the floor outside.

'Mighty commander 462!' he barked. 'We are following the puny human vessel! Their inferior instruments have not detected us!'

Slowly, 462's long neck swung around. As his features came into view, a wave of awe spread over the adjutant, strongly tempered with fear. 462's eyes focused on his minion with the intensity and kindness of headlamps. He threw back his head and shrieked with laughter. 'Ah-hahaha! Good, good. And the other human craft, the battleship?'

'We are being followed by a British cruiser, named the *Tenacious*. The human cruiser does not know we are aware of its presence. Forgive my individual thought, but I believe it expects us to attack the *John Pym* and is waiting for us to make the first move.'

'Excellent!' 462 rubbed his primary hands together. 'Ready all weapons and prepare to execute a rapid turn. Once we have destroyed one we shall take the other as we wish.'

'Yes, Captain! We shall destroy them utterly!'

'Of course.' 462's pincer arms rose up behind him, the claws rubbing together in anticipation. 'Prepare for war! Hahaha!'

Two hours away from New Fran, Smith found a curious artefact on the floor between his chair and Carveth's. It looked like a glass tube with a pipe sticking out the side, rather like the condensers he had used as a child in school. 'What's this for?' he asked.

The pilot was reading *On The Road*, one eye on the instruments, occasionally taking deep swigs from her tea. She turned to him, and her eyes widened. 'That's mine!' she said. 'I bought it on New Fran. It's an... an ant-farm.'

Smith fished in the device and found a small plastic bag. 'What're these bits of leaf in the little bag?'

'They're for the ants to eat. Obviously.'

'Fair enough.' Smith sat back and turned to his own book: *Heroes of the Empire, Volume Eight*. He had finished the page when a thought struck him. 'We don't have any ants.'

'Not yet we don't,' Carveth said somewhat mysteriously, and took the object back from him. 'How's the flower lady?'

'You mean our guest.'

'That's the one.'

'I assume she's fine. I was going to check on her, actually. Thought I'd make us a sandwich and see if she wants some.'

'Careful. She's probably vegetarian.'

'Good point.' Smith marked his page and left the cockpit, strolled down the corridor and knocked on Rhianna's cabin door. There was no reply. Smith knocked on Suruk's door.

'Enter.'

The alien was crouched on his stool, folded up like a gargoyle. His tiny eyes opened as Smith came in. 'Greetings, Mazuran.'

'Hello. Where's Rhianna?'

'The woman with tendrils on her head? She rests in the lounge.'

'Thought I might see if she wants something to eat. Coming to say hello?'

'No.'

'I see.' Smith glanced around. Suruk had brought some of his favourite trophies with him and laid them out around his spear. 'I like what you've done with the skulls there.'

'Thank you. I believe it says both "modern chic" and "senseless brutality". I will stay here for now. I find the new woman strange.'

'Well, she is foreign.'

'Indeed so,' Suruk replied, and he lowered his tusked head again and went back to sleep.

Smith closed the door behind him. 'Bit unfriendly,' he said, and he ducked through the doorway and entered the long room that served as both kitchen and lounge.

Rhianna Mitchell sat in the middle of the battered mock-leather settee, sandals on the floor and legs folded under her. Her hands were clasped loosely on her lap and she seemed to be asleep.

'Hello?' said Smith.

Her eyes flicked open. She had removed the green jacket and wore a white T-shirt with some kind of Chinese character printed on the front. Smith thought she dressed very oddly: had Rhianna been Imperial, she would have been wearing a skirt and corset, with black ankle boots. That said, her loose, floaty clothes seemed to suit her personality. In fact, she didn't look bad at all, if you liked pixies.

'Hello, Captain Smith.'

'Hullo. Sorry to interrupt.'

She smiled vaguely. 'Not at all. I was just resting.'

'Meditating, eh?'

Rhianna raised an eyebrow. 'I didn't think you had meditation in the Empire.'

'We have lots of things. We have thought-exercises to concentrate the mind, for fighting and what not. I did once try meditation, though, to help me relax.'

'Did you not take to it?'

'I took to it too well: I fell asleep.'

'I suppose it must seem like nonsense to someone like you.'

'No, no. Suruk always says that there's great wisdom in knowing how to rest as well as how to fight. That said, Suruk also says there's great wisdom in the words to "Jump Around" by the House of Pain. I really came down to see if you needed anything to eat.'

'I'm fine for now, thank you. I am a vegetarian, though. I should have mentioned that earlier. Is that okay?'

'I should think so. The food here's so bad, even the Welsh Rarebit doesn't include anything I'd call meat. You'll be fine.'

'Sure.' She stood up gracefully and padded barefoot across the room. Quietly, she closed the door and returned to her seat. 'Captain Smith, I need to talk to you.'

'I run an informal ship. Just call me Captain.'

'Captain, then. You understand that this is all rather unexpected. I was of the impression that a transport was going to arrive in a couple of weeks' time, not now. And that the ship would be much, well... bigger.'

'Bigger?'

'You know, a warship. I thought I'd be going on a ship that was armed.'

'I thought you people disapproved of guns.'

'Well, yes, I do. But I'm prepared to waiver if I'm getting shot at.'

'Well, we're not getting shot at.' Smith glanced around, suddenly worried. 'We're not, are we?'

'No. It's just that I was given the impression it would be a bigger ship.'

Smith frowned. 'How come?'

'Well, I was waiting for your Mr Khan to contact me. He was due to send a ship in a couple of weeks' time. He must have felt that it was urgent, seeing how you're ahead of time.'

'Should it be urgent?'

'I don't know. I'm not paying for the flight.' She sighed and leaned back in the chair. Smith could see her ankles.

He didn't see many women's ankles. They were shapely. He kept his eyes on her face and reminded himself of the soppy nonsense in her shop. Who'd want a wife who rubbed her body with essence of kelp? What was kelp, anyhow? *Rubbing*. Stay on target, Smith.

She was saying some stuff.

'You see, Captain Smith, I was worried by the current political situation, and decided that I should head into Imperial space, in case the Ghasts decide to annex New Fran. Mr Khan is a good friend of some people I know. Important people. They say it's only a matter of time.'

'I see. And you didn't know who they'd send.'

'Well, no, I guess.' Rhianna yawned. 'So I didn't know to expect you. I knew someone was coming, just not then – and in a bigger ship.'

'Well, this is it,' he replied, irked by her wish for a more impressive carriage in which to travel. 'It may be small, Miss Mitchell, but it suits us fine – and to us, it's home.'

'Ow, crap!' Carveth shouted from down the corridor. 'Bloody low ceiling! Bloody pissing heap-of-crap ship!' She appeared in the doorway, rubbing her scalp. 'Boss, trouble.'

'One moment.' Smith stood up and paced to the door. 'What is it?'

'Signal on the scanner,' Carveth said. 'We've got multiples, closing fast. From the way they're moving, I'd say void sharks.'

'What, again? I thought you said they were rare!'

'Not rare enough. I say we endanger them.'

'Captain Smith?' He turned – it was Rhianna. 'Can't this be dealt with without all this killing and violence?'

The dreamy, insipid part of her voice seemed to have got louder.

'Possibly,' he said. 'But it wouldn't be the Imperial way.'

He closed the door behind him, annoyed. 'How long till they reach us?'

'Two, two and a half minutes,' Carveth said. The corridor was small: they were near to one another and it felt close, uncomfortable. Carveth turned away and hurried into the cockpit, trying to rub her eyes into life. 'They must wait around New Fran, looking for junk. Either that or they smelled the rust.'

In the sitting room, Rhianna exhaled and closed her eyes. Clear your mind, she told herself. Feel the stress slip away. Reach out with your soul. Think of the whales...

'I'll weave around,' Carveth said as Smith opened the weapons locker. 'That should confuse them a bit.'

Smith pulled out the Maxim Cannon and checked the ammunition counter. Two hundred and fifty six rounds in this drum and the full thousand in the other. Hefting it in both hands, he carried the thing into the hall, eager for zero-gravity to take the weight away.

The suits were stored in the corridor, in a cupboard opposite the cabins. He laid the gun down and hauled out his suit as though dragging an unconscious man. The jointed limbs flopped awkwardly as he laid it down. The ship yawed, and Smith lurched drunkenly, keeping his footing with an effort. 'About a minute!' the pilot called over her shoulder. 'It's void sharks alright!'

'Keep weaving, Carveth. I'm going out.'

One leg in, then the other, and the body closed around him like a suit of armour. His fingers slid into the gloves, and he picked up the gun and quickly fastened it to the side of the suit.

Helmet in hand, he strode down the corridor and through the lounge where Rhianna sat cross-legged on the sofa ignoring him, doing her exercise. He yanked the far door open and strode into the hold, slammed it behind him and saw the pressure needle spring up in the gauge. He was sealed in.

Smith climbed the steps onto the walkway. He put his helmet on, checked the seals and activated the suit radio. 'Carveth?'

'Very soon, Cap.' The ship lurched as he reached the airlock. 'I can't outmanoeuvre them. You'll have to go outside.'

'I'm ready at the hatch. Can you give me a reading?'

'Lidar says they're in front, coming in on an intercept. I'd say twenty seconds.'

Smith readied the Maxim cannon and checked the umbilical line. 'I'm going out.' He reached out and put his gloved hand around the lever.

'Wait.'

He froze, arm outstretched. 'Carveth?'

Her voice was a crackle beside his ear. 'Wait, Smith.'

'What is it?'

'They've stopped.'

'How do you mean?'

'They're circling us. They're not coming any closer.'

He stood there, waiting. 'What're they doing, waiting to attack?'

'I don't think so. They're just… staying away. I don't get this. They're pulling back.'

He listened. 'What do you want me to do?'

'I don't know. You're the captain.'

'I'm staying here. Call me if they go.'

Smith lowered himself awkwardly and sat down on the floor beside the airlock. He stared out across the empty hold, at the chains and pulleys that dangled from the roof, and the rear door big enough to accommodate a truck. He waited. Five minutes passed.

'Are you coming back soon?' Carveth said over the radio. 'You said you were making a sandwich about half an hour ago, and I'm still hungry.'

Smith pulled himself up and stomped back to the corridor. Rhianna did not seem to have moved throughout the incident. He unbuckled the suit and hung it in the locker, then he made some tea.

'Biscuit?' he said, returning to the cockpit. 'Here's some tea.'

'Thanks, Cap.' Carveth still held the controls, moving her hands along with them as the autopilot returned the ship to its programmed route. Smith put the Maxim cannon back in the weapons locker.

'Don't ask me, because I just don't know,' Carveth said as he sat down. 'God only knows why they decided to go away. Just be glad they did. That could have been a real crisis.'

'I doubt it would have bothered our guest,' Smith replied. 'She's been sitting there half-asleep all through it all.'

'So you're not sold on the space cadet?'

'I don't know. I mean, she's attractive and pleasant enough, but I find it hard to warm to the kind of stuff she believes in. Sappy nonsense, all this pagan stuff, listening to trees and tying bits of string on dolphins.' He stood up. 'Now, if you'll excuse me, I'm going to have a sleep.'

Smith lay on his back, staring at the ceiling and trying to think. He missed the Captains' Lounge back at the company. This time he would have a story or two to tell: his battle with void sharks, his experience of the Franese and his strange near-miss with a second pack of creatures that would normally have been trying to chew through the hull. Funny business, all that.

He had put up a couple of pictures, the same ones he always took on missions. There was a map of Known Space, with the Empire a broad swathe of pink running across the centre, and a reproduction of Waterhouse's *Lady of Shallott*. Now, he thought, there was a proper woman, not a weed like Rhianna or an oddment like Carveth. The Lady sat in her boat, her damsel-sleeves almost trailing in the water, staring out and awaiting rescue. She wouldn't give you sarcastic backchat, or spend hours on the sofa staring into space. She would be appreciative, and awed, and good at cakes. She might smell of small onions, though. He drifted off into sleep.

Smith dreamed that he was in the Captains' Lounge, sitting on a wicker chair under the stuffed monocorn head that jutted from the wall, a souvenir of Wickton's expedition to claim the Outer Systems. He was describing to a rapt, mainly female audience how he'd defeated the void sharks. He looked around, and Carveth and Rhianna were in the room. 'That's not how it happened,' Carveth said. 'No, it really happened like this,' Rhianna said, and Smith awoke.

The intercom rang and a copy of *Tales of Adventure* fell off the shelf next to it and landed on Smith's head. Muttering, he stretched out and switched on the intercom. 'Yes?'

'Come up here, now,' Carveth said, and for once there was nothing flippant in her voice.

He reached the cockpit in his dressing gown. The others were there already, the alien and the visitor standing behind the pilot's chair. 'What's going on?'

'Look,' Carveth said.

Something turned lazily in the middle of the screen. From here it looked like a shard of sooty porcelain or a scrap of bone, a snapped, shattered, ragged thing. It was partly hollow, like broken honeycomb. Little fires winked around its edges. Without air to feed them, the explosions were tiny, like the glow of embers.

'We picked up the call on emergency frequency while you were asleep,' Carveth explained. 'Probably an automated distress call. That used to be a frigate. There would have been fifty people on board.'

'My God,' said Smith. 'Is there anyone alive?'

New lights flared up along the stricken ship. Its systems were in their final, terminal throes. The core computer would be burning out, the doors no longer sealing, the oxygen stores leaking away. It was dying.

'From a wreck like that?'

'Check, Carveth.'

'What's the point?'

'Just do it, woman!'

'It is dead,' Suruk said.

She nodded and pressed buttons, turned dials. 'The emergency kits would have beacons attached, on the lifeboats and the suits...' she said, studying the controls. 'No beacons.'

'Fifty people,' Rhianna said from the back of the room. 'That's awful.'

A piece of metal from the hull floated past. It must have been the size of the *John Pym*, a huge sheet of plating wrenched into a pretzel shape. Smith lowered himself slowly into the captain's chair, like an old man. Numbly he realised that his dressing gown was not covering his knees, and he pulled it closed.

Carveth looked down the binoculars and held them out for Smith. 'The *Tenacious*,' she said. 'It's one of ours.'

'What happened to it?' Rhianna asked. Her voice sounded lost, disembodied.

'The engine's still intact,' Smith replied. 'Its missiles must have gone... or somebody torpedoed it.'

'Nothing on the signals,' Carveth said. 'I say we go.'

'Check again.'

'Right.' She looked back to the dials, very slowly turning one of them with her hand. They could hear the click of the dial as she explored the band, from top to bottom. Nothing.

Smith said: 'Is the emergency signal still going?'

'Yes. It's two hundred miles away from the main wreckage, moving away fast... Probably blown clear.' She turned and looked at Smith. 'Boss, I know this is bad, but there's nobody left alive out there... And

I don't think it was a malfunction that did for them.'

Smith ran a hand through his hair. Technically speaking, there could be people on the ship, survivors whose suit beacons didn't work, or who were unconscious, or too shocked to put them to use, or a hundred other reasons why, waiting for help, hoping that somebody would come. *Technically*, but they all knew otherwise.

'Take us out of here,' he said. 'There's nobody alive. Set the co-ordinates and put us back on course.'

'Right,' said Carveth. The *John Pym* rumbled: they heard the soft whine as the thrusters swung to push them backwards, away from the scene.

A light flashed on the radio. 'Hang on,' Carveth said. 'That must mean something. It's picked something up.'

She pressed the headset against her ear. 'It's a standard S.O.S. transmission,' she said. 'Wait, there's something on the end... it's in code.' She looked around at Smith. 'Why is it in code?'

'Run the code *6079Smith* through the decoder,' he said.

'Is that their code?' Rhianna asked.

'It's the only one I know,' he said.

Carveth pulled the console down on its jointed metal arm and typed. 'Then it's for you. I think you'd better hear this.'

The loudspeakers crackled at the edges of the room and a voice filled the air between them, like the voice of God. It took up the cockpit, a deep, actor's voice, the voice of a man who was not quite elderly.

'This is Bentham Cartwright, Captain of HMS *Tenacious*, fleet number 2305. If you can hear me, I am assuming two things: firstly, that I am addressing Captain Isambard Smith and the crew of the *John Pym* and, secondly, that our mission to protect you has been a failure. For that I apologise.

'Captain Smith, no doubt you have wondered as to the purpose of your flying to New Fran to collect a seemingly unimportant dissident, to rescue her from the possibility of that colony being annexed by the Ghast Empire. You are presumably on the way to deliver Miss Mitchell to the city of Midlight, on Kane's World. It is vital that you continue with this mission. You are to proceed with all possible speed to your destination and to stop for no reason whatsoever. It is absolutely imperative that she reaches the destination intact and unharmed. The only higher priority is that you prevent her from falling into the hands of the Ghasts or their allies.

'You employer, Mr Khan of Valdane Shipping, has long had links with the Deepspace Operations Group of Great Britain and its Colonies. He gave you this task because your ship was unimportant, less likely to be noticed than a larger, military vessel. He arranged for us to follow you and protect you – which, if you are hearing this, we have been unable to do.

'Mr Khan believed that you would be less likely to reveal yourself or make any errors if you did not know you were being shadowed. It was a mission where ignorance was vital, a mission for which you were the ideal choice. Now, however, you are no longer safe. You are exposed, and it is you and you alone on whom the safety of your ship relies...'

'We're stuffed,' Carveth said.

'... I can only wish you good luck. May your ship prove up to the task ahead.'

'Yep, we're stuffed all right,' Carveth said.

'... I am merely hoping that your crew can deal with this responsibility and see you through with honour and success.'

'So am I,' said Smith.

'Good luck, Mr Smith. And remember, on no account must Miss Mitchell be passed to the enemy. In the event, you know what you must do. Goodbye, and carry on.'

The message ended. The four of them were quiet, as if they had been listening to a funeral address. Smith broke the silence. 'Get us out of here, Carveth. Top speed.'

The *John Pym* raced through the dark of space, away from the murder-scene. Smith sat grimly in the captain's chair, his eyes fixed on the instruments. Carveth said nothing as she worked the controls. Rhianna had gone back to the lounge, presumably to pray to whatever it was she worshipped. Suruk was peering into the hamster cage.

'There is one good thing,' Suruk said.

'What's that?' Carveth said, not looking round.

'At least we may have a proper fight before we get home.'

'You know,' she replied, 'you may find this surprising, but I really would prefer not to have to bother.'

'Quiet,' said Smith. 'How far have we gone?'

'From the *Tenacious*? About six thousand miles.'

'Good. Keep going. If we stay on this course and at this speed, we should be fine.'

Something exploded behind them. The whole ship lurched forward and Smith was thrown back in his seat, knocking the air from his lungs. In the living room,

Rhianna shrieked. Warning lights broke out across the console. A siren howled in the corridor.

'Something's wrong!' Smith yelled.

'Really?' Carveth shouted back. Teeth gritted, she was wrestling the control stick as if fighting a cobra. 'Do you think so?'

'Dammit, we're hit! What's the damage?' cried the captain.

'Serious hull weakening on the port! Engine's shutting down to prevent overheating. We're down to forty percent efficiency.'

'Hell! Can't you override it?'

'Not unless you want to be in two galaxies at once. Much more and it explodes.'

'Dammit to hell!' Smith pinched his brow.

Feet pattered on the floor behind him, and he heard Rhianna say, 'I fell off my chair. Is something wrong?'

'Just a bit,' Carveth called back. Panting, she released the stick. The ship stayed level. 'Torpedo up the poo-chute.'

'Oh Gaia! Is it – like what happened to the other ship?'

'Looks that way.'

The loudspeakers squealed. Suddenly the room was full of bitter, raucous sounds, as though they had tuned by accident into some frenzied squabble in a duckpond. The voices barked and hissed at one another, like geese struggling to express human anger. In the stillness after the explosion, all four of them stared up at the speakers like prisoners waiting to hear the sentence passed.

'What is that?' Rhianna breathed.

'Ghasts,' Smith replied.

'Attention human scum!' the loudspeaker screeched. 'Attention human scum! Ghast Empire calling!'

Very slowly, Isambard Smith picked up the intercom. 'Put me on, Carveth.'

'Right.'

'Ghast ship, this is Captain Isambard Smith of the Second British Empire. What do you want?'

'The destruction of the entire human race! Space shall be cleansed of the human taint!'

'Anything we can do, or are you just generally annoyed?'

'You will deliver the woman from New Fran to us immediately. Failure to do so will result in your swift and ruthless annihilation!'

The three crew watched Smith's pallid face. A light sheen of sweat had appeared at his hairline. He swallowed. 'You may not have this woman. You are outside Ghast space and acting illegally.'

'Silence! There is no law! There is only strength! You will surrender immediately and pass the woman to us, or we shall destroy you all!'

'You are making a very grave mistake,' Smith said quietly.

The voice gave an insane, wild laugh. 'We do not make mistakes! Surrender at once! Resistance is fertile!'

'Don't you mean futile?'

'... That's what I said! Surrender or die!'

'How dare you! Do you think I would give up a woman, someone who I am honour-bound to give safety on my ship, just because the arrogant minions of an alien despot hurl threats and abuse at me?'

'Well, yes, we do.'

'Alright then, give us ten minutes.'

'Hahaha! Puny weaklings surren—'

Smith hung up.

'Oh no.' Rhianna closed her eyes and put her hands out in front of her. She was breathing with difficulty. 'Channelling positive thoughts. Positive thoughts. In with the good, out with the negativity. In with the good—'

Carveth looked around the room. 'Ah, crap. Any ideas, anyone?'

Rhianna said, 'Okay, let's make a Calm Circle. Let's all join hands and try to visualise—'

'Get the guns,' Smith said. 'Carveth, go down to the engine rooms and bring up a gallon of petrol and some rags. Suruk, fetch your spear and sharpen up your knives. Rhianna, just put your shoes on. We're going out fighting.'

There was silence as Smith got to his feet. Suruk gave a low and dirty chuckle. 'War! That's the best news all holiday!'

# 3

# Smith Defies the Space Ant Horde!

Five minutes later Smith was in the kitchen area, a bottle of beer in either hand, pouring the contents into the sink. Two empty bottles stood on the draining board beside him.

He looked at the bottle in his hand. The beer flowed away so quickly, he thought. Like time, like the years of his life flowing away, all to end on this wretched ship.

Glug, glug. And what had he achieved? Any meaningful relationships? A career that would bring him fame and success? No. Years of being the only non A-grade student at Midwich Grammar followed by a brutal upbringing in Harcourt Park School for Boys had led straight into an insipid career as a minor space pilot. If he died now, would he get into heaven? Probably by default, he reflected: his life had been so mediocre that God probably wouldn't have bothered watching it.

'Oh my God,' he cried, 'what a waste! What the hell am I *doing*?' He stopped pouring and drank the beer instead. 'Fancy pouring good beer away. Bally idiot.'

Suruk entered the room, his spear in hand. Smith looked up and said, 'All set?'

'I have everything I need,' the alien said, counting on his fingers. 'Machete, parang, kukri, stiletto, Bowie knife, wakazashi –' he moved onto his other hand – 'and the spear of my ancestors. All set.'

'Good. I'm making petrol bombs. I'm also getting drunk and angry.'

'Tell me, Isambard Smith: how many Ghasts are there on a Ghast warship?'

'I don't know. Three, four hundred?'

Suruk thought about it for a moment. 'We are going to die, then.'

Smith realised that he was damned if he was going to surrender. He did not fear the Ghasts: after six years in a minor prep school north of Harrogate, he felt that he could take anything. An arcane hatred was stirring in him, the atavistic urge to stick something pointed in creatures who did nothing other than stand in lines, shout and try to tell him what to do.

'They're not having my people, Suruk. I know she's a wishy-washy nuisance, but she's a woman, and she's on my ship, and they're not having her. My crew matter to me. Same goes for whatshername. The pilot.'

'Death in battle. Hohoho! Are you resigned to it?'

There was a simple answer. Despite his inability to remember a part of his life that had not been rubbish in some way, Smith felt that he had a lot more to offer the world: more precisely, certain parts of him had a lot to offer attractive women. He felt that he deserved to live: he still had a lot to prove to the world. 'I don't know. I would rather stay alive. But I won't give in.'

'It is not necessarily so.'

'How do you mean?' So far, he had assumed that they had a straight choice of being forced to go down fighting or being murdered once their captors had tired of them. But if Suruk the Slayer was saying this, perhaps there was an alternative, a way of surviving, of snatching some kind of success from the jaws of glorious defeat.

'I have a plan, Mazuran. But we will need to delay our enemy for it to work. Then, we will carry out great and terrible slaying: we will fight like warriors, but will live to fight again. Then the prize female will want to breed with you. Perhaps the short annoying one as well, if your ancestors favour you.'

'I'll do it anyway. What do we need?'

'So,' said Narzak the Despoiler, 'I'm like, "This kill is mine", and he's like, "No way! This kill is so mine", and I'm like, "N-uh! Check out the spear before you start hassling me, alright", and he's like, "Back off, little warrior," like he's totally amazing or something.'

'Some people just need to cool down,' Azrag Blood-hammer said from the other side of the room. 'So what did you do?'

'I told him to get off his high horse and chill. Then I cut off his head. What's that flashing thing on the panel?'

The control panel of the good ship *Smashface* was hidden, like much of the craft, under a thick layer of bones, red paint and things no longer edible. Azrag shoved the junk aside and his small eyes peered through the gloom at the controls. 'It's a message,' he said. 'Says it's from Suruk the Slayer. Apparently he's looking for Thador Largan.'

'That's way uncanny,' Narzak said, 'because he's on this ship.'

Azrag skim-read the message. ' "Join us for a mighty battle. War... killing... honour... party of the decade..." Fetch the guys! This is going to rock!'

Carveth rested the shotgun on her hip and began to push cartridges into the breach. She zipped up her waistcoat and emptied the spare shells into the watch pocket.

'You know you can have the Maxim cannon if you want,' said Smith.

'Nah,' she said. 'This'll do as much good as anything else. I'd rather give the big gun to someone half-competent.'

'Don't talk like that,' he said. 'We're going to give them a good show. Suruk, did your chaps say how long they'd be?'

'I do not know. But their spacecraft has a larger engine than this, and their pilot is much less fat. They should not take long.'

'Then we'll hold them as long as we can. How long do we have before the Ghasts dock?'

'Two minutes,' Carveth said. 'And I'm not fat. Can I have a bit of that beer?'

'Oh, sorry.' He passed it over. 'There you go.'

Carveth took a swig and passed it back. 'Whoa! Bracing.'

Rhianna stepped into the corridor. She was holding the wooden practice sword from her bag. 'I'm ready to fight,' she announced.

'Like that?' Smith said. 'These are Ghast stormtroopers. You've got flip-flops and a stick.'

'They want me, not you,' Rhianna said. 'I ought to help.'

'You could always go on your own and we could get away,' Carveth suggested. She met Smith's eye and added, 'Just a thought.'

'I would have suggested it,' Rhianna said, 'but I knew he wouldn't let me.'

'Point,' Carveth said.

They had pulled up some of the empty cargo boxes from the hold to use as a barricade. Smith and Rhianna stood behind the boxes on one side of the door, Suruk and Carveth on the other.

'Are you ready, men?' said Smith.

The loudspeaker crackled into life.

'Ghast Empire calling! This is warship commander 462 addressing you, weakling human Earth-scum! Warship *Systematic Destruction* is preparing to dock with your puny craft. On hearing the docking tube attach, you will open the hatch and surrender immediately!'

'Hang on,' said Smith. 'We've got a problem.'

'What?'

'We have a, um, a highly contagious terminal disease. We need at least half an hour to get better.'

'We are immune to disease! Only weaklings succumb to disease, and weaklings must be destroyed! We will board now!'

'Let's just kill them all,' Suruk said.

'Open the door or we will train lasers on your feeble craft and slice it in two!'

Smith quietly passed two petrol bombs to Carveth. 'Did you bring a lighter?' he whispered.

'Not for this,' she replied, snapping it out of her pocket. 'This isn't exactly how I was planning to get wasted.'

'Ghast ship? We'll open the door,' Smith said into the radio.

Something hit the ship with a dull, metallic clang that reverberated through the hull. 'That's them,' Rhianna said.

They waited.

Carveth stepped out from the boxes, over to the door. 'Let's get this over with,' she said, reaching to the airlock.

'On three,' said Smith. The pilot wrapped her hands around the wheel. 'One.'

'Two,' Carveth said. Smith braced himself.

'Three!'

She spun the wheel; it whirled and the door opened with a squeal of metal.

They looked down the Ghast docking tube: a corridor, full of mist, stretching off into somewhere that they could not see. The walls were ribbed, vaguely organic. Somewhere behind the mist, a light shone towards them.

'What's all that?' Carveth whispered.

Suruk turned to her. 'Small woman, wait.'

Smith flexed his fingers around the rear grip of the Maxim cannon. It was strapped straight to his belt, and it was heavy. He felt tired already, although whether it was from the weight of the gun or from fear, he did not know.

The light in the docking tunnel flickered as something ran past it. 'Dammit!' said Smith. 'Can't get an aim!'

The light vanished, came back on, and suddenly it was a strobing, pulsing beam as something scuttled past, then another, and another—

'Dozens of them!' Smith exclaimed.

Suddenly Carveth sprang up and fired the shotgun into

the docking tube. 'Come and get it, tossers!' There was a screech of rage, and a muffled thump of something falling to the ground. The tube was silent. She looked back at the others. 'So much for the cat and mouse stuff,' she said sheepishly.

Lights flashed in the dark, bolts of light coming for them. 'Down!' Smith cried, and the wall exploded above his head, the metal corrupted and bubbling.

Smith leaned into the entrance and let rip. The Maxim cannon roared like steel sheets being torn, sending bullets thundering down the tube. Shadows screamed and fell. In a great horde the Ghast boarding party rushed at them.

Bullets and white beams turned the docking tube into a maze of light. Carveth saw something rush out from the mist, limbs whirling, and she racked the slide and shot it in the chest. It roared and fell, and a thing like a vast insect rushed along the wall, and she blew that apart before it could clear the mist and she would have to look at it. Smith's gun ripped out and a row of them fell, more of their comrades scrambling into the gap. Rhianna screamed.

The round counter spun down to zero and Smith tore out the ammo drum and slapped a new one into place. 'Score one for Blighty!' he yelled, and he opened fire. Disruptor shots hit the box beside him and it melted and collapsed.

Something new appeared in the fog: sparking lights, the business ends of shock-sticks. 'Aha!' Suruk cried. 'Proper fighting!', and for the first time one of the Ghasts cleared the fog and leaped on them.

Carveth only caught a glimpse of it – the goggling eyes

in a skull-like face, the long coat, the antennae poking through holes in its steel helmet – and then Suruk whirled in front of her and sliced off its head. They kept firing: the enemy swarmed forward, frenzied.

No time for aiming now. Smith kept his finger down and raked the corridor from side to side. The light in the docking tube was blocked out by the rush of Ghasts. Suruk hurled a knife into the horde, Carveth pumped and fired until her gun was dry and her terrified fumbling fingers snatched the revolver from her belt.

Smith threw the cannon down. 'I'm out!' he cried, and they heard the hiss as he drew his sword. Suruk held out a bomb to Carveth, she lit the rag and he hurled it into the corridor. There was a flash of fire, and he threw another, and suddenly there was nothing alive in the docking tube.

Silence from the Ghasts. Nothing moved in the passage except smoke. Smith looked at his crew. 'They know we're out,' he said.

Rhianna was bolt upright and shaking. 'Why don't they attack? Why don't they attack?'

'They wish to make sure,' Suruk said, and as he did a fresh batch of raiders ran into the light and charged at them.

Suruk roared and leaped into the gap. Blades whirling, he felled one and then another as they tried to swarm over him to the humans beyond, calling out the names of the techniques he used as he cut down his enemies. Distantly, he heard Carveth's revolver going off and sensed Smith at his side – but that did not matter. He was in the spirit world, running with his ancestors, feeling them guide his spear.

A trooper leaped the boxes and knocked Carveth to the ground. The revolver bounced out of the simulant's hand. The Ghast grinned down at Carveth, flexing its pincer-arms. Carveth gave in to fear and howled.

Rhianna stared at it, horrified. Something happened to her with the slow certainty of a dream. The wooden sword rose in her hands, drew back, and she dropped in a position she knew only from Tai Chi. The sword whipped out and struck the Ghast in the head.

The trooper stumbled but its claws lashed out for her. She did not move – the geometry of the universe shifted – and somehow they missed, swiping through air where her body should have been. It lurched aside and, as Carveth grabbed the revolver and swung it up, the trooper's head was in her sights.

The world was slowed: to Carveth, it seemed like a dream. She fired, killed one Ghast and blasted the next as it lumbered into range. Suddenly it was rather easy, and somehow, she knew that Rhianna was making it so.

Rhianna blinked and was awake again. The enemy were gone. Smith was calling to them all, asking who was hurt. Suruk stood surrounded by spidery bodies, bellowing in triumph. Carveth had a finger up her nose. And voices were answering Suruk's calls – not Ghasts any more, but the M'Lak, his friends.

'It was most excellent,' Thador Largan told Suruk forty minutes later. 'We got the prow right in place and caught them really smooth. We like cut straight through and then, well, you know, honour and stuff.'

Narzak and Lorgan had joined the humans in the *John Pym*. In an attempt to flush out the invaders the Ghasts had simply opened several of their airlocks, and the M'Lak were forced to take shelter while the *Systematic Destruction* pulled away. Now, the Ghasts had fled, and the *Smashface* had docked with the *John Pym* to collect Suruk's friends.

'It was indeed good work,' Suruk said. 'The pinkies here were about to be overcome. You were most fortuitous with your timing.'

On the other side of the lounge, Carveth was pouring beer down her neck. To Smith, sitting opposite her, it seemed as if she had disengaged the need to swallow, and was just tipping the stuff down the chute.

'I'm telling you,' she said, pausing just long enough to speak, 'it was really strange. There she was, just standing there, and suddenly everything went weird and they sort of stopped trying, so I shot them. It wasn't like she did anything fancy either. She just stood there. It was almost as if they *couldn't* hit her. That's almost as impressive as frogboy over there.'

Smith was finding it difficult to concentrate. In the last fifteen minutes he had celebrated his continuing existence by drinking three bottles of beer. As a result, his vision was slightly uneven and his front marked by a stripe of spluttered lager. 'So what do you reckon?' he managed, quickly turning back to his bottle as it began to froth. 'Do you think there's something wrong with her?'

'My considered medical opinion? She's a killer mentalist with knobs on.'

'She might just be trained.'

'Trained in what, psychic ninja death? Why should she be? She's the first ninja I've met who spent their free time listening to whale noises. That said, she *is* the first ninja I've met full stop.'

'Well, it does seem odd that a pacifist who works in a health food shop might turn out to be some sort of mystic assassin.'

'Well, yeah. I doubt they get many samurai attacks at Veggie-world. Besides, it wasn't quite like all that. It was more... it's not easy to describe.'

'Go on.'

'It wasn't martial arts. It was more that things changed around her. She suddenly seemed to be in the right place at the right time. Not that she disappeared or anything like that. Blimey, I'm an android and *I* can't work out how to explain this.'

'I think I understand.'

'Smith, those void sharks. She was meditating all through that and they didn't attack us at all.'

'Yes. But I don't see... hold on... no... what're you saying?'

Carveth sighed. 'I'm not sure, Cap. It's too strange for me to describe properly. I'm an android, a simulant. I'm pure rationality. I don't even drink alcohol, let alone believe in magic powers. Well, not much alcohol. But what if she's right? What if she really is in tune with nature or something?'

'I see what you mean.' Smith frowned, rubbing his chin. 'My God. Think of the unholy power you could unleash with such abilities. It would be just like Doctor Dolittle all over again.'

'Yes, I suppose so. You do know that was just a book, right?'

'Figure of speech.'

'But you remember that bit in *Snow White* when all the animals come out and dance around with her?'

'I don't watch children's films.' Smith shrugged and stood up. 'I'll have a talk with her, see if she wants to say anything. Good work with the shotgun back there, by the way. Bagged a couple of good'uns. Thanks for that.'

'No problem,' she said, and her shaking hand reached for another bottle of beer.

Suruk was bidding his comrades goodbye in the corridor. Smith glanced through the open hatch and caught a glimpse of their ship; crudely painted with symbols he could not recognise, the walls hung with trophy racks. 'Good plan back there, Suruk. You saved our skin.'

'I thank you. Besides, I have always owed you a debt.' Suruk drew a machete. 'Now, if you do not mind, the skull one of these alien stormtroopers will make a charming paperweight.'

Smith left Suruk to it and knocked on Rhianna's door.

'Hi, who's there?'

'Smith. Can I come in?'

'Sure,' she said, and he walked in. Rhianna was sitting up on the bed, reading a book about Tibet. The room smelt of joss sticks. She had brought cushions with her, it seemed – a choice that seemed both offensively new age and irritatingly feminine. The cushions had swirly patterns on them that seemed subliminally to invite him to throw them out the window.

'How're you?' she said. She looked very Bohemian, in an insipid way, and he rummaged through his mind, trying to establish who it was that she resembled. 'Well,' Smith began from the doorway, unsure of how to approach this situation, 'that *was* exciting, wasn't it?'

'You can close the door,' Rhianna said.

'Right.' He closed the door and stood in front of it.

She pulled her feet up and patted the end of the bed. 'Sit down if you want.'

'Absolutely.' He sat down. Smith suddenly realised who Rhianna reminded him of: Miss Brooke, his art teacher when he had been eight, and the first woman to whom he had ever been attracted. He had discovered this attraction shortly after Miss Brooke had found him stealing pencils, for which she had slapped him across the back of the head and paraded him in front of the class. He hoped the incident had not affected his psychological development. It would be unfortunate if he were only able to achieve sexual satisfaction by culminating a relationship in front of an audience of twenty jeering eight-year-olds.

'Well, that was something. Always good to have a crack at some alien types. Most of the time they deserve it, too.'

She nodded.

'Dangerous sort, your Ghast. Ferocious and organised. No moral fibre, though,' he added, feeling for reasons he could not pin down that he was digging himself into a hole that he could not yet see. 'Your Ghast's like your foreigner, you see – clever enough, in a low cunning sort of way, but ultimately not the ticket, not at all.'

Rhianna raised a finger. 'Can I just stop you there, bearing in mind that I *am* a foreigner?'

Ah, so that was it. His satisfaction in having located the hole was mollified by the knowledge that he had just jumped into it. 'You don't count, of course,' said Smith. 'I mean, it's not like you're French or anything. You're just … just… unusual, that's all.'

'That's sweet of you.'

'Thanks.' Smith was wary of being called 'sweet': like many men, he had always interpreted it as a euphemism for 'emasculated wimp'. Yet from Rhianna the usual undertone of being a spineless, easily-manipulated cretin was not there. He wished he knew how to deal with women. Life had not offered him much opportunity. Most of the girls on the Captains' Training Course seemed to have stepped from the work of either Tolkein or Wagner – sometimes, cruelly, both.

'I mean, my point is that your Ghast is not the right type at all. Were any of us bound to fall into his hands, he would treat us without a shred of decency. Whereas, of course, were you bound and falling into my hands, you can rest assured that I would never think of behaving indecently with – to – you. Quite.'

'Uh-huh?'

'Absolutely. So do you have magic powers?' he demanded, going in for the kill.

'Does Wicca count?'

'Baskets? No.'

'Then no. Why?'

'I just wondered.' A more subtle approach was required. 'Rhianna, when you go for walks, do animals come and dance round you?'

'Like in *Snow White*?'

'Exactly.'

'No. Isambard, did you get hit out there? In the head, perhaps?'

'No, I'm fine, thanks.'

'Thank you for defending me.' She shifted position, folding her legs under her, which had the effect of sliding her towards him slightly. Smith wished this conversation could be carried out in a larger room, preferably around a table and through intermediaries. 'I owe you, and your crew. Thank you.'

'Not at all,' he said. 'Not at all. And don't think you have to repay me in any way, financially or, otherwise. You are a guest on my ship, and your passage will remain free from my interference.'

She moved slightly, towards him. Smith sprang upright and lurched to the door. 'Right, see you later,' he said, and left.

The M'Lak ship was gone, and so were the Ghast bodies. There were only clues left to hint at the fight that had happened here: the wreckage of a couple of crates, patches of melted metal where stray disruptor bolts had hit the walls and the stain of oily Ghast blood on the floor. Smith hastened to the cockpit.

'Well, I think that covered it,' he announced, dropping into to the captain's chair.

Carveth was studying a clipboard. 'You were gone a while. Did you pump her for or in exchange for information?'

'Yes. Apparently she's not Snow White and she isn't magic either. Although she may be lying, of course. Didn't think of that. What've you got there?'

'It's a list of all the things wrong with this ship.'
'Bad news?'
'They could bring it out in paperback. That torpedo hit us hard. We've got serious damage to the thrusters, heat-warping in the secondary camshaft and the right-side emergency jet's completely knackered. We can't thrust, our shaft's bent and we'll probably never shoot off from the right hand again.'
'What sort of engines do the thrusters use?'
'Multi-stroke Wankel-rotary. Why?'
'Just wondered.'
'But that's not the worst of it. We've got no Supralux.'
'What does that all mean?'
'Well, we don't have a hope of repairing the damage unless we reach civilisation. But we can't move between systems and at our current state we won't get home for about thirty years.'
'Blast!' said Smith. 'We should have asked those Morlocks for help.'
'Are you kidding? They'd have given us a push straight into the sun. I don't know what their ships run on, but I wouldn't want to share jump-leads with them.'
'Good point, I suppose. What about the Ghasts?'
She shrugged. 'I don't know. If they're anything like I think they are they'll be sorting themselves out ready to come back for another go. You know, we could really do with a mechanic.'
'Aren't you the mechanic?'
She frowned. 'I'm the pilot. I can't be flying this thing and sticking it back together at once. Don't you know about spacecraft design?'

Smith shook his head. 'Nothing bigger than Airfix, I'm afraid. Balls: out of the frying pan and into the fire.' He sighed and checked Gerald's water. 'What do you suggest?'

'We've got no options. We'll have to put down at the nearest civilised world and see what they can do. If not civilised, then we'll have to make do with inhabited.'

Smith nodded. 'So we can make planetfall?'

Carveth said, 'Fall in the sense of dropping out the sky, yes. I'll try and steer us down, but we sure as hell won't be getting up again without a boost.'

'Right. Well, I suppose that's all we can do in the circumstances. Soon we'll be in Republic of Eden territory. They may be a bunch of trigger-happy fanatics, but they're mad enough for the Ghasts to stay out of their way.'

'How do you mean?' she said.

'I'll show you on the navigational computer. If I can find which bank of consoles it is.'

'There's a machine for locating it.'

'What, a satnav for the satnav?' The console bleeped, and Carveth pointed to a screen on which a three-dimensional mock-up of the galaxy spun slowly. Smith zoomed in on their position.

'We're still in New Fran's space, right?' he said. 'The sooner we cross the border into Republic space the better. The Franese are so wet they wouldn't raise a finger if the Ghasts started a war in their territory. But if the Ghasts start destroying neutral ships – like us – in Republic of Eden territory, they won't be welcome at all. The Republic's so heavily policed that the Ghasts won't dare attack us once we're in their space. You see?'

'That's smart,' Carveth said. 'But you know it's a bad week when you're looking to those tossers to keep you safe. Still, what choice have we got?' She sighed. 'Right you are, Boss. I'll set us a course straight for the border. Into the fire it is.'

462 sat in the captain's chair of the *Systematic Destruction*, drumming his pincers on the armrest. A minion stood beside him, polishing his helmet. 462 reached up and prodded the intercom.

'Praetorians to bridge!' he barked.

'We obey!' voices yelped back. He settled back in his seat and gloomily sipped at a glass of reddish liquid. It was pulped Ghast, made from one of his servants who had failed to display the requisite level of efficiency while performing some task. Behind him, hooves clanged on the floor as his personal guards arrived. His helmet-polisher cringed.

They were the Ghast elite-caste, bigger and darker-coloured than the crewmen who scurried about on the bridge trying to look busy and avoid being noticed. Under their helmets they had no faces, as such: just piggy little eyes and teeth. Their antennae stood to attention.

'Damage report!' 462 ordered.

'Damage severe, Glorious One! Craft mauled by M'Lak rabble! We fought them off, but they have caused extensive damage to secondary systems. The engineers report difficulty in repair.'

'Shoot the engineers,' 462 replied instinctively.

'We obey!'

The praetorians spun around, their hooves crashing down, and took one marching step away, coats flapping. The helmet-buffer breathed out again.

'Praetorians halt!' 462 yelled.

They stopped, stock-still.

'You can turn around,' he added.

The brutish heads faced him, waiting for him to speak.

462 bared his fangs in an evil smile. His eyes narrowed slightly. 'Cancel that last order,' he said. '*Threaten* to shoot the engineers.'

'A brilliant plan! Always we obey the genius of our commander!'

462 reflected that it was ideas like this that elevated him above the crowd.

The intercom burst into life with a trumpet-blast of martial music. 'Glorious 462, this is adjutant 7835—'

'Spare me the time. Your batch number is unimportant.'

'Of course! The Republic of Eden craft *Fist of Righteousness* approaches. Shall I hail the puny human scum?'

'No.' He stood up and pulled his coat closed. 'I will communicate with the weaklings myself. They shall be of use to us. After all, it is only proper that allies should speak face to face.' He chuckled to himself. His laughter grew in pitch and volume and, out of fear, the surrounding crew joined in like an orchestra backing its first violin. The bridge rang with cackling: it echoed around the weapon-racks, the huge picture of Number One, the banners and posters that decorated the walls.

'Your helmet is shined,' said the minion. 'Further orders?'

462 stopped laughing and looked at him. 'Prepare for victory!' he replied, and, laughing again, he strode off to meet his guests.

# 4

# One Night in Paradis

The *John Pym*'s working engine stuttered into life, a lonely, flickering light at the side of the ship. Gradually, the spaceship built up speed and swung towards the tiny Alcesdis system, at the very edge of Republic of Eden space. In the window, a blue dot appeared. Through the binoculars, Smith saw that it looked like a reshuffled Earth. The Haynes manual helped Carveth divert power from the broken engines to the working one and the ship approached in a loose, long arc until the whole of the window was taken up by cloud and the nose-cone glowed red as they began their descent onto a world called Paradis.

'We're in the upper atmosphere,' the pilot called. 'It's going to get rough. If you want to pray or use the loo, now's the time.' She turned to the captain. 'Anywhere in particular you'd like me to dump the ship?'

The *John Pym* cut deep into the layers of cloud. It rattled.

Smith typed at the console, searching the *Pym*'s onboard database. Something struck the underside of the ship, rocking it. 'I've got the *Rough Guide*,' he said. '"Paradis boasts fascinating bars where locals meet to discuss the crayfish harvest. Downtown has been rather overdeveloped and would appeal only to package tourists."' The toy soldier on the dashboard fell over. A storm raged around Parliament in the paperweight as Smith searched through the pages. 'But where are the bloody docks?'

Rhianna entered, pulled down one of the emergency seats and strapped herself in. 'Is everyone okay?' she asked.

'Great,' Carveth said between her teeth. 'How're you?'

'I have every faith in your abilities,' Rhianna replied, ducking and covering her head. The ship wobbled alarmingly. Wind buffeted them and flames lapped around the nose-cone.

'I've found the map!' Smith said. 'We're over land. Try to put it down just off the coast. Should there be all that fire at the front?'

'Don't look at me!' Carveth shouted back. She checked the scanners. 'This is looking bad, Cap. We'll have to ditch into the first lake we come to. Boss, I'm passing water now!'

'Cross your legs, woman!'

'Emergency parachute out!' The ship lurched as the parachute snagged the air, but it ploughed on. Carveth wrestled the control lever. At the edge of the windscreen, there was fire. 'Collision imminent – five, four—'

'Duck!' Smith cried. He threw his arms around his head. The ship hit something, twisted, struck something else and smashed into the water. The impact threw him forward and the seatbelt hit his chest as if he had been tossed against a fence; he coughed violently, flopped back again and gasped before he realised that he was still alive. Red lights flashed in the cockpit, a broken siren died with a slow, parping fart and then the room was full of the sparking of the control panel over his head.

Suddenly able to move again, he snapped open the straps and half-rolled, half-climbed out of his seat. Smith staggered over to the pilot's chair and pulled Carveth back.

Her eyes swam in her head. 'What ho, Captain,' she said uncertainly, and she groaned and rubbed her temple.

'Are you alright?'

'I'm fine. Look at the magic princess.'

Smith assumed she meant Rhianna and he lurched towards the door. Rhianna had curled into a ball in her seat, knees in front of her face. Slowly she unfolded. 'Are we done crashing yet?' she said.

'Yes,' Smith said.

Suruk looked around the doorframe. He seemed mildly curious. 'My ornaments have fallen down,' he said. 'Are you deceased?'

Rhianna unbuckled the seat harness with numb fingers, blinking. Smith offered her a hand and she got up.

Carveth had pushed a finger through the bars of the hamster cage and was wiggling it to get Gerald's attention. Smith reflected that after what must seem an earthquake to a small animal, the last thing Gerald would want to see would be a gigantic worm come to prod him back to life. Still, Gerald's trauma could wait. There were more important things to do.

'I'm going to scout around,' he declared.

'Use the top hatch,' Carveth said. 'We're floating.'

Smith paced out of the cockpit and down the corridor,

pushing his way past fallen wires like an explorer passing through fronds. He crossed the lounge and stepped into the hold. Smith climbed the steps to the airlock, glanced round and was surprised to find Rhianna behind him. 'Hello again,' he said, taking hold of the lever that opened the roof hatch. 'Are you alright?'

She looked slightly concussed, which was no change from the norm. 'I'm fine,' she said. 'How are you?'

'Been worse.' Struggling to remember when, he pulled the lever and the hatch swung open, revealing a circle of shockingly blue sky. A blast of fresh air hit him like some drug too potent for his system to take on board, leaving him reeling from its purity. 'Let's have a look around.'

He climbed the rungs and scrambled out onto the roof, into the clean air. Rhianna followed and he leaned down and held his hand out to help her up, getting a full view of her cleavage, such as it was. As she climbed out it suddenly occurred to Smith that the ship might still be hot from entering the atmosphere and he checked lest Rhianna's flip-flops melted onto the roof. It was merely warm, and she climbed out and stood up next to him.

They were on the edge of a lake. It was a warm day in Paradis's equivalent of early summer and the light was hard and bright. Conifers stood on the bank. Geese flapped across the sky toward a slow-moving alien creature that looked like a cross between a pterodactyl and a handkerchief. A light breeze stirred Rhianna's flares.

'What a view,' Smith said.

Rhianna stood on tiptoes and took an enormous breath, tossed her head back and threw out her arms with alarming enthusiasm. 'God, I love being outdoors,' she proclaimed.

'Yes, absolutely,' said Smith. 'Bit of fresh air, eh?'

'Oh, yes!' Her eyes were closed and her sleek, elfin face turned towards the sun. 'I really feel much closer to everything – to the world – like this. I love being in touch with nature.'

'Well, yes. Rather pleasant, really.' Smith agreed with her, but he felt uncomfortable in this line of talk. His own view of nature was intrinsically linked to hiking boots and the smell of waxed canvas in jaunty, masculine company. Most of the women he knew who claimed to love the outdoors were stocky beings called Hillary, who enjoyed shouting 'Come on, then!' at Labradors. Rhianna's idea of getting in touch with the countryside, he suspected, might well involve getting in touch with herself in a countryside setting. This, although appealing, was rarely covered in *The Rambler's Periodical*. He kicked and shoved his brain onto cleaner thoughts, like a riot policeman encouraging a sit-down protester to 'move along'.

'Alright up there?' Carveth yelled from below.

'We're both fine,' Smith called back, sounding slightly guilty.

'Got a dinghy here,' Carveth said. 'I found it in a locker. You'll need it to row to the bank.'

'Good idea.' Smith climbed through the hatch and back into the greasy atmosphere of the hold. A large yellow dinghy lay inflated by Carveth's boots.

Something occurred to Carveth and she looked down at

the dinghy, which was about four feet wide, and then back up at the hatch, which was two feet across.

'Oh, *arse*,' she said. 'I knew I was doing something wrong when I blew it up.'

Carveth rowed the dinghy to the riverbank. Rhianna watched the other three from the roof of the ship.

Smith stepped out onto dry land. Rhianna waved and he waved back. 'Good luck!' she called.

'Thanks!'

'Yeah, good luck,' Carveth said from the dinghy. 'You know,' she added, 'we're forty miles from the nearest town on the map. Are you guys sure this is a good idea?'

'I'm sure. We'll try to get to higher ground and put a signal out. If anyone wants to find us, it'll be the signal they pick up, not the ship.'

The pilot frowned. 'I suppose so. Look, Captain…'

'Yes?'

'It's Rhianna they want, isn't it?'

He looked back at her, sunning herself on the blackened back of their ship. 'I think so. That's why she's staying here with you. Out of danger.'

'If you two need anything… ' Faced with the novelty of expressing helpfulness, Carveth's vocabulary ran dry. 'You know what to do.' She reached into the boat and passed him the shotgun.

'Thanks, Carveth. But I got us into this, and it's my job to get us out.'

'*They* got us into this. The Ghasts, I mean.'

'Yes, mainly.' He gazed back at the ship, his eyes vacant. 'You know, the Empire really sent us out here as a decoy, a lure to draw the Ghasts out, like a goat left out for a tiger. But the Ghasts were smarter than they thought and blew up the *Tenacious* before it could get them. So now there isn't any hunter any more. It's us, the goat, against the tiger.'

'I know,' she said. 'But you're doing alright, considering.'

'Let's get going,' Smith said. He turned and stalked into the woods, Suruk strolling by his side.

Four hours later, Smith returned.

'Burning,' Suruk said.

It was approaching dusk and the light was deep and ripe. Insects made the air shudder. The white, battered tail of the ship stuck into the air like the fin of a shark that has let itself go and turned to beer and pies.

On the bank, Carveth and Rhianna were sitting on packing crates. Several beer bottles and a good deal of food wrappers lay around their feet. Carveth glanced up and passed Rhianna the strange device she had acquired on New Fran, the one she had described as an ant farm. There was an odd smell in the air, like paper and spice being cooked together, a dry, herbal smell.

Carveth looked up. 'Hey, Captain. You joining us?'

Smith strode towards her.

'Find anything? Settlements? People? Pirate treasure?'

Smith got close, and his face was hard. 'What on Earth is this?' he demanded.

Carveth blinked. 'Nothing much. We're just having a bit of… ' she glanced at Rhianna hopefully.

'Quality time,' Rhianna said.

'Right. Quality time for us ladies. You gentlemen are welcome to join us, of course.'

'Certainly not! You are a British naval operative, and you are quite obviously drunk! You should be manning a lookout, or building a house out of sticks or something.' He paused and sniffed the air, turning his neck as if to inspect a halo. 'And it reeks of marijuana.'

Carveth said, 'Among the cognoscenti, one does not pronounce the J.'

'Well I'm not the cognoscenti, thank you, and I intend to complete this mission without being pot-crazed on blow reefers. While you have been tripping the fantastic light with Jenny Spliff—'

'Mary Jane,' Rhianna said quietly.

'Whatever – I'm not a drug fiend – *I* have been out on a recce to get this transmitter set up. I have had to climb every mountain—'

'And ford every stream?' Carveth asked. She sniggered.

'Right! That's it! I've walked an awfully long way just to come back and find you lazing around off your head. What've you done to help, eh, other than get squiffed and blow bubbles in your ant-farm?'

'It's not an ant-farm, it's a bong. Christ, Captain, just try to relax, would you? Calm down.'

'I will not calm down! I am a British officer—'

'I know that. And I'm not.' Suddenly, she seemed very calm. The bank was silent other than the lapping of water against the ship. Far off, geese honked. 'Please, sit down. God, Cap, if you get wound up any more your head'll pop. Just sit. We'll talk about it.'

'Alright,' he said. 'But I don't condone any of this,

young lady android, not for one moment. And I think you're a disgrace to your job, taking illegal substances when we have a duty to repair our ship.'

'Can I say something?' Rhianna said.

Smith lowered himself onto one of the boxes. 'Well, alright. I suppose so.'

'Why don't we just talk it through, okay? We don't have to fight. Come on, guys. Let's be nice about this, huh? Let's just calm down, find our happy space, make a truth circle and begin to deal with our issues through dialogue instead of shouting, okay?'

'Bollocks to that.'

'Excuse me.' Suruk stepped forward. They had forgotten about him, all of them. The alien seemed dignified, oddly civilised for having avoided the argument so far. 'May I make a suggestion? Among our people there is a custom for resolving disputes of this sort so that all have an equal chance to make their point, and none lose honour by doing so.'

'Does this by any chance involve an arena and sharp knives?' Carveth said.

The alien said, 'You've done it too?'

'Let's take it easy,' Carveth said. 'Talk first, decapitations later.'

'Huh,' Suruk replied. 'There is a reason why we refer to you as *puny* humans.'

'Captain Smith,' Rhianna began, 'I can understand you're in a difficult position at the moment. But I really think you ought to make an effort to relax—'

'She's right,' Carveth put in. 'No offence, but you're pretty anally retentive. I'd put big money that you've sat on a broom before and found it was gone when you stood up. If your arse gets any tighter you'll crap spaghetti.'

Rhianna smiled. 'Well, perhaps that's a bit hard, Polly.'

'Only if you're a repressed neurotic.'

'Right!' cried Smith, leaping to his feet. 'I am not a repressed neurotic and I don't want to talk about it ever again!'

He stormed off into the trees.

'Curious,' Suruk said.

Rhianna started to put her shoes on. This took a lot of concentration.

'I'll do it,' Carveth said. 'You stay here.'

Smith had gone ten yards before he realised that there was nowhere to go to, but he was obliged to go thirty more before he could stop and try to work out what to do. He wondered what it was that had sent him storming out of the group like a pellet shot from a rubber band. Only as he stood here, the midges buzzing around his head, did he realise that he couldn't tell what was driving him.

Carveth's obvious incompetence? No. He did not even think she truly was incompetent. She had made an excellent job of landing a crippled ship. No matter how irritating she might be, it was largely due to her flying skills that they had landed without being reduced to the consistency of Marmite.

Of course, that didn't stop her from being a lazy pain in the arse.

And then there was Rhianna. Rhianna, with her nonsense about holding hands and chanting to the great pixie, her meditation and lentil food, her nice ankles and long brown hair. She meant well, of course, and that was the problem. Her motives were good – and her physique, he suspected, was excellent. And he had no idea how to get her, either. For all that it mattered, she might as well have been on the other end of the galaxy.

He stood there, the hot night air close around him like a blanket, and realised where his anger really came from. Fleet control had set him up. He had been given this mission not because he was a brilliant captain but the opposite. Khan had chosen him as the kind of fool who would negotiate space with the casual grace of a toddler in a bathtub, leaving so many bubbles in his wake that the Ghasts could not fail to notice. Then the Ghasts would make their move, and then the *Tenacious* would spring on them, save the day and reveal the predatory attacks the aliens were making on Imperial shipping. And in the process, save the idiot crew of the *John Pym* from their own stupidity. It was not him who was supposed to protect Rhianna at all. He had never been expected to do anything except look like an easy target. That knowledge stung.

'Boss.' Carveth approached, a beer bottle in each hand. 'Fancy a bribe?'

'Please,' he said. He took the bottle she held out. 'Thank you. You've not poisoned it?'

'Absolutely not.' She waited until he took a swig and said, 'Spit isn't poisonous, is it?'

Smith whirled around and she grinned at him. Smith forced a smile back.

'You know, you'd be right about all of this,' she said, 'all this stoned on the job stuff, if I really was a pilot.'

He stopped smiling. 'What? I don't understand,' he said.

'I'm not a pilot – at least, not a qualified one. My documents are forged. I'm self-taught.'

'I don't see what you mean.'

'I'm a fake, Smith.'

'But you're a simulant. You're built to be a pilot. They wouldn't make you otherwise.'

'They made me for a purpose,' she said. 'But it wasn't that.'

He took a very small step back from her, turning a little. The sword was on his belt; he could draw it more easily with his right side facing her. 'Then what are you?' he said.

'I'm a sex toy.'

'What?'

'I'm a custom built sex toy.'

'But you – you can't be. I mean, you don't look sufficiently…'

'Inflatable?'

'No, that's not what I mean. You don't look like you'd be… sufficiently…'

'Attractive?'

'No, no. That's not what I meant at all. No. You're not unattractive in the slightest – you're just, well – *different*. I didn't mean to imply that you wouldn't be attractive enough to qualify as – sod it, yes, that's exactly what I meant.'

He looked at her. Carveth was watching him keenly, as if worried that she might miss him do a trick. 'Well?' he demanded. 'What?' It seemed profoundly unfair that he was now feeling the need to apologise for having criticised faults that were self-evidently true. How did women manage that? 'It's just that I... ah... happen to look upon you as a crewmember, and I find it difficult to envisage you not as a fully rounded person, but as a mere sex object.'

Carveth stuck her hands out like a cartoon robot and made a huge O with her mouth. 'This help?'

He shuddered. 'Rather too much, actually.'

She lowered her arms. 'You're right, though. I'm hardly *my* type, let alone anyone else's. I was developed for one particular man. They custom-made me according to answers to a questionnaire. Apparently I'm exactly the girl he was looking for. Except for the hair, of course. I dyed that over the sink.'

'I did wonder.'

'So there you go. I overheard them discussing it: they talked about it outside the tank they grew me in. First chance I got, I overpowered the head scientist and got out. Luckily there were some items of restraint nearby.'

'But what about your pilot's licence?'

'I forged it.'

'But it has a signature from the Ministry of Trade.'

'Me.'

'And a picture of the Minister.'

'Me in a hat.'

Smith stared at her in the growing dark. Never had she looked so sincere, or so pretty, strangely enough. She had never talked like this before: the jaunty, facetious part of her was gone, lifted up like a shell to expose the rawness beneath. 'I believe you,' he said.

'I just thought I'd mention it. I mean, the Ghasts'll be looking for us, and, well, it's good to get it off my chest.'

'That's quite alright,' he said.

'Sorry to piss you off.'

'Don't worry about it. You're a very good pilot, by the way.'

'I downloaded the information straight to my cerebellum. Well, most of it. I was in a hurry.'

'Who ordered you to be made?'

'Paul Devrin, from the Devrin Corporation. They're rich beyond anything either of us will ever know. There are planets that they run. That's how he was able to get away with it. Apparently he's so depraved no normal woman will sleep with him. Typical, eh? The man I was made to meet would freak out the Marquis de Sade.' She sighed. 'So, er, there you go. Let's get back, shall we?'

'Did they mess with your mind? I know simulant personalities are pre-built.'

'I'm not sure. I'm surprised how independently-minded I am. Perhaps they did tamper with my head.'

'Probably just dropped you on it.'

'I don't know. I have a feeling there is something there, some kind of behavioural inhibitor. Sometimes I find it difficult not to make innuendo, for instance – not just sexual stuff, but anything childish and crude. I'll be talking normally, as we are now, and all of a sudden it just flops out in front of everyone. Before I know what's happening it'll be gushing in full flow and I'll have made such a mess that it's hardly worth trying to zip up again.'

'True. So is Carveth your real name, then?'

'In as much as any.' She shrugged. 'I chose it myself. Pollyanna Carveth. What do you think?'

'Very good. Fancy building someone, a real person, just so you can do perverted things to them. Now that,' Smith said thoughtfully, 'that is the lowest thing I have ever heard of anyone doing.'

'Apparently he can go much lower, once he's got the right props.'

'Well, as far as I'm concerned, you're *bona fide*. You're the pilot, and that's that. Although I'd appreciate it if you would download the rest of the pilot's manual.'

'Cheers, Boss.'

'If ever we work out how to get out of here, I'll do everything I can to see that you don't go back.'

'And I'll make sure that we do get out of here. So we're friends again?'

'Yes. Let's go and have a drink, shall we?'

'Aye aye, Captain,' Carveth said, and they turned back to the ship.


Morning jumped on Isambard Smith and bashed him awake. Suddenly he was alive again – too much alive, for the colours of the sitting room burned into his head as though he'd fallen asleep against a neon sign. He staggered upright like a poorly animated marionette and his brain shifted alarmingly inside his skull. Something fell off the front of him and stupidly, like the living dead, he turned round to see what it might be. It was Carveth's boot.

Carveth herself was stretched out on the sofa opposite. So why was her boot on him? He remembered their argument last night. Had she given it to him as a token of friendship or, more likely, mistaken him for a doormat? Perhaps she had simply flung it at his head. That seemed like a satisfactory explanation. Like the sole survivor of an apocalypse emerging from underground, he wonderingly surveyed the wreckage around him and decided to leave it well alone. It was Carveth's mess and so she should clear it up. It was probably hers, anyway.

In the bathroom he started brushing his teeth, then discovered that the toothpaste tube looked very similar to something of Rhianna's called *Balsamic Foot Salve: For Calloused and Hard Skin*. He resumed his search for the toothpaste with renewed urgency.

Teeth cleaned, Smith decided to get some air. Yes, that seemed like a good idea. He reached the main airlock before he remembered that opening it would sink the ship. Lucky one, that, he thought as he stepped back from the door. You can't fool me. I'm the captain. Sharp as a razor. He shambled towards the hold.

Rhianna's door was open and she slept, fully clothed, on top of her bed. She looked pretty, apart from the small pool of dribble that had accumulated at the corner of her mouth. There were three empty bottles on the shelf. Odd, Smith thought, that she would drink. Ah yes: it was that organic stuff he'd bought on New Fran.

Wasn't organic beer supposed not to give you hangovers? What charlatan had said that? He left the room. In the hold he climbed the rungs, swaying on them like an old salt approaching the crow's nest in a storm. Hot light caught his face as he struggled out onto the roof of the crippled ship.

Suruk crouched on the roof, his back to Smith. The

alien was looking out across the lake, almost totally immobile. The air was fresh and seemed to carry in it a little of the life-force that had oozed out of him and been replaced with beer. On a small island in the lake, a heron peered quizzically into the distance, surrounded by reeds.

'Greetings, Mazuran,' Suruk said.

'Hello,' he ventured.

'I knew your footsteps. It is a fine morning, friend. I find that the rhythm of life flows well in a place like this. All seems connected.'

'It'd be better if my brain wasn't pickled in hurt.'

'Indeed.' Suruk stood up smoothly. 'How are the females?'

'Asleep.'

'Did you spawn with them?'

'Certainly not!'

'Humans. You have a very complicated breeding system.' He shrugged. 'Being asexual certainly has its advantages. I do not have to bother with lengthy courtship rituals.'

'Must be good,' Smith said, rubbing his head and staring across the water.

'It is. Although at times I have returned from meeting fellow warriors and asked of myself, "What time do I call this, reeling in drunk to my own bed? How can I be the humanoid I married years ago?" '

Smith pinched his brow. It sounded like the plot of a Phillip K Dick novel he had once tried to read. 'Don't. You're making my head spin. We've got to work out how to get this ship repaired.'

'True. But there is a more urgent problem, Smith.'

'Really? What's that?'

'Listen.' Suruk cocked his head. Smith listened and, in the stillness of the morning, he heard it too: the sound of a boat engine becoming louder as it approached. 'Friend or enemy, Mazuran, they come for us.'

# 5

# Taken Up the Bayou

The boat was small and low, hardly larger than a rowing boat. A tubby black man sat in the bows, steering the craft. Behind him, a thin white man in a baseball cap took a drag on a rolled cigarette and glanced left and right, a rifle hanging from his shoulder.

By the time they drew close, Suruk had gone. 'Don't hurt anyone unless I say,' Smith said as Carveth and Rhianna joined him, hoping that Suruk would hear.

Carveth had the shotgun. 'Here, Boss. Just in case.' She slipped him the revolver and he pushed it into the back of his trousers.

'Hey there!' the pilot of the boat shouted over the chugging engine. 'How're you doin'?'

'Hello!' Smith called back. 'Very well, thank you, except that our ship won't fly.'

'Wondered what got you down here,' the steersman said. 'Crash land, did you?'

'That's right.'

He cut the engines. The thin man threw his cigarette into the water. 'We're the law,' the thin man said.

'Police?'

'They don't bloody look like it,' Carveth muttered.

'Local militia,' the thin man said. 'If that thing sinks, we get salvage rights.'

'Now, Francois,' the black man said. 'That's no way to say hello. He's right, though. My name's Andy Delacroix, and this here's Francois Laveille – my deputy. Welcome to Paradis.'

'Careful, men,' Smith whispered sagely. 'They may not be trustworthy. This Francois fellow sounds rather French to me.' He cleared his throat and declared: 'I am Isambard Smith, captain of this ship. This is my crew. We need to get our ship running again,' Smith called. 'Do you know of any shipyards that could help us get into orbit?'

The two men looked at one another and conferred. Francois shrugged and spat into the water. Smith turned to Carveth. 'Definitely French,' he said.

'You've got what's known as a problem,' Andy called back. 'Sure, there's places you could get fixed up, but you won't be able to get off-world without payin'. And there's a tax on that.'

'A tax?'

'Air pollution,' Francois said, and he gave a short, snorting laugh. He took off his cap and studied the inside.

'Hell,' said Carveth.

'This is a bad thing, right?' Rhianna asked.

Francois nodded. 'You people want to get off-world, you've got to get past the defence grid, otherwise you get a missile in the tailpipe. And the man who controls the grid'll want to squeeze you people till your pips squeak.'

Andy nodded. 'My deputy is right. For the right price, we could fix up your ship ourselves. But it would be useless to you 'less you pay Corveau to let you go. And he's a hard man to bargain with.'

'Who's Corveau?' Carveth demanded.

'Some other Frenchie,' Smith said.

'*Governor* Corveau,' Andy replied. 'You don't wanna argue with that guy. He answers straight to Edenite authority.'

Smith frowned. He had spotted Suruk, pressed against a tree that overhung the ship. Slowly, like a spider, the alien was crawling out across the branches, ready to drop into the boat.

'Could you take us to a shipyard?' Smith asked.

Francois grinned. 'We can take you to the next best thing. Hop on in. That's what I do, see, repair machines. We can take you there right now.'

'I thought you said you were militiamen.'

'God no. That's just what we have to do.' Francois looked at his rifle and shrugged. 'You don't think I carry this round for fun, do you?'

The boat chugged and spluttered along the length of the lake, keeping close to the shore. Smith and Carveth stood at the back, watched by Francois: Andy, in his role as captain, steered. Carveth carried the shotgun, and the revolver was stashed in Smith's belt, hidden by his coat. Carveth leaned in and whispered, 'Is this a good idea?' The engine hid her voice from the two men.

'Which part of it?'

'Pick one.'

'Probably not. But we don't have any choice.' Smith glanced up and saw that Francois was watching them, his rifle lying across his lap. 'Look, we need to get the ship running as fast as possible. These people may be able to help.'

'And if they choose not to help? If they decide to sell our ship for scrap?'

'We'll just have to shoot them, I suppose. Anyhow, we need to get out of here before the Ghasts come looking for Rhianna. The Republic of Eden may be neutral, but that won't stop the Ghasts trying to sneak down here.'

'Fair enough. I'm not sure we should have left Rhianna back there with the big frog, though. They're a pair of space cadets.'

'Making you a space expert, I suppose.'

'Comparatively, yeah. There probably won't be a ship left by the time we get back. No offence to your friend, by the way.'

'None taken.'

Carveth looked up. Francois was watching her. 'You folks enjoying the ride?'

'Oh, absolutely,' she replied. 'I've often thought that I don't get taken up the bayou frequently enough. Dear God, save me from my stupid mouth.'

Up ahead they saw the trees part to make room for a slipway. Behind it, a set of long, metal buildings sat in the long grass like the outhouses of a farm. Smith squinted through the trees, trying to make out the purpose of the buildings as Andy turned the boat. A washing line hung between a large shed and a second building shaped like a giant glasses case.

'Not quite salubrious,' Smith said under his breath.

'Sure puts the fab in prefab.' Carveth fingered her

shotgun. 'I'd feel safer carrying a much larger penis substitute.'

'You think this is dangerous, Carveth?'

'Look at this place. It couldn't get more hairy if it shacked up with a mammoth. I can hear the banjos already. These people probably have one surname per thousand miles.'

Smith whispered, 'I'm sure they're fine.'

'I just hope you're well up on your pig-squealing, that's all.'

Andy spun the wheel, and as the boat came in close they saw a woman by the slipway, throwing a toy for a speckled, stubby-headed dog. The dog leaped on it, shook it, and tossed it under a squat, four-wheeled bike. Behind the buildings, Smith caught sight of a small crane rising above the complex like the neck of a dinosaur. Andy waved at the woman, and she blew an extravagant kiss. The boat chugged to the land and Francois hopped ashore to tie it up.

Andy motioned for them to get off. 'Y'all go on ahead. We won't bite you or nothin'.'

Smith and Carveth stepped onto dry land and stood awkwardly beside the boat. 'Hey there, Marie!' Andy called, and he strode up the slipway and embraced her.

'Hey. Who's this?' the woman demanded. She was tanned, about forty, wearing jeans and a short-sleeved shirt. Her hair was thick and brown.

'Some English guys who crashed a ways down,' Andy said. 'We were out on patrol when we heard 'em. Sounds like their ship needs fixing.'

'Ship, uh?'

'That's absolutely right, madam,' Smith said, stepping forward. He put out his hand. 'My name is Isambard Smith, captain of the spaceship the *John Pym*. We were attacked in an act of piracy and forced to crash-land here. As it stands, we're very badly damaged, our Supralux drive is broken, and we are unlikely to be able to leave this world until full repairs are carried out. And I'm informed by these gentlemen that this is the right place to have them done.'

She gave a quick snort of laughter. 'If you're flyin' a lawnmower. You happen to have any engines made out of a vacuum cleaner, you should be okay.'

Carveth leaned across to him. 'I don't think we do,' she whispered. 'But I'm not positive.'

'That ain't fair now,' Francois called as he walked up from the boat. 'I ain't saying I can fix their drive, sure. But it ain't just tractors. Jets, stabilisers, I know all about them. You remember that car I fitted up last year?'

'That lawnmower?' Marie said.

'That weren't just any lawnmower: it was jet-powered. It cut the grass fine, but I gave up using it. Burned my shins.' He looked at Smith. Smith's eyes moved from one to the other, across the faces of the three locals to the doubting expression on his pilot's face.

'Righty-ho,' Smith said. 'We'll bring the ship down to you right away.'

Suruk and Rhianna passed an interesting hour together in the hold. Indeed, they were getting on so well that neither paid much attention when the upper hatch opened and Carveth looked inside.

'Holy cack!' she exclaimed. 'He's throwing knives at her head, Cap!'

Smith put his head through the hatch, next to Carveth's. 'You there!' he called. 'Stop throwing knives at Rhianna, Suruk.'

The alien looked up. 'But—'

'Right, that's it. If you two can't be nice I'll just have to come down.'

Smith climbed down the rungs and into the hold. It was an odd sight, more suited to a circus than a spacecraft. Rhianna sat against the cargo doors, eyes closed in concentration. A number of knives were scattered around her, including most of the ship's cutlery. Suruk, always a tad freakish at the best of times, stood at the far end of the hold beside a tray full of forks.

'It seems I can't leave you for five minutes without the carnival coming to town,' said Smith. 'What the Dickens has been going on here?'

Carveth jumped down behind him. 'Hello Rhianna, hello Thing.' She peered at the blades laid out around Rhianna's feet. 'Looks like you've been playing patience with sharp objects. You've got a two-pair of flick-knives there.'

Smith folded his arms and tapped his foot. 'Well, Suruk?'

'The woman is immune to blades,' Suruk said.

'What's that supposed to mean?'

The alien flexed his tusks. 'She appears to be able to deflect the weapons as they approach. The knives you see around her are ones I threw to test this theory. She entered a state of concentration and my blades could not strike.'

Rhianna opened her eyes. 'It's totally weird. He throws, and I think, and it just goes away! Really weird. You look kind of sceptical.'

Smith said quietly, 'Does this ship carry sedatives, Carveth?'

'Even if it did, they'd be in me by now.'

'Well, that's odd,' the captain said. 'Dangerous, though. I think you'd best stop in case Rhianna loses concentration and you give her antennae by mistake. And pick up the cutlery, would you? I don't want that going back into the dresser unwashed. We're going downriver, by the way,' he added, striding towards the living room. 'There's a couple of chaps there who think they can repair the jets.'

As he reached the door, Carveth called, 'Captain?'

'Yes?'

'Sorry to stop you there. I know you're busy. But, just out of interest, has anyone else noticed that this woman is an unnatural freak?'

'No,' said Smith.

'No,' said Suruk.

'I prefer "alternative",' Rhianna said.

Carveth raised her hands and made a placating gesture with her palms. 'Right. Alright, then. I'm clearly in a minority. I appreciate that my views may seem out of place, or even extreme – *but this is really really weird!*' She looked around the room. 'Doesn't this whole magic force-field thing strike anyone as wrong?' she concluded, piteously.

Smith rubbed his chin. 'See your point there,' he said. 'But we do have a spacecraft to get going. We can test this out later, but first we need to get the ship moved. Carveth, you're the expert. On paper, anyway. Which you forged. Could you steer us downriver, please?'

It was raining. It never stopped on Carver's Rock. Rain sliced across the rooftops, over neon signs and the backs of vast apartment blocks, steady and relentless as if God was trying to wash the sin from the dirty streets.

God might be omnipotent, Rick Dreckitt thought, but He'd never manage that.

He pulled his coat close around him and wandered through the street, past pedestrians of a thousand different sorts, guilty of a thousand different crimes. He thought about the gun in his jacket, warm against his side.

A floating billboard crawled across the sky above his head. 'Go to a different off-world colony!' it cried. 'Why stay here when you can begin again?'

Dreckitt paused at the entrance to Joleen's. 'Damn right,' he said at the billboard.

'So go already!' it replied, and he ducked under the lintel and stepped out of the rain and into the smoke.

A Nick Cave record was playing on the jukebox at the wrong speed. Mr Cave was describing, in elaborate and unnecessary detail, how he had single-handedly slaughtered the patrons of a bar not unlike this one. He was currently killing a man with an ashtray as big as a really big brick. Dreckitt glanced at the ashtray on a nearby table. Some other time.

Behind the bar, a thin woman slowly rubbed a towel along a row of dusty glasses. The ceiling fan turned lazily, just fast enough to prevent anyone throwing a rope over it. A fat man sat in a booth, weeping.

'Home,' Dreckitt said. He walked to the bar. 'What kind of rye do you deal in a two-bit joint like this?'

'Same as last night, pal,' the woman said, not looking up.

'Same as last night, then.' He took his drink and sat down, alone. Nobody joined him. He sipped.

Someone prodded him in the back. 'Rick.'

'Waldo,' he said, not looking round.

Waldo was sweating: his dirty face seemed to drip the stuff. He wore a dirty hat and a dirty leather jacket wrapped around his gut. He was quite dirty. Dreckitt looked around. 'You're dirty, Waldo,' he said.

'Good to see ya, Rick.'

'Sit down,' he replied. 'You're blocking my view of some dead flies.'

Waldo sat down. 'I saw what you did last night, Rick. Impressive piece of work.'

'Yeah.'

Waldo glanced around the room. 'You celebrating, then?'

'Yep. I'm throwing a party. Jim Beam's here already and I'm expecting Johnny Walker to drop by later on.'

'You and Jim Beam, huh? That's good. You always were a funny guy, Rick.'

'Yeah. Drinking here, while in the neon city outside the rich get richer and the bullets cut the night. Where everyone bets on the long shots and tomorrow never comes. When I sit here and remember things I wish weren't real.'

'You do know it's happy hour down at Hooters, don't you?'

'You think I want to spend my time with a bunch of other people, drinking cheep beer and staring at waitresses' tits all night?'

'Yes.'

'Waldo, I look at them and I see death. I see a whole load of blood.'

'Tits? You're unwell, Rick.'

'People. I've gone down this dark street a long way, Waldo. Too long, further than any android ought to go. And it's getting to me. I don't know what to think in this fake town of cheap dreams and broken futures.'

'You ever think of taking a break from the juice, Rick?'

'I'm taking a break alright. From this. From the killing. For good.'

'What're you telling me?'

'I'm quit.'

'What?'

'I'm quit. I'm an android. I shouldn't be doing this. I should stick my elbows out and say pansy things about protocol, not go round killing people.'

'Hey, don't give me that! You do what you're made to do!'

'The four I killed last night . . . they could have been me. That last one, the guy in the suit – I shot him, and I looked into his eyes as he died. He could have been an android, just like me. There was nothing there: no soul, no mercy, just coldness. Less human than human. Like me.'

'Which one was he?'

'The lawyer.'

Waldo shrugged. 'Well, that explains it. It happens to a

lot of androids, Rick. They kill some human with no morals or compassion, and they think it could be them. You're not the first.'

'I look at these people and think, they could be simulants.'

'You're not quitting, Rick. You're the best. I need you to work your magic on somebody.'

'No way.'

'Yes way. Because things happen to androids who don't help. Androids who start with this crazy talk about seeing humans like machines. Who start to see no feelings when there's feelings there. You want to be careful, Rick, turning me down like this. You might wake up one morning and find a severed head gasket on the pillow next to you.' Waldo wiped sweat from his brow. 'The target's a woman. Full of life. Friendly, instinctive, humane. All the things you're not. Nothing like an android.'

Dreckitt looked up, but he said nothing. He waited.

'She's a human,' Waldo said again. 'A meatbag. The company wants her dead.'

He passed Dreckitt a photograph. Dreckitt studied it, committing the face to memory. It was a pleasant, quirky-looking woman, quite pretty but not remarkable. He tilted the picture to get a better view of the sides of her face, and turned it over so he could see the back of her head. He had a feeling that she would be small.

'What did she do?'

'What do you care? Company wants her dead. And Company means Republic round here. And Republic means a one-way ticket to the scrapheap for godless androids who don't play ball.'

Dreckitt snorted. 'I'll do it. But this is the last, and I mean it. This dirty city sickens me. Don't you think I get tired of the blood, the corruption, the Panama hats? I'm getting out, Waldo. I've got savings. I'm going to retire somewhere warm, get me some metal claws and carry off some dames.' He downed his drink and stood. 'But until then, I'll do it. Make sure there's a ship down at the strip.' He peered at the name under the photograph. 'Polly Carveth. Too bad for you, Miss Carveth.'

Waldo watched Dreckitt disappear into the rain, and then walked down the road to Hooters.

They climbed out of the roof hatch and looked at Andy's farm.

'Hey boys,' Andy called, strolling over. 'What's going on?'

'Not a lot,' Smith said.

'Got some fish on the barbecue,' Andy said. 'Way I see it, if we're going to get custom like yours, might as well make sure you come back a second time.'

Carveth glanced back at Smith as she climbed down onto the wing. 'How're we paying for all this?'

Smith whispered, 'I'm working on a plan for that.'

'This doesn't involve shiny used rifle cartridges, does it?'

The ship lay in the water like a boat, and Andy walked to the edge to help the crew step onto land. 'Ma'am,' he said, nodding to Carveth.

Smith gestured back towards the ship. 'And this is Miss Mitchell, a friend of mine.'

Andy nodded. 'Pleased to meet you, Miss Mitchell. I trust – *Sacre merde!* What the hell is that?'

'Suruk the Slayer, doom purveyor,' the alien proclaimed, kicking the hatch closed behind him. His first thumbs were hooked over his belt, his tusks lowered in a friendly greeting. 'Son of Agshad Nine-Swords, grandson of Urgar the Miffed. I offer you my hand in friendship and my blade as a warrior. You name it, I'll maim it.'

Andy chuckled. 'You learn yourself all that?'

'It's teach. And yes, I did.' Suruk bowed.

Thoughtfully, Andy shook his head. 'Well, he sure is something. What, I'm not quite sure. Thank you, Mr Suruk. And I'm Andy Delacroix, victor of absolutely nothing. Over there's Francois Laveille, lord of the lawnmower. It's a pleasure, all of you.'

'Thanks,' said Smith. 'It's good of you.'

Francois wandered over, half a sandwich in his hand. He stood there, studying the four of them, his mouth moving slowly as if chewing the cud. 'So now,' he declared, 'which one of you's ship's engineer?'

'Me,' Carveth said. 'At least, I've been in the engine room.'

'Any chance of the tour?'

'Why of course,' she replied. 'Hop on.'

Smith watched as Francois climbed onto the *John Pym*. Then he turned and walked up the bank with Andy, Suruk and Rhianna at his side.

'Here,' Andy said, gesturing to a plastic table and some chairs. ''Fraid it's probably not what you're used to, back in your ship.'

'Well, it's not rusty, but I can get used to it.' The four of them sat down in front of what seemed to be Andy's house: a long metal building like a scaled-up, polished

Nissen hut. It looked at once ancient and advanced, like a 1950's idea of what the future might be.

Marie strode over. She was tallish, with handsome features and quick, clever eyes. 'You people hungry?'

Andy slapped his large belly, setting his T-shirt rippling. 'Sure am.'

'Food'll take a little while. We should be ready about four.'

'Thank you,' said Smith. 'Very good of you.'

'That's alright. Besides, this is the only place you'll get something to eat outside Dulac, and that's a half hour away.'

'A town?' Rhianna said.

'About the only one. I'm being a bad host.' Andy stood up, walked to a cool-box and opened it. 'Y'all drink beer?' He set four beers on the table, took out a penknife and opened one for Marie. She wandered back inside.

Andy swigged and sighed. 'Ah, that's good. Dulac's the only real settlement on this whole rock. Most of the rest's just farms, and most of them're automated. Only two things happen round here, to be honest: farming and wrecking. They say living on Paradis is like getting cheap breast implants: you stay put and you just get weighed down – try to run, and you end up with two black eyes. As for us, we stay put. We live off of repairing the farm machines, most of the time.'

Rhianna was examining the label on her bottle. She shrugged and took a cautious sip. 'So, if you don't mind me asking, how come the names of everything here are French?'

'This used to be a French world,' Andy said. 'Back in

the war – War of Disarmament, that is – the Republic of Eden grabbed a hold of it and haven't let go since. If I had my way, we'd be with the United Free States, but that's how it goes. The Republic must think four thousand people on a rock like this is worth something.'

'It is if they can get ships down here,' Smith said.

'True. We're on a trade route, and you'd be surprised how many touch down near Dulac for supplies. They've got a shuttle pad there and everything. Then the crews find that they're locked into the missile grid, and if they want to get out, they have to pay up. Simple, but nasty.'

Smith frowned. It reminded him of the stories he'd heard about wreckers in Cornwall. He'd read about it in a Daphne du Maurier book: something about gnomes in red coats wrecking boats with killer birds. That kind of stuff.

'But dammit, that's not on,' Smith said. 'It's a dirty trick to pull on a man. Why doesn't someone send a warship and bomb the place from orbit? Dreadnought diplomacy: that's how we'd do it in the Empire. Teach the buggers some courtesy. Or just blow them up.'

'No way. Governor Corveau's got serious backing. 'Sides, wouldn't that be a breach of airspace?'

'Ah. That. Good point there.'

The dog stood up and wandered over. Rhianna leaned over and beckoned it, and it flopped against her side.

'It's sewn up tight,' Andy said. 'More's the pity. You okay with the dog, there?'

Rhianna glanced up and smiled. She looked pretty, Smith thought. 'Oh, I'm fine. My cousin's got a dog. All he does is lie around and scratch himself.'

'My cousin does that too,' said Smith. 'So, how should I go about meeting this Corveau fellow, then?'

'Meeting him?'

'Of course. I'll need to persuade him to let us go. Or is he off-world?'

Andy shook his head. 'He's here alright. There's no way of leaving, even for him. The Democratic Republic's careful who they give interstellar travel to.'

'Then perhaps we could arrange to give him a lift to somewhere better.'

'They wouldn't like it.'

'They wouldn't see.'

Andy laughed. He threw the dog's toy across the grass and it bounded after it.

'You don't like the governor, do you?' Rhianna said.

'Nope, not one bit. He's everything about Eden that I don't like, and I don't like anything about it anyway. They've always hated me and Marie being together, so I reckon I've got a right to hate them back for it.'

'Why don't they like that?' Smith demanded. 'You seem like a reasonable sort.'

'Take a look,' Andy said, gesturing at himself. 'See what's wrong?'

Smith looked at him closely. 'Well, you're a bit of a fatty, I suppose.'

'I think he means on account of him being black, and Marie being white,' Rhianna said. 'I've heard that the so-called Democratic Republic of Eden isn't fond of inter-racial marriages.'

'Oh yes, so you are!' said Smith. 'You know, I really didn't notice that. Very sharp, Rhianna.'

'We ain't even married,' Andy said, grinning. 'That's a trip to hell twice.'

For no obvious reason, Suruk had pushed almost all of a beer-bottle into his mouth. 'Humans are stupid,' he declared, pulling it out. 'Petty prejudice does not interest my people. A wise warrior once told me: "Respect your brother M'Lak, no matter what shade of greenish-grey he may be."'

'Those are beautiful words, Suruk,' Rhianna said.

'– "Then, while various races of stupid human are fighting one another, you can steal their goods. And cut off their ridiculous little heads. And laugh. In their blood."'

'Those words are also' – she groped for the right word – 'honest.'

Suruk shrugged. 'Many colours of skin are there, many different shades of face. But if you look within, deep inside a person, human beings are all alike. Red and squelchy.'

The alien chuckled. Andy looked into his beer. Rhianna said: 'Um, has it got colder out here?'

Smith slapped his hands together. 'Right then, on a slightly less alarmingly macabre note: where do we find this Corveau chap?'

Meanwhile, Carveth was showing Francois around the ship. 'This is the cockpit.'

'Hell of a ship you got here,' Francois said, ducking through the door.

'It's not so bad. It goes pretty quickly, when it's going. Through there is the Captain's cabin, this door here leads to mine – no, don't open that – and that one is, well, it's full of skulls.'

'Whoa,' said Francois, gazing into Suruk's room. 'This where the alien guy lives, huh?'

'Yes.'

'This his little shrine?' Francois pointed to a small pyramid of bones piled in front of Suruk's spear, the weapon of his ancestors. 'He's like a samurai, right?'

'More like a raving nutcase, but there's probably an overlap.'

'Whoa. That's *beaucoup* serious.' Francois bent down and picked up a shallow, rectangular dish, full of carefully raked sand and little pebble-shaped objects. He lifted one out. 'This his little Zen garden?'

'I'd put that down, if I were you.'

'Sacred, huh?'

'Not exactly. It's his litter tray.'

They left Suruk's room, Francois wiping his palms on his overalls. 'Now, through here is the engine room,' she announced, opening a small door beside the entrance to the living room. 'It's down these steps. Careful.'

He ducked down and followed her into a dim, red corridor. It looked like something from a submarine: twin rows of pistons stood still on the edges of the room, waiting for the second to plunge down and fire the Supralux drive. A long rod stretched down the last third of the engine room, bent out of shape and covered in soot. Copper-coloured boilers hung above their heads. From one, a shorted and blackened control panel dangled on half a dozen wires. It smelt of burning.

'Looks like you got it bad,' Francois said.

'They had us over a barrel,' Carveth explained.

'Sure looks that way. Still, I reckon I could get the outside jets goin', no problem. Never seen a Supralux drive up close before, though. How's it work?'

Carveth frowned. 'Well, it's pretty complex. Basically, it's a tacheon shunt that causes acceleration up to maximum realspace velocity, and from then on, the plotting computer adds or decreases mass to regulate speed relative to mass index. In layman's terms: it just works because it does, alright?' She reached up and pointed to the burnt-out console, dangling from the roof. 'Thing is, that's the device that does the plotting.'

'So it's that thing that makes the drive work.' Francois scratched his head, loudly. 'And without a new plot device, you can't fly.'

'Not faster than light.'

'That stuff's way beyond me. Who did this to you, anyhow?'

'Ghast raiders. One of their warships attacked us without provocation, so we were forced to crash-land in neutral space.'

'Attacked you?' The bad, red light threw Francois' face into hard relief. 'How come?'

'It's a long story. But if you want to know I'll tell it to you just like it happened.' Carveth crossed her arms and leaned against a bulkhead. She took a deep breath, hoping that she was not about to have one of her sexbot moments. 'Well, we were cruising, hardly looking for action at all, when suddenly the Ghasts jumped us from behind, stuck a torpedo up our back end and blew our motors out. They must have seen that we were exposed at the rear because they stuck out their tube so they could come inside, but the captain ordered us to get our tools ready and beat them off if they tried to enter us by force. They all came at us at once down the passage, but what with Smith shooting off from the hip and me pumping my piece for all I was worth, we were able to give them a good seeing-to until they had to withdraw. We were knackered, though. We could hardly pull off, let alone thrust, so we saw this lake and decided to dump in the water until we were able to repair the ship and get it up again. That's pretty much the size of it.'

'Ouch.' Francois took off his cap and smoothed his hair. 'And you're still walkin'?'

'Stiff upper lip, my friend. Stiff upper lip.'

Andy finished his beer. 'Corveau is no problem to find: he'll be at his house in town, holding court. That's what he does pretty much every weekend of the year. But he's one *menchant* son of a bitch. He's had men killed before, I know it. You'll get to see him easy, but if you want to get away, or even argue with the man, that's a different story. He has a lot of people, and whatever decent guns there are on this world, they're his. Not that we don't keep our own pieces, but he's got serious stuff and men to hold 'em.'

'What kind of house does he have?'

'A pretty fancy one. I tell you, the place is plush. It's got grounds all done out, and more staff than anybody could use for anything. He must have a few spare asses to need so many people to wipe his butt.'

Smith glanced at Rhianna to make sure that she was not offended. She smiled.

'Sees himself as a little king,' Andy said. 'People come to him to get their noses browned, looking to get some money off of him. Most of the cash that gets made farming goes to him as well, as protection money, pretty much. There's a lot of folks who'd like to get shot of Corveau, but most of 'em ain't brave enough to try.'

Smith nodded understandingly. 'It happens a lot abroad.'

'Plus, if you're thinking of waltzing in there strapped, forget it. The dress code's black tie and no weapons. It's a strictly no-tools do.'

'I need no weapons to slay with my hands,' Suruk declared. 'I *am* a tool.'

'Quite,' said Smith. 'But we won't be going in to kill. I don't want a bloodbath.'

'Like on your lawn at home?'

'No, that's a birdbath. Because, Suruk, I am a civilised, cultured person who objects to mindless violence. We're going to talk to this Governor fellow, and ask him nicely if he'll lower the missile grid to let us through. And if he doesn't—'

'We tear off his limbs?'

'Well, alright then.'

Andy's barbecue was excellent, and that evening Smith and his crew walked back to the ship drunk and full. Crickets and frogs made the warm night noisy, and above them the stars glinted, tiny but bright, as if to remind them that home was still there, and that they were a long way from it.

'Whoo!' Carveth cried, delighted to hear her own voice echo around the lake and hills. 'This is really something!' She slipped, and Smith caught hold of her. 'Blimey, Cap, I think I might have overdone it. The stuff they brew here's pretty strong. I never would have thought you could squeeze so much alcohol from a single cane toad.'

'It seems you can. How many fingers am I holding up?'

'On which of your many hands?'

They climbed onto the ship with difficulty. Smith helped Rhianna and Carveth on board and Suruk climbed up on his own. Smith watched Rhianna open the hatch and climb inside, the alien following, and Carveth watched him doing so.

'Careful on the rungs, Rhianna. And no more knife throwing!' he called after them.

A hand touched his arm. Carveth stood back a little, her neat little head tilted to one side like a puzzled bird. 'You like her, don't you?' she said quietly.

Carveth seemed very sober and still, or perhaps Smith's wobbling vision was in sync with her wobbling body.

'I like some things about her,' Smith said. 'Others I'm not sure about.'

'Rhianna seems alright, I suppose. But she's weird, Captain, weirder than just lentils and listening to whales. I don't know what they've saddled us with, but the Ghasts wanted her for a reason. And if you ask me, it's a very strange one indeed.'

Smith paused. 'I know,' he said. 'I see what you're saying. But we have to get off this planet. That's the first thing. Everything else can wait. Unless you think she's a danger to us all.'

The simulant stared out across the lake, the water black as velvet. 'No, I don't think she's dangerous. Not like that. Just weird.'

Rhianna poked her head out of the hatch. 'Are you guys coming inside?'

'Yes,' said Smith. 'I'll be with you in a moment. We'd best get to bed, Rhianna. We've got a lot to do. Tomorrow, that is. Not in bed or anything of course.'

'I'll turn in soon,' Rhianna said. 'I just want to get some air.'

'I'm off,' Carveth said, and she climbed into the ship. A moment later Rhianna emerged. She walked over to Smith, looked up and sighed. 'It's a beautiful sky.'

'Certainly is.'

'I find the stars so romantic,' she said. 'Sometimes, when I look up at them—'

'Cup of tea?' said Isambard Smith.

'What?'

'Would you like a cup of tea, Rhianna?'

Wrong-footed, she said, 'Uh, yes, please, I guess. I find the stars—'

'Righto.' Smith turned and left. Rhianna pulled her shapeless cardigan tight around her and waited. She sat down on the hull, drummed her fingers on the metal, huffed and looked up at the sky.

After a few minutes, she heard footsteps behind her.

'I find the stars so romantic,' she resumed. 'When I was a little girl, I used to believe that they were the lights put there by a fairy princess, up among the heavens.' She leaned back and shook out her hair and laughed. 'Seems funny now, to be so innocent and naïve.'

'I think I am probably not your intended audience,' Suruk the Slayer said. 'Isambard Smith told me to bring you this.'

He shoved a cup at her. 'Oh,' she said coldly. 'That's really friendly of him.'

'I too enjoy looking at the stars,' the M'Lak said. 'I see meanings in them. Some, these brighter ones, make me think of my ancestors, shining warriors to whose deeds I aspire. This group here, further away, makes me think of us: bound close, alone in the void of space. And this one on its own I call Isambard: quite large, and not especially bright.'

'Wow. I never knew you knew so much. Do you know the constellations?'

'Indeed.'

'What's that one up there, that looks like a little tree?'

'With the small wings, like an angel? Braves call that one Doomblade.'

'And the one next to it shaped like a rabbit?'

Suruk pointed into the sky. 'Gorehammer. Then the Pile of Guts . . . and Bloodweasel . . . and then the Plough.'

'The Plough? Isn't that a bit innocuous for you?'

'Not if it is ploughing into Bloodweasel's head.'

'Is your *entire* culture based around violence?' Rhianna asked.

'That and folk dancing, yes. There's also some macramé, but it's mainly violence.'

'I find that quite hard to square with my principles of

non-violence,' she said, sipping at her tea, 'Still, it can't be easy, being a person of species in a human-dominated galaxy. I suppose violence is a natural response to persecution.'

'Is persecution where people seek to fight you for no good reason?'

'Yes, that's right.'

'Ah yes. Fun, that.'

Half an hour later the *Systematic Destruction* slipped into a high orbit around Paradis. In his chair on the bridge, 462 waited.

The Ghast Empire had no say in the running of Paradis. His instinct was to land and have his troopers tear this worthless planet apart to find the *John Pym*, but he knew that was not possible. To violate Edenite territory would be very foolish, especially as there were other, more democratic nations to annex first.

There were more subtle ways. 462's contacts in the Republic of Eden could bring Smith to him. And with Smith would come Rhianna Mitchell, their prize.

The next morning they got to work. Carveth was up remarkably early, and as Smith was getting dressed he could hear the thin whine of electric drills as she and Francois began to repair the jets. Andy fetched parts from a barn he used as a garage, dragging them down on a quad bike and trailer. At midday, with the basic directional thrusters repaired, they were able to fire the engines of the *John Pym* and fly it twenty yards onto dry land.

Smith helped out, but he was troubled. As Carveth shot

rivets into a piece of plating that Suruk held against the side of the ship, he sat in his room and tried to work out a plan. By twenty past two he had the plan worked out, and he announced it over sandwiches.

'We're going to a party this evening,' he announced. 'By my reckoning it's a Saturday, which I gather means that Governor Corveau will be holding court tonight. We'll smarten ourselves up and put on a good show, and if he asks, we'll say that we're representatives from the Empire. Question, Carveth?'

'Will there be any nice blokes?'

Francois was leaning against the ship, chewing. 'What about security? Say he don't want you there – or don't want you leavin'?'

'I've thought about it. I'm going to claim we're a diplomatic team, which will grant us a certain amount of immunity. Hopefully it'll make him think we've got warship protection. He may not do of course, and that's why Suruk's coming. People ought to think twice about getting nasty with him as our bodyguard.'

Suruk displayed his teeth. 'I look forward to it.'

'But remember, Suruk: we're going to this party to talk to the Governor, not because we hunger for the flesh of men. That goes for you too, Carveth. I'm expecting at least some attempt at dignity. Remember you're all repre-senting your country, and you ought to behave as the Empire does.'

'So we can kill and loot at will, steal their goods and claim the planet as our own?' Suruk said.

'Not exactly, no. And by "exactly", I mean "at all". Alright?'

Rhianna raised a hand. 'What about clothes? You've got your uniform. Captain Smith told me I wouldn't need an evening dress.'

'I didn't think it was necessary for space,' Smith replied.

'I'm sure Marie can lend you something,' Andy said. He nodded slowly, appraising them all. 'Then it's a plan.'

# 6

# Ho-Down of the Damned

'Mr and Mrs Harding Walters!' barked the loudspeaker mounted at the entrance to the main hall. The queue shuffled three feet forwards. 'Mr and Mrs Richard Milford and their son Paul Milford!' Another shuffle. 'Doctor and Mrs Wainwright!'

Carveth yawned. In front of them about fifteen couples stood in a long line that stretched the length of the Corveau entrance hall. Servants moved down the line, collecting coats and offering drinks.

'Well, that's something,' the simulant said, taking a large glass of white wine from a waiter and swallowing a third of it in one gulp. 'Four more of these and I won't mind standing in this queue.'

'Two more and you won't be standing at all,' said Smith.

'Maybe. Anyway, how am I looking? Too hot to handle?'

'Well, I wouldn't touch you,' Smith said, and she shot him an evil look. Carveth had borrowed an impressive blue dress that reminded Smith of a device used by his maiden aunt to conceal toilet rolls. She wore long boots: they were her workboots, and the only footwear they could find that had fitted her. 'You look like a bell,' Smith said. 'That is to say, *the* bell. The belle of the ball. That's it.'

'I don't believe you,' she said with annoying perceptiveness.

'You're very distinctive,' Rhianna said from behind. 'I mean, you really stand out.'

She had fared somewhat better, choosing a floor-length skirt and white shirt with a dark jacket borrowed from Marie. It made her look like a cross between an explorer's wife and a Pilgrim Father, minus the boots and buckled hat.

Carveth scowled at her. 'Go boil your crucible.' Rhianna was one of those irritating women who naturally looked good. She was intrinsically, annoyingly graceful, Carveth reflected, and could probably manage to look sexy in a clown outfit with a dung-spattered lampshade on her head.

'We all look nice,' Rhianna persisted. 'Even Suruk here. You certainly look the business, Captain Smith.'

'Well, yes, I do try.'

Carveth crossed her arms, determined to vent her irritation on someone. 'What difference does it make if we've got Scary Alien with us? You could at least have done something with your hair.'

Suruk snorted. 'I am a warrior, not a butterfly. Dreadlocks are very last hunting season.'

'Your names, sir?' a servant asked at Smith's side. 'I don't believe you've visited the estate before.'

Smith gave their names.

'I see, sir. And the greyskin? Is he your houseboy?'

'He's my friend.'

'We don't get many non-humans here, you see. They tend to exist in a serving capacity.'

'So do you, my man,' Carveth said, holding out her empty glass. 'So get to it. More wine for the lady, please.'

'Of course, Miss. And where might the lady be?'

Finally, the couple in front were announced and they stepped up to the doors, looking into the hall. 'Captain Isambard Smith and Miss Rhianna Mitchell! Miss Pollyanna Carveth and Suruk the Slayer, son of Agshad Nine-Swords, Victor of the Plain of Useth, and – how much of this crap is there?'

They stepped inside. 'Whoa,' Carveth said.

The hall was three storeys high and thirty metres square. In it, several hundred people talked in groups or danced in a restrained manner. A small band played in a corner of the room. Men in suits and smart string ties kissed the hands of women in long dresses. Above the music came the steady tinkle of glass and high-class laughter.

'I take it all back,' Carveth said, her head rolling back to take in the roof. 'This is way out of my league. I ought to throw myself out now and save someone else the trouble.'

'Nonsense,' said Smith. 'You're as suited here as anyone. Come on. Let's see if we can find this Corveau.'

'Why don't we split up?' Rhianna suggested.

'Of course,' said Smith. 'Ladies, we'll stop cramping your style. Come and fetch me if you see our host.'

Poor Carveth, he thought as she headed for the bar. Under all that cynicism, there's, well, more cynicism, but under that, someone who's hardly seen the world at all. She deserves to have a good time. Oh, and just look at Rhianna's lovely little arse.

Stop that, he told himself. There was business to be done. He slipped between two chattering groups, who fell quiet as Suruk passed them by. 'Just look at him,' someone whispered loudly, 'greenish-grey as your hat.' Without doubt the alien was not welcome here. In the Empire he would have seemed unusual; on this backwater he was not just out of place but something to be driven away.

Up ahead a dozen or so men stood clustered around someone. They looked well-dressed and serious. Smith caught a glimpse of a white suit. He turned to his friend.

'Suruk, I think I've just spotted this Corveau chap. I'm going to have a look. Would you mind waiting here a moment?'

'Not at all, Mazuran. But be careful. I see many guards here among the frivolous ones. I shall await the call to war by the drinks table.'

'Well, have fun – but not too much fun. See you later, Suruk.' Here we go, Smith thought grimly, and he strode towards Corveau.

Suruk watched Smith go and strolled over to the food table. It looked interesting, if needlessly elaborate. Everything was very small. It was difficult to think with all the noise going on behind him. Stupid human mating rituals. The only thing on the table that was a decent size was a metal cup of some yellow stuff, surrounded by bits of twig. He picked up the warm cup and drank. Cheesy.

'— not as good as before,' a woman said to his right. 'They had a fondue last time, and finger food.'

He turned at her and tried to look friendly. 'Very true,' he observed. 'This finger food clearly contains no fingers.' Rudely, the humans hurried away. He finished the cup and put it back.

Someone prodded him in the back. 'You there, boy,' a fat female was saying. He looked down at her. After the yellow stuff, he felt quite peckish, and in different circumstances she would have been quite suitable. 'Take my coat, boy.'

'Thank you,' he said. A man behind her dumped a top hat in his arms. 'You are too kind, sir.'

'At least it knows its place,' the man said to the woman, and they walked away as Suruk put on the coat and hat and admired his reflection in his new clothes. He smiled at the mirror. Not a bad party so far.

Smith found Corveau in the centre of the group. The governor wore a white linen suit and a cream shirt, open at the neck. He looked like a crow, Smith thought, thin and black-haired, with bony hands and long grooves at the sides of his mouth. His skin was loose and very tanned, as though the sun had withered his fat away.

'— worth twice the price off-world,' he was saying, and men nodded as he spoke. Lower than the music, a little rumble of approval ran though the group. 'Which is why the trade lanes matter so much to commerce here.' Corveau had a slow, drawling voice, as if he should have been wise and gentle. It belied the quickness of his eyes. Smith stood at the rear of the group with his glass of wine, sipping and waiting for a way into the conversation.

Corveau lifted his head and looked straight at Smith. 'And here's just the man to ask. Gentlemen, I believe this is Captain Ichabod Smith.'

Smith put out his hand. 'Isambard. It's Isambard, actually. Pleased to meet you, Governor Corveau.'

'I'm glad you recognise me. Sorry; Isambard.' Well-fed faces turned to Smith, nodded and smiled to him. 'Mr Smith here is from the British Empire. He's a trader, am I right?'

'That's right.'

'Just landed, I understand.'

'Absolutely,' said Smith. 'You don't miss much, Mr Corveau.'

'I don't. There's not much to miss on a world like this.'

'Well, I'm not planning on staying long. I've got rather a tight schedule to cling to, I'm afraid.' The merchants emitted an understanding, wordless murmur as he spoke. They sounded like an avante-garde performance piece about beekeeping. 'I'm planning on lifting off as soon as possible. It's a shame, since this seems rather a pleasant sort of world.'

Corveau smiled. 'It is indeed splendid. *Spiffing*, you might say.'

The audience smiled too: deep smiles that stretched their faces, although their lips stayed closed. Smith moved on.

'That's actually what I wanted to talk to you about, Governor. I gather than there's some sort of tax on air-space round here.'

'There sure is, old boy. Jolly bad luck for a chap, but there you go.'

147

Smith knew then that Corveau was making fun of him. The chorus of merchants lapped it up; their smirks turned to outright grinning.

He glanced about, looking for support. Suruk was standing in front of a mirror, for some reason admiring himself in a top hat and fur coat. Carveth had disappeared. Rhianna was dancing with a military-looking man. Smith felt a jolt of envy and, looking back at Corveau, remembered that he was being mocked.

'I understand that you have some sort of tax for leaving the surface,' Smith said. 'I'd like to negotiate.'

'I'm sure you would. Your people must be keen to get back every ship they've got, what with the Ghast Empire breathing down your necks. Awfully bad luck, old fellow,' Corveau said. 'The offer's not open to negotiation. Way I see it, you're not in a negotiating position. That's bad business sense. Am I right, fellers?'

There was a rumble of agreement from the sycophants.

'You know, you're not much of a haggler at all, Smith. I'd be surprised if you were much of a captain either.'

'At least he's not a jumped-up hick,' a woman said.

It was Rhianna. She stood on the edge of the group with the military man. Her eyes were cold. The military man was looking elsewhere. Suruk had turned from the mirror and was watching them, thoughtfully rubbing his tusks together, waiting for the real fun to start.

Carveth was circulating the room, still awed. A nice, rugged-looking fellow passed by and she smiled at him, for which he shouldered straight past her without meeting her eye. 'Nice to meet you too,' she muttered glumly.

There were some chairs at the edge of the room and she sat down, her large dress billowing out around her like a pool of swell. Waltzing couples rolled past, as if part of a carousel. A tall girl in a significantly better dress was talking down a spectacled young man at the edge of the dance floor. A few of her friends stood behind her, as if expecting to have to pile in to settle the matter with fists.

'As if I would ever!' the tall girl said vehemently. She had the sort of groomed, made-up features that would have looked good thirty feet further back: this close, they looked as if they needed to be thirty feet away. 'Like, you'd be lucky if I told you the time, let alone dance with you.'

The man made no reply. Obviously, he had not expected whatever verbal battering he had just received. 'Smack her in the chops,' Carveth said to herself, and finished up her wine.

'Excuse me?' Carveth had been staring into her glass, and looked up to see the thin girl standing over her. 'Did you just say something?'

'Hello,' Carveth said.

'I asked you a question,' the girl said.

Carveth felt confused. She blinked. Thrust at her, the girl's groomed face had become ugly and tough. 'I can't remember. Why don't you leave me alone?'

The princess snorted. 'Boo hoo, Bo Peep. Did you leave your sheep at home?'

'Knowing this planet, they're probably with your brother.'

The intake of breath was almost sufficient to vacuum the ribbons out of Carveth's hair. 'How dare you? Have you got no breeding?'

'None at all,' Carveth said gaily, getting up. She felt happy again.

'Disgraceful.' The thin girl spun around and stalked away.

'I do have boobs, though, pancake girl,' Carveth added, but she was not sure that her opponent heard. She turned to the nice man in glasses. 'Hello, nice man in glasses. I'm Pollyanna. Want to teach me how to waltz?'

Corveau looked at Rhianna. 'And who might you be?'

'Rhianna Mitchell. I came here with Captain Smith.'

'I see.' A servant stopped at the group with a silver tray. Amid the wine glasses was a single can of beer. Corveau took the beer, cracked it open and swigged. 'So you're a relative of his, I presume?'

'Just a friend.'

The military man frowned. He said, 'Where I'm from, a decent woman doesn't go out unless her husband's taking her.'

Smith was about to point out that Rhianna could go where she liked, but she beat him to it. 'We're not really into marriage where I'm from.'

'Nor piety, so I hear.' The man's face remained in-expressive, but his tone disapproved.

'I believe in spirituality as opposed to organised religion,' Rhianna said.

'Which makes you a hellbound unbeliever.'

'Now then,' Smith said. 'You're talking to a lady here.'

'Perhaps you should have discussed this on the dance floor.' Corveau looked tired. 'Then again, I'm not sure

God and getting down go well together.' His cronies smiled.

Smith turned to the officer. 'May I ask your name, sir?'

'You may. Captain John Bradley Gilead, Navy of the Democratic Republic of the New Eden. You must be Smith. Pardon me, but I only shake with believers.'

Gilead's face, Smith realised, was almost immobile. The man had the permanent look of mild surprise that characterised senior officials of the Democratic Republic. This, Smith knew, was the result of what he had once heard one of them call 'hyper-repeatmented plasticated surgification.'

'You're excused,' Smith said.

Gilead's very square jaw moved slightly. 'So, I understand you're the captain of the ship that got stranded here. The *John Pym*, am I right?'

'That's right.'

'What kind of name for a ship is that, anyhow? Was he someone famous?'

'He was an early democratic campaigner. He fought for the people against the king.'

'Communist, eh?'

'I didn't say that.' The atmosphere seemed heavy suddenly, charged. He decided to lighten it. 'Besides, it's not the strangest name I've ever heard for a ship, by a long way. I used to know a Yorkshireman who named his ship the *Norfolk and Chance*. I used to say, "Why did you call your ship *Norfolk and Chance*?" and he'd reply, "Because there's *Norfolk and Chance* she'll get off the ground!" Haha! Ha! Ha. Ha? Oh.'

The band tuned their instruments. On the lawn, a cricket rubbed its legs.

'Well then,' said Smith, glancing round for an exit route as desperation rose up within him. He had been hoping to leave in a civilised manner, preferably via conversation with someone else, but right now he was tempted to run shrieking and gibbering down the length of the room, immediately prior to flinging himself through the French windows and emptying his shard-lanced bladder onto Corveau's lawn as a gesture of contempt.

'Rhianna!' he said delightedly. 'Care for a dance? Please?'

'You're wearing spacesuit boots,' Carveth's man said as they danced.

'Damn right, Hector,' she said, grinning. 'Want to know what else I've got?'

Rhianna did not seem very happy to be dancing. Smith, on the other hand, was overjoyed: not only had he escaped ritual humiliation at the hands of a religious bigot, but a very attractive woman was dancing with him. People passed by, possibly under the impression that he and Rhianna shared the same bed.

'Are you having a good time?' he asked.

'No. You're on my flip-flops, Isambard.'

'Sorry.' He adjusted his stance. 'Still, must be better than dancing with that Gilead fellow. What a tosser!'

'He's a fascist and a sleaze,' she replied as they whirled past Suruk. Smith was surprised by her vehemence: he had expected something about negative energy. 'He spent the whole time with his hand on my ass.'

Smith's own hand stayed very still on her waist. 'You should have told him to take it away.'

'How could I? He's Republic military. Round here his word is more law than the Governor's.'

'Arsehole. I should have socked him one for that,' Smith replied, regretting the fact that he had not trained to be a specifically evil space captain. He felt bitterly cheated by this news.

'You realise violence doesn't solve anything permanently, don't you?'

'Except for lowering the galactic arsehole proliferation rate. I'd settle the Governor's hash at the drop of a hanky as well.'

'They're staring at you.'

'Look, we're going to have trouble here. When I said we should reason with these people, I didn't know we'd be strolling into a pan-galactic prat convention. I think we should consider going.'

'What're you going to do about getting off-world?'

'Looks like Suruk and I will have to deal with it on the sly. We can come back here tomorrow night—'

'Oh no!' Rhianna's eyes were fixed on something over his shoulder. 'They've got Carveth!'

Smith glanced around. Two large guards stood either side of Carveth and a man he did not recognise. She looked worried.

'I'll be back in a minute,' Smith said, and he strode across the room, Rhianna hurrying after him.

'What's all this?' Smith demanded, drawing near.

'Drop the attitude,' said the guard. 'We found this

woman in the private rooms, with this man. Attempted sex outside wedlock carries five to ten here.'

Smith said, 'Everything is under control. This is my niece. She suffers from a rare genetic condition that makes her into a complete fathead. I'm very disappointed in you, niece, wandering off like that. I'd best be getting her back home, gentlemen. We're leaving,' he told Carveth.

'Leaving? But I hardly got started!'

'Better keep her on a leash, neighbour.' One of the guards chuckled, and they stepped aside.

Smith leaned in close. 'Dammit, Carveth, what were you thinking of?'

She looked genuinely apologetic. 'I'm really sorry, Boss. I only wanted to get some willy,' she said miserably.

'We're getting out. I've had no luck with the governor. There's some nasty customers round here.'

'I can handle myself. I've got a pistol in my smalls, Cap.'

He tugged her arm. Carveth waved at her gentleman as the three of them hurried towards the main doors.

Corveau was waiting in the hall. Two men stood against the far wall, their faces brutal and blank, shotguns held across their chests.

'Captain Smith!'

Smith hissed to Carveth, 'How fast can you get to your knickers?'

Corveau laughed. 'Got to get back home urgently?' He stepped forward with a fresh beer in hand. 'I know what you need, Smith. I'll talk terms. If you want to get off-world, it can be arranged. Come to Gadster's Farm at, let's say, midday tomorrow. We should be able to sort something out, provided you're there.' He shrugged. 'I've got to get back. You two have a good evening, now. Or do I need to tell you that?'

He gave them a condescending smile and turned back to the party.

The air was cool on the porch. Outside they happened on a surreal sight: Suruk crouched on a picnic chair wearing a top hat, sharing a heaped plate of vol-au-vents with two waiters and a dog. He sprang down as they approached.

'We are leaving?'

'We're leaving all right,' Smith replied.

They walked down towards the gate. Suruk turned his collar up and listened as Smith explained what had been going on.

'So what do you think happens at this farm?' Rhianna asked.

'Sounds like bad news,' Carveth said. Suruk adjusted his hat as he strode along beside her. He and Carveth looked like characters from a production of *Alice in Wonderland*, as performed by the criminal underworld.

Smith licked his fingertips and checked the shape of his moustache. 'Well, and bear in mind this is just an opinion, I'd say that's where they are going to try to murder us.'

Andy laid out the map on the living room table. 'Gadster's farm's been abandoned nigh on six years. It's got a load of outhouses and a farmhouse, probably stripped bare by now. These two rectangles are storage barns. The towers to the north are for observation or somethin'. I'd put a man up there with a rifle if I was Corveau.'

'Sounds like we could do with a recce,' Carveth said. 'It doesn't look friendly.'

'It ain't. Word is it's where Corveau does his dirty work. The place has a bad rep: Sheriff Parker went missing up there four years back, when he tried to get them to throw the Governor out for taking bribes. All they found was a badge and a couple of fingers. He's probably down the well.'

Francois whistled and approached the table. The six of them made the ship's living area seem cramped. 'Yep, that there's your bona-fide one-stop chopped cop drop-off shop,' he said. 'Walk in there without a decent gun an' I reckon you're screwed.'

'Thanks,' said Smith. 'I appreciate the help, and the map. Shame it's 1:50,000, but you can't have everything.' He peered at the tiny markings. 'We're going to need a good plan if we're to disarm Corveau.'

Heads were lifted from the map; eyes met across the table. 'Disarm?' Carveth said. 'You want to get him alive?'

'We'll need him to shut down the missile array so we can get off-world.'

'But alive? You're actually suggesting that we walk in there, heavily armed, and ask him to surrender? What are we, the Mild Bunch? I say we go in and blow the bastard away, and what's more I say you go in and blow the bastard away and I pick you up afterwards. Now, that's a *proper* plan.'

'Lady's got a point,' Andy said. 'The man has troops.'

'I'm with Andy,' Carveth said.

Smith raised a hand, silencing her. 'Fear not, Worrier Princess. Corveau may have the advantage in terms of numbers and positioning, but we have the skill and moral fibre to see this though. Once they understand what they're dealing with they'll fold over just like that.' He snapped his fingers.

'Only from laughing,' Carveth said.

'Now, here's the plan. Suruk, you know about knifing people from behind, what with being foreign and all. I'll need you to skirt the edges and take out any snipers they may have. Think you can carry that off?'

'Easily.'

'Good. Now, looking at the map, we can expect Corveau to take up a position near the farmhouse, which is this tiny square next to the two miniscule ones. I'll be going in to the farmhouse, where I expect Corveau will try to signal his men to get the jump on me. But he's not going to be able to, because Suruk will have dealt with them by then.

'I will get hold of either the controlling device or Corveau himself and shut down the grid. Carveth, you will be in the ship for all of this with the engine running. As soon as I give the signal, you fly to Gadster's Farm and pick us up. Now, does everyone understand what they've got to do?'

There was a murmur of agreement. Suruk croaked and flexed his fingers.

Rhianna put her hand up. 'Erm, what do I do?'

'You're probably best off in the ship,' said Smith.

'I think I ought to go with you,' Rhianna said.

'Why?'

'I might be able to talk some sense into him. I can't help feel I'd be better at persuading people than you.'

Smith frowned. 'I don't know. You are a woman after all.'

'With magic powers,' Carveth whispered into his ear.

'I don't know. It's hardly safe.'

'She might be able to – you know – *help*.'

'Very well,' said Smith. 'Rhianna, you can come with me if you want. Carveth, I'll need you to scan this map into the main computer. Then all we've got to do is arm ourselves.'

Andy said, 'Question: say you guys get captured, or killed. How then do we get paid?'

'Yeah, paid,' Francois said.

'Well,' said Smith, 'that's a good question. A very good question. You see, you don't like the Governor, do you?'

'No.'

'Now, if this goes well, not only will we be able to leave the atmosphere but you will be able to choose a new Governor and join the Free States. Either one of you could stand for the job.'

'I see,' Andy said. 'So you weren't meaning to pay us at all.'

'Not in money, no. But in services, yes! Andy, this is about more than money now. This is about liberty, about freedom, about overthrowing a corrupt and tyrannical elite. We must join forces to defeat the Governor, and then you can hold your own elections, make your own decisions without fear of retribution – and even apply to the United Free States to become one of their members. And in the generations to come, your children will thank you for making Paradis paradise once again.'

'So no money.'

'Yes.'

'Francois, get the rifle.'

'We could always have a whip-round,' Carveth said.

'Now, there's no need to be uncivilised about this –' Smith began as Francois left the room. They heard his boots clatter on the steps, going down, and then rising again. Suruk's tusks moved into their fighting-position.

'This here's a 308 Morgan Plainsman,' Francois declared as he stepped into the room. A long, wooden-stocked hunting rifle was in his hands. 'They call it the Frontier Special, out on the frontier. Everywhere else, they call it the Special. Ammo's stored in the stock, here, or loaded individually in the breech. It takes up to eighteen supercharged .45 rifle shells, chambered by cockin' the hand-guard Winchester-style, like this.' He flicked his hand forward, then back, the metal finger-guard sliding back into the gun with a loud and satisfying *clack*. 'One shot from this'll go straight though a safe door, and you can get ten off in so many seconds. It's quite a gun. So take good care of it.'

He held out the rifle. Smith took it. Carveth breathed again. Smith cradled the weapon in his hands, lifted it and looked down the scope at the far end of the room.

'Best bit's the scope,' Andy said, grinning. 'Made that m'self. You've got a night-sight and composite thermal imager there, with a motion detector. Hell of a piece.'

'Does it have a name?' Smith said.

'Heck no. Do I look like a redneck gun nut to you?'

'Well, your neck's not actually red, in a literal sense . . .'

'It's very kind of you,' Rhianna put in. 'Sharing spreads harmony and peace.'

'Very true. I could blow a man to bits with this,' Smith said. 'Excellent. Andy, Francois, thank you. I appreciate this.'

They got ready. Smith found two suits of light body armour on the ship, thin enough to wear under a coat. He fetched one for himself and one for Rhianna, and checked his weapons as Carveth scanned the map.

'Captain,' she said quietly as he was strapping the sword to his side.

'Yes, Carveth?'

'I saw something funny last night. It was when I went in that room with that bloke I met.'

'Last chipolata in the value pack, was it?'

'No, no, not that. We went into a billiard room, you see. It was dark, and I didn't notice to begin with, what with being preoccupied, but there were nameplates on the walls, the names of ships.'

'Ships?'

'Yes. Spaceships. Trophies of the ships he's destroyed. This really is a wrecker's planet. He must have put them up there, like the stuffed animal heads you have at home.'

'You've never seen my home.'

'I just know.'

'Gosh, that's eerie.'

'I bet there's some tweed there too. Anyhow, the point is: I've not seen anyone round here who looks like they're not local, if you see what I mean.'

'You mean he killed the crews.'

She shrugged.

'My God. He lured ships down here and murdered their

160

crews to strip them for scrap. This fellow doesn't know what he's got coming, Carveth.'

She paused, arms folded. Her small face frowned. 'You be careful, Boss. Make sure you and Rhianna get back all right.'

'I will.'

In the midday sun, Gadster's Farm was as white as bone. Towers jutted from the uneven ground, a propeller turning in the wind on one of them with a noise like a rusted hinge. The barns were holed and empty and echoed with the sound of crows. The windows of the farmhouse looked like eyeholes in a skull.

Smith passed Rhianna the binoculars.

Around the edge of the farm, like crashed airships or the skeletons of dinosaurs, the spacecraft lay. They were huge, stripped down to the ribbing, robbed of glass, heat shielding, motors and steel plate, monuments to the folly of those who had presumed to land on Corveau's world. Half a dozen shuttles lay on their bellies and sides, ruins now. Smith saw a Spanish flag on the front of one, a Japanese Chrysanthemum on another, the emblem of Indastan on a third.

'One of them's British,' he whispered. 'The dirty swine.'

Rhianna lowered the binoculars. 'This place is huge. It's like a little town. They could have men anywhere.'

'Suruk'll find them. How long's he had?'

'About half an hour.' She dusted herself down. In flares, sandals and a long white shirt with flowers on the sleeves, Rhianna was not dressed for combat. They stood in the shadow of an outcrop of rock, fifty metres from the edge of the lake where Andy had dropped them off. 'You and he are really close, aren't you?'

Smith nodded. 'We've known one another for a while, if that's what you mean. He's a decent sort.'

'You seem like good friends. Although it's quite hard to tell.'

'I suppose.' Smith looked round at her, rather irritated to have to bother with all this. 'He'd better come back alive.'

'I know. He means a lot to you.'

'He's got my bloody penknife. You'd think someone like that would bring enough knives, wouldn't you? Typical alien. You can see why we have to run space for them.' He dropped the binoculars into his coat pocket. 'Right. We're all set. Still sure you want to be in on this?'

'Yes. I think I can help.'

'Maybe seeing a woman will soften them up, weaken them a bit. Let's go.'

They walked out into the farm.

On one of the towers a man with a rifle watched them approach. He wore sunglasses and below them his face was set and hard.

The road to the farmhouse was flanked by barns. Smith's eyes flicked between each barn and its neighbour, where the long high walls made alleyways. Behind the barns, a buggy crept along, keeping pace with them. There were three men in it. It looked light and fast.

Smith held the rifle in both hands. His coat swished out behind him.

'I don't like this,' Rhianna said. 'They've got people everywhere.'

'They know we're not idiots,' Smith replied.

A man stepped out of the dark mouth of the house and yelled, 'Hey, idiots!' He cupped his hands to his mouth, his grey coat flapping around his boot-tops in the breeze. 'In here!'

'I'm scared, Isambard.'

'Don't be. You've got *me* here. It'll be fine.'

A crow screeched and then everything was silent. The stillness of the world seemed to swallow them as they approached, as if one loud sound might shatter it. The man in the grey coat stepped inside the house.

Smith said, 'I shouldn't have brought you out here. This isn't a place for you.'

'For a woman?'

'For you. Listen, if it gets nasty, I want you to run, alright? I'll make damned sure I settle his goose, but I don't want you getting hurt. Run and call for Suruk.'

'Captain Smith?'

'Yes.'

She stood on tiptoe and kissed his cheek. 'Thank you for giving me a lift.'

'Let's settle some hash,' he said, and he pulled back his coat and strode inside.

Corveau sat at the back of a long whitewashed room, empty apart from a table and a chair. He wore the same white suit: it looked as if he'd slept in it. There was a very thin cigarette in his hand, and no can of beer in front of him.

Two men stood behind him. They held their shotguns

loosely, ready to raise and use. Behind Corveau's chair there was a door.

'Mr Smith.'

'That's Captain.'

'Sure.' Corveau yawned. Behind him, one of the men spat onto the concrete floor. 'Sleep well last night?'

'Like a log.'

Corveau snorted. 'You think like a log as well, walking in here. One man against three. Or maybe a little more than three.'

'What do you want?'

'It's more what you need. Which, I believe, is this.' His hand snaked down to his suit pocket. Smith's fingers tensed, ready to grab the revolver at his side. 'Here,' Corveau said, and he placed a small black device on the tabletop, the size and shape of a television remote control. 'What you're looking for, I believe.'

'Yes. How much do you want to get off-world?'

'Nothing.' Corveau shrugged. 'Things change. That's why I've got you here, in person.'

'Why's that?'

'To inform you of a change of plan. I don't want money any more. I want her. The girl goes with us.'

'What?'

'With us.' It was a new voice, but familiar. Smith's eyes flicked to the door. Smart in his blue-grey uniform, a sash around his waist, Captain Gilead stepped into the room and stood beside Corveau. 'Change of plan, Captain Smith. It's your lady friend we need.' His thumbs were hitched over his belt.

'What the devil do you want her for?'

Gilead smiled. On his tight-stretched face, the expression looked unnatural. 'I have my reasons. In three days time, the Republic of Eden will sign a formal non-aggression pact with the Ghast Empire. Then, as a gesture of our goodwill, we will hand this woman over to them.' He held out one hand. 'Come with me, woman.'

'My God,' Smith exclaimed. 'You'd willingly hand over a woman to depraved aliens? What kind of degenerate are you?'

'The smart kind. Now, Captain Smith, give your hussy to me.'

'Certainly not,' said Smith. 'Terribly sorry to phlegm in your teacup, but I can't let you have the lady.' Light slanted through the window, onto his face.

'No?' Gilead glanced down, and Corveau turned in his seat to look at him. 'Yeah,' Gilead said to Corveau. 'Do it. This has gone on long enough.'

Corveau clicked his fingers, as if calling a waiter.

They looked at one another. Seconds passed.

Smith broke the silence. 'Thought you'd try a dirty trick like that,' he said, a smile forming at the side of his mouth. 'I had my alien chap do a bit of scouting, you see. Your man with the rifle's probably taken a Blighty one by now.'

'Then I'll just have to kill you myself,' Corveau replied.

Smith's hand sprang to his side. Corveau lunged into his jacket and half-drew a huge revolver before Smith's gun cracked out and threw him against the wall. Gilead leaped out of the door. The man in the long coat raised his shot-gun and the heavy boom of his weapon rang through the room as Smith threw himself to the ground. Rhianna screamed and Smith shot the coated man from the floor, rolled around and fired twice into Corveau's other guard. Outside, men's voices yelled and motors tore into life.

The room stank of cordite and smashed plaster. Smith stood up in the middle of it, rifle in one hand, revolver smoking in the other. 'There!' he snarled. 'How d'you like that, *old bean*?'

Propped against the wall, Corveau said, 'Not… very … much.' He slid down the wall, fell onto one side, and died.

Smith grabbed the remote control, flicked it to 'missile defence system - off' and pulled out his radio. 'Carveth!' he yelled into the handset. 'Immediate lift-off required! Pick us up right away! Carveth? Dammit, she's not responding! I knew she couldn't be trusted!'

'Other way up,' Rhianna said.

He turned the handset upright. 'Carveth, we need immediate evacuation. Do you hear me?'

'I'm coming,' she replied.

'Then come fast. It's about to get pretty spicy down here.'

'Drop 'em!' John Gilead stood in the doorway, a stubby machine pistol in his hands. 'Drop 'em and get face down, or I'll send you both to Hell!'

'It's you who's going to Hell,' Smith said, but he froze, outgunned.

Gilead laughed. 'Full marks for trying, Smith. You fight pretty good, for an ungodly sonofabitch.' He raised the gun. 'So long, sucker!'

Gilead pulled the trigger. Rhianna stepped in front of Smith.

'*No!*' he cried as a dozen bullets ripped through the air.

Smoke and dust swirled through the room. Rhianna stood beside the desk, her hair brushed with plaster. Her eyes were closed.

Smith blinked. 'Oh. You're alive. Good-oh.'

'Damn!' Gilead dropped the gun and ran out of the room. 'Backup, get me backup!'

Smith holstered his own revolver and picked up Corveau's gun. 'Let's walk,' he said, and he stepped out into the blinding sun.

Smith shot the first person he saw, who luckily happened to be one of Corveau's thugs. Rhianna screamed. 'Stop screaming at things!' he shouted. A buggy raced out, throwing dust behind it. On the back, a gunner stood over a black, long-barrelled weapon.

'Laser – get down!' Smith called, and a red beam sliced the air above their heads, cutting a line across the wall as the buggy roared past. Sand turned to glass as the beam touched it and suddenly the gunner shrieked and fell, a knife-hilt jutting from his neck. Smith glanced upward. Suruk stood on one of the towers, chuckling.

The buggy spun round and the man on the passenger side pushed a magazine into his gun. Smith ducked between two barns and pulled Rhianna after him. In the shadow of the barn, he checked the rifle and passed the remote control to Rhianna. 'Hold onto this.' He took out the radio. 'Carveth, where the bloody hell's the ship?'

'Near here.'

'Where's here?'

'Give me one minute.' A pickup truck rushed past the barns, men hopping down from the back. Someone ducked around the corner of the barn and fired, missing them before ducking back.

'Stay here,' Smith told Rhianna. 'Don't move unless you have to. If they throw in a grenade, run. And try running with your arms down. It helps.'

A figure leaned between the barns. Smith pulled up the rifle and fired before the man could react, throwing him dead onto his back. He jogged towards the edge and peered out.

There were people everywhere. Corveau must have twenty men, Smith thought. Seeing him, the buggy swung out to make another pass. Smith raised the rifle, closed one eye and activated the scope. A bullet whined over his head. Moving target, short range, weaving . . .

He pulled the trigger and the driver dropped over the wheel. The buggy lurched, veered off and slammed into the house, disappointingly failing to explode. Smith ducked back into the alley, a rattle of gunfire following him.

He found Suruk waiting for him next to Rhianna. 'Greetings, warriors!'

'We're surrounded,' Smith said. 'I put their buggy out. We might be able to get it working, but they've got a car of their own out there and it's a long way back.'

'Where is the ship?'

'I don't know. I told her—'

His sentence was lost in the roar of engines. The *John Pym* tore over the farm, its jets blasting downward, turning in to land.

They ran to the edge of the barn. Corveau's men scattered, panicked by the arrival of this huge machine, but as the ship aligned itself Smith saw the pickup dart into its shadow, where the onboard cameras could not pick it out. On the back of the truck a man was loading a long-barrelled artillery-piece.

Smith recognised it: a railgun, one of the few infantry weapons strong enough to crack open spacecraft armour. If that hit the jets, it could send the *John Pym* crashing to the ground – or even make it explode.

'Carveth! Car under you with a railgun!'

'I can't see anyone!' she yelled.

'Dammit, he's in the blind spot! I'm coming to help.'

He ran out, head down, towards the ship.

'Where is he?' Carveth called.

The man with the railgun pushed something into place and lined up his shot, sights fixed on the ship's underbelly.

The *John Pym* dropped out of the sky. It fell straight onto the pickup, and with a deafening crash of metal vehicle, men and railgun disappeared. 'Where's the car?' Carveth cried.

Smith stopped running. 'I wouldn't worry about it,' he said. A great cloud of dust was rising around the ship, hiding it like a sheet. As the dust began to clear, the side hatch flew open and Carveth sprang out, the Maxim cannon strapped to her body. It was slightly bigger than she was.

'Come on!' she yelled, lumbering down the steps. 'Who wants some? Come and get it, arseholes!'

She saw Smith standing there and stopped. 'Well?' she said, panting under the weight of the gun as she looked around. 'Where've they gone?'

A thin trickle of red ran from beneath the hull. 'They're

under the ship,' Smith said. 'You landed on them.'

Carveth took this on board. 'Right,' she said. 'Landed on them. Right. I meant to do that, you realise? Works every time. So, have we won?'

'We have indeed,' said Smith. 'We've done very well. I recovered the missile controller and picked up this rather nifty pistol as well. Good show, everyone.'

'And I got you this!' Suruk added proudly, holding up a plastic bag.

'Erm, what's that?' Carveth asked. 'It's kind of dripping.'

'You said you wanted our enemies disarmed.'

'Yes. So what's that?' said Smith.

'It's their arms.'

# 7

# Is Rhianna A Weirdie In Disguise?

It fell to Carveth to make the victory speech that night, purely by a process of elimination. Smith was fetching himself another drink, Rhianna already too drunk, and it was generally felt that providing Suruk with a microphone would be like giving Genghis Khan directions to a discount axe emporium. So, in front of the town hall, before the new interim mayor of Paradis and a crowd of wellwishers, Carveth tried to express her thanks.

'Best ship inner world,' she said. She rocked a little as she spoke, giving her voice a weird stroboscopic effect not often heard outside progressive rock. 'We are a happy island breed from another Eden. We're great. Thank you Paradis! We liberate planets from tyranny and oppression and – the other one. Frog-boy over there cuts heads off things and the captain? Captain can kill a man just with his moustache. Best captain ever. Proud to be under him. Not that I've been under him at all – but ladies, you could be. You know what they say about men with big moustaches, right? Damn right. Best ship in the world. Hey – what're you doing?'

Smith picked her up and placed her at the side of the

stage. 'Thanks, everyone, very sorry. Thanks for having us. And for dinner.'

'I'm not sorry!' Carveth persisted as he removed her. 'Great big tash! You remember that!'

Smith deposited her out of the way and climbed off the podium. Rhianna was waiting at the bottom.

'So, is it true, then?' She grinned.

'Well,' said Smith, his tongue loosened by alcohol and praise, 'it has been remarked that I'm doing rather well in that regard. Of course, I don't want to blow my own trumpet – although I probably could if I tried – but back at the shower room in Woking Cricket Club they did sometimes wonder if a baby elephant was on the loose.'

'I don't understand. How does having the best crew in the world help you get mistaken for a baby elephant? You've got the wrong number of knees.'

Smith fought down the sudden urge to flee. 'It was... well... near Woking zoo. Anyway, I do indeed have an excellent crew, despite it consisting solely of Carveth, technically speaking. Consider yourself an honorary member.'

Rhianna smiled. 'Thanks.' She saluted. 'Right-ho, Captain! Is that how it goes?'

The sight of Rhianna attempting an English accent and saluting him sent a wave of lust through Smith strong enough to leave him nearly nauseous. If she did that again, he might be overwhelmed and puke on her flip-flops. Which would be a major *faux pas*. 'Something like that,' he said weakly.

'I normally don't condone violence,' Rhianna went on, waving a hand to illustrate her point. 'But I appreciate you being good at it. I mean, everyone's got a talent, I believe, and it's important to nurture that. Yours is just, well, kind of negatively assertive.' She sighed. 'You know, if someone had described you to me a week ago, I would have assumed you were just another colonialist bigot spoiling for a fight. But I would have been wrong.'

'You'd have to be foreign to think a thing like that. More drink?'

But Rhianna had been distracted by some local dancing and had wandered off, leaving Smith feeling that he had missed an opportunity. He looked into his cup and sighed. Andy was waiting for him at the bar. 'That was one hell of a job y'all did,' he said for the fourth or fifth time.

'Thanks.' Smith spun the tap and watched his cup fill with beer. 'Good of you to lend me that rifle.'

Andy shrugged. He wore a tuxedo jacket over his red T-shirt to reflect the gravitas of his new role as mayor. 'It's no problem. Keep it. Listen: we've got a solution to you getting off world.'

'Surely we can just fly away now, can't we?'

'Sure. But Gilead'll be sitting in orbit, out of range of our missile grid. Soon as you clear atmosphere, he'll come for you all guns blazing.'

'Oh, I see. Yes, good point. I hadn't thought of that.'

'Well, me and Francois came up with a plan. I've got the boys to fix us up a rocket of our own, a decoy. We programme it to break atmo on the other side of the planet, and while Gilead's chasing it, you guys can make a break.'

'That's not bad,' said Smith. 'Not bad at all. Wait a moment. What if they scan for lifeforms? It'll just show up as a metal tube.'

Andy grinned. 'That's where we get smart. The nose-cone is hollow. We're gonna put a bunch of plants inside.'

'Plants? Won't they be a bit small?'

'Not these. Genetically modified cauliflowers. We got a load spare. Not like we'll miss 'em, anyway: nobody eats GM food down here.'

'Taste bad, do they?'

'No idea. Nobody's caught one yet. But I reckon we can drive a few into the cone, so long as they don't stampede. Then, all we have to do is fire up.'

Smith took a sip of his beer and rubbed his chin thoughtfully. 'But do you really think the Ghasts will mistake us for a bunch of vegetables? No, don't answer that. How long will this take?'

Andy started pouring himself a beer. 'I reckon we can get launched tomorrow morning. We should be able to stick the rocket up at eleven o'clock, say, if we can get it crewed up by then, and then you'd need to give it about an hour to get around the planet and start transmitting... You could go at noon.'

'That sounds like a jolly good plan,' Smith agreed. 'Alright then, twelve it is. Goodness knows we'll need all the time we can get.'

In his chamber, 462 ran a digit along the spines of his video collection, deciding which speech to watch today. The morning's Shouting In Lines had finished, his torture devices were already polished and there was a little while before *Listen with Glorious Number One* came on the radio. He could spend a human hour or so watching the first fifth of one of One's speeches. He had the complete set.

It was not easy to choose between the lively motivational quality of *You Too Can Become an Assault Brigade Leader Today* or the moving emotional intensity of *Crush All Humans Now*. Who could forget the touching moment when Number One forgot how to speak and simply shrieked like a broken siren, overcome by dribbling rage? Nobody, because anyone who had dared forget it had been shot.

The intercom trumpeted. 'Glorious 462!'

'I hear!' he barked. 'Speak!'

'Puny human Republic craft *Fist of Righteousness* is docked! Human captain approaches!'

'Ahahaha! Prepare for me to address him on the bridge.' He sprang up and pulled his limbs into his coat two at a time.

When Gilead strode in, 462 was waiting for him in a high-backed chair. Gilead marched into the centre of the room and stood there straight-backed with his hat under his arm. The Edenite captain looked ill at ease in the control room, with its ribbed, organic walls, slimy control panels and lack of cruise control.

Ah, humans, thought 462. So foolish, and so weak. They clambered over one another for the chance to make allies of the Ghasts, to curry favour with the beings destined to destroy them. He looked at the newcomer and saw pride, cunning and an ambition that nearly matched his own. This particular human, this Gilead, had his uses.

'You have not captured them,' said 462.

'No.'

'I am disappointed. Saddened, even. It is regrettable that you were deceived.'

'They used a convincing disguise,' the human said.

'Convincing. I have my doubts.' 462 reached down to a box beside his chair and lifted out a very large cauliflower. A crude, smiling face had been drawn on the front of it with a marker pen: two wide, vacantly happy eyes and a broad grin. The face stared at Gilead with banal happiness as 462 held it up. 'You will forgive me, but I do not believe humans are often green?'

'No,' Gilead said.

'No? You are a fool!' 462 sprang from his chair. 'Were we not allies I would have you shot! Your stupidity is intolerable! If you were under my command I would – I would – *ngh*!'

Choked with fury, he pulled off one of his gloves and belted one of his adjutants across the face with it.

'Ow!' said the adjutant.

He turned to it. 'Is there a problem, adjutant?'

'Yes, there is! You just hit me in the face with a glove!'

462 felt that the world was imploding around him. 'Smith is at large. We have scanned the vicinity and have not been able to locate his ship. No doubt the puny humans have been using the opposite side of this pointless world as cover. Now, watch.'

His skinny arm reached out and thumbed a knob on one of his chair's four armrests. An orifice opened in the wall beside Gilead, and with a squelching sound a screen slid out. Images appeared on the screen: planets. It was a map of the system, with Paradis in the centre and the sun at the edge.

'This is the world from which Smith has escaped,' the Ghost explained. 'His craft appears to be a Sheffield class ship, with a damaged supralight tacheon shunt drive and, it seems, working thrusters. Assuming that he has travelled at full sublight speed, here is the maximum radius of distance that he could have reached by now.'

A sphere appeared in the centre of the map, centred around Paradis.

462 barked, 'So, we must calculate where he will be. He is somewhere within this sphere, obviously. But where? If you were Isambard Smith, what would you do?'

'Request a refund.' Gilead rubbed his chin, staring at the map. It glistened.

'You seem unable to provide a location,' said 462.

'No, I know alright. I just don't want to touch a computer that's come out of your spaceship's anus.'

462 turned to one of his praetorian guards. '*Ak! Ak snak nicnak!*' The praetorian saluted and strode off. 'I have ordered light refreshments for us,' 462 explained. 'So, where will our quarry be?'

'He'll need to sort out his ship. The light drive will need repairs.' Gilead smiled. 'There's only one place within range that's got good enough facilities. Deuteronomy.'

'I have not heard of it. What planet is that?'

'It's not a planet. It's a city, the capital of one of our production worlds. Callistan 4. Up there.' Eager, he jabbed the screen, then looked at his fingertip. 'Ugh, mucus. Do you have a handkerchief?'

'Deuteronomy. I look forward to paying this Callistan 4 a visit. Ready the port officials. Be there in person. You will bring him to us.'

'Now listen.' The Ghast's tone galled Captain
Gilead. 'We're partners,' he said. 'I don't take any orders
here.'

'Oh yes you do. There are no equals here, only
hierarchy. There is always one who gives the orders and
one who takes them. Your sect is wise to side with us,
Captain Gilead. Very soon we will be giving the orders to
the whole of the galaxy. If we've not decided to destroy it
instead. We will have our territory, and you will receive
the help you need to carve you own little empire, in the
shadow of our own.'

An aide appeared at the side of them, holding a tray.
462 took a transparent, unwholesome-looking device that
squirted reddish liquid into his mouth. Gilead's drink
came in a plastic cup. 462 watched him take a sip.

Gilead smiled. 'Your alien food isn't bad. Kind've like a
smoothie. Anyhow, it's *you* who are lucky to be coming
along with *us*. Soon, my friend, those of us made in the
Image will begin our great crusade to wipe impiety and
disobedience from every settled planet in the universe. The
galaxy will burn from the light of a billion roasting
heathens, and we shall cast them asunder like the
Moabites, to gnash their seed on stony ground.'

He had been staring out the window while he delivered
this speech, rapt with the notion of barbecuing people. A
hissing noise behind him made him turn and he saw that
462 was sniggering.

As much as his face could, he looked offended. 'What's
so damned funny?'

'Your naïve religious fanaticism amuses me. You fail to
understand that there is no great power behind the

universe. There is only force. Force, and the ceaseless struggle for survival between all living things.'

'Cut that out. That sounds like Evie talk.'

'Of course. The survival of the fittest. That is how space should be run. You or I are greater than the servants you see around us and deserve to triumph where they fail. The rulers must prey on the ruled. It is for that reason that you and I are currently drinking the pulped remains of one of my minions and not the other way around.'

'Phflawgh!'

'But it is vital that you capture this man – and his crew. We must have the woman who travels with him.'

Gilead nodded grimly. 'I know how important she is – better than you do.'

'Good. Then you understand that you must use every resource you have to succeed. This is serious business, Gilead. There can be no room for error. Remember, it is no mere childish game we play.'


'Miss Carveth? In the boiler room, with a piece of piping,' Rhianna said, pointing down the corridor.

'Righto,' said Smith, and he strolled down, opened the door and put his head inside. 'Carveth? Coming up for Scrabble?'

She was staring up at the remains of the plotting computer, a section of tubing in her hand. 'Up in a minute, Boss. I seem to have some pieces left over from the repairs. What we technicians call a "Lego moment".'

The other three were waiting around the table in the living area when Carveth arrived. 'Right,' she said, 'let's get cracking, eh?'

'We will,' Smith said a little gloomily, as if he had something unpleasant to announce. 'But first, Rhianna has something to say.'

They were silent. The only noise was Suruk crunching nonchalantly on something.

'That's right,' Rhianna said, leaning over the table. 'Firstly, I want to thank everyone for dealing with the problems we've experienced so far in a professional way. Now, while I don't necessarily approve of violence, or consider it a solution to problems rather than a problem in itself, I'd like to thank everyone here for looking after me during my time on this ship. Thanks, everyone.'

Smith looked flustered. Carveth caught his eye and waggled her eyebrows, conveying some message whose details he could not read but whose main thrust he knew to be crude. Suruk looked unconcerned and rooted in a little bag for something else to eat.

'Well,' said Smith, 'that's very good of you. Thank you, Rhianna. Very decent. I mean... I, and I think I speak for all of us when I say "I", do try to—'

'We rock out,' Carveth said. 'Anyone second me on that?'

'Rock,' Suruk said.

Carveth nodded. 'Motion carried. We're all pretty super. If anyone's feeling bashful about that, I'll tell them they're great and they can tell me back. Next point?'

Looking a little surprised, Rhianna pushed her hair behind her ears and said, 'Oh, well, I thought now might be a good time for us all to talk.'

The other three studied one another suspiciously, as if a visiting sleuth had just announced that there was a murderer in the room. 'Talk?' said Smith, in the manner that one might say 'Bugger an owl?'

'Yes. I thought that now, while we're together, would be a good time for us to share whatever feelings we might have, that we might want to air with the rest of the group.'

'Does this involve emotions?' Smith said warily.

'Yes, if you'd like.'

'Er, no, I'm fine thanks.'

From the vantage point of his stool Suruk said, 'I constantly want to kill things. Is that an emotion?'

'It could be,' Rhianna said. 'Is there something you'd like to say about that? Something you'd like to get off your chest, to share with the rest of the group?'

'It is brilliant.'

'Okay, silly question... anyone else? Polly?'

'Fine, thanks,' Carveth said.

'Mustn't grumble,' said Isambard Smith.

Carveth slapped her hands together. 'Well, that's that. We're all great. Let's get on with – oh, wait a moment. There *is* something I want to say.'

Rhianna nodded. 'Okay. This is your space. Take your time.'

'Are you an alien?'

'I'm sorry?'

'Look,' said Carveth, 'I've been thinking, right? I'm a simulant, an android, and I'm not too bad at thinking. It's something that's been dawning on me for a while. I reckon there's something really wrong with you and I think it's time we knew the truth.'

Suddenly Rhianna looked afraid, frozen. Her face

hardly moved as she spoke. 'I don't really see what you're getting at.'

'Well, I've made a list. Hold on.' Carveth pulled a bit of paper from her back pocket and unfolded it. 'Right. This is my list of all the weird things you've done. Ready?'

'Ready, I guess,' she replied.

'One. When the void sharks attacked us the second time, they suddenly pulled away just before the captain went out to deal with them. You were meditating at the time.'

'I don't see—'

'Nor did I, at the time. Now, onto the next. The fight with the Ghasts. When they tried to board us, you were next to me. One of them got close, and was about to attack me with its claws. Remember that?'

'Yes, I do.'

'Something happened then, something weird. I can hardly explain it: it was as though a ripple ran through the universe and sort of shifted everything around. Like a burp in the space-time continuum. Do you know anything about that?'

Rhianna shrugged. 'Why should I?' She sounded defensive, hurt.

'You were there. You did it. You made it happen.'

'Hey, I don't have to take this! What is this, Fascist oppression hour? Why should I be called to account because of your negativity?'

'Easy on her, Carveth,' said Smith.

'I am easy.'

'This the galaxy probably knows,' Suruk said.

'Back off, frog. I just want to know the truth, on the off

chance that Rhianna is a space monster in disguise. I think that's pretty reasonable. Now, may I continue?'

'I shall hear you out,' Suruk replied. 'Then possibly knock you out, but go on.'

'Next, that whole knife-throwing thing. What's all that about? I leave the ship for ten minutes, and I come back to find you've grown a force field. Not natural. And what's more, either Suruk and Captain Smith are a pair of absolute chronic idiots or you've done something to their minds to make them think it's all perfectly normal and above board. Eh?'

'I didn't do anything to their minds.'

'Well, alright then. But you are immune to knives, and that ain't right. And, the cap tells me that you stood in front of him in that gunfight down on Paradis and that Edenite officer bloke fired a whole magazine at you and none of the bullets hit. That's not just weird: that's Kate Bush territory. Explain that.'

The ship hummed around them. The three faces turned to her. Slowly, Rhianna opened her hands and shrugged. 'I don't know,' she said.

'You don't know?'

'I really don't. I mean, I've always believed in Karma. Does that help at all?'

'You must have been doing some bloody good works in your past life to turn bulletproof,' Carveth replied.

Smith said quietly, 'Rhianna, have you always been able to do this?'

'Always?'

'As in "all your life",' Carveth put in. 'Look, I don't know what you really are, but I've got a shortlist. And none of the options is looking good.' She turned her piece of paper over and peered at writing on the back of it. 'Here's my shortlist. One, you're an alien; two, an assassin reprogrammed by the government – it happens, I saw it on TV – or, three, some sort of magic person with psychic powers.'

'Oh, please,' Rhianna exclaimed. 'Enough persecution already, little miss witchfinder. Come on, do I *look* like an alien?'

'You might be. An alien could look exactly like a person except for some extra stuff stuck on its head. The difference could be very small.'

'Unlikely,' Suruk said.

'Rhianna,' Smith said gently, 'can you remember anything from your past that's been like this? Have you always been able to do unusual things? Your parents, for example. How about them?'

'Well, they were hippies. They fled the Republic of Eden just after the War of Disarmament. They ended up on New Fran, but first they went to Earth and followed the old 1960's trail: Woodstock, Tangiers, Morocco, Brighton, Skegness – they didn't really do maps.'

'I see. What else *did* they do?'

'Acid. And they looked into crystals and stuff. They were Vorl nuts.'

'What, little round things?' Carveth said, screwing up her face in puzzlement.

'*Vorl* nuts,' Smith said. 'Vorl is the name of an important alien race.'

'No wonder I've never heard of them,' Carveth said. She sighed. 'I don't see the connection. Who are these Vorl, anyway?'

'The guardians of space,' Rhianna said quietly. 'The most advanced race our galaxy has ever seen. Creatures so attuned to the cosmos that they became one with it, free from the constraint of earthy bodies, free to live forever amongst the stars.'

Suruk had been listening with his head tilted to one side, quietly crunching. 'I have heard of such things,' he said. 'The floaty woman speaks only half the truth. There are many legends spoken of the Vorl: we of the M'Lak believe that they once walked amongst us. To those who they called friends, they gave honour. But to those who they called enemies, who sought to bend their power to evil ends, they brought doom. It was said that they could throw down lightning from the sky itself, and melt the very flesh from a man's bones as if it were wax. Of course, they said it about the M'Lak, not men as such, but the point remains.'

Smith shrugged. 'It's all nonsense, if you ask me. There're two very good reasons why nobody's found the Vorl: firstly, space is infinitely vast, providing a sentient being with limitless opportunities to hide, and secondly, they're not real. I suggest we just get back to repairing the ship and forget all this made-up science-fiction stuff. The positronic versifier won't transfibulate itself, after all.'

'Perhaps my parents knew something about the Vorl,' Rhianna said. 'I guess that would explain why the Ghasts are after me.'

'Perhaps the storkoid left them a little bundle under the cosmic gooseberry bush,' Carveth said. 'Perhaps you *are* a Vorl.'

'Stop that,' said Smith. 'Look, Rhianna. What Carveth

says is true: there's no doubting that you have special abilities, which make you... special. That's fine by me. It's variety that makes the Empire great. That and dreadnoughts. And tea.

'When I was at school, one of my best friends was unusual. He used to eat crayons, but we all thought he was smashing. He'd always have people round him, in spite of him being, um, special, especially if he was eating a crayon at the time. We'd all say, "Look, there goes Crayony Dave again", and everyone would laugh, and so would he. Everyone was happy. So you see my point.'

Rhianna said: 'You want me to eat crayons?'

'Goodness no!' Smith laughed. 'It's that you may be weird as hell, but you're one of us, no matter what you are. In all honesty, even I don't know what you are myself!' He laughed again, in what seemed an oddly silent room. I hope to God you're not psychic, he added to himself. That could be embarrassing. Especially what with you being a very fine bit of filly indeed. God, the number of times I've thought about parping your boobs... If you're listening, Rhianna, I didn't say that. 'And besides, the fact is that whatever your parents' connection to the Vorl may be, it seems that someone out there thinks you're worth capturing. Beer, anyone?'

He stood up and fetched new bottles. Smith lined them up and began to open the caps. 'It doesn't really matter, though, in the long run. The fact is, you're a woman in need of help and you're on my ship, and if anyone wants to kidnap you while you're on board, they'll have to fight their way past me first. I'm sure the crew agree. Right, crew? Crew?'

'I agree,' Suruk said.

Carveth ran a hand through her hair. 'Looks like we're all in this together,' she said. 'Just don't fry anyone.'

'It was melt,' Rhianna said.

'Ah, so you admit it!'

'I'm only repeating what Suruk said.'

'Well, alright. Now,' said Carveth, 'has anyone got anything else they'd like to raise, or can we move on to Item Two on the list – Scrabble? Nobody? Right then, let's Scrab. Where are all the letters?'

'Mint, anyone?' said Suruk, holding out the bag.

'Oh, for God's sake!' Carveth grimaced, mouthed some words and sighed. 'Right then, Scrabble's off. It's chess or Mousetrap.'

'Mousetrap,' said Smith. 'I wouldn't play chess against a Morlock if I were you.'

'Will he rip my arm out of its socket if he loses?'

'I don't know. He never loses. That's why I wouldn't play chess with him.'

'Fair enough. Mousetrap it is. But don't go crazy, now: we've got two days to kill.'

The next day, Carveth was on the bridge with the captain, reading. A light flashed under the main navigation dials and she turned around in her seat. 'We're coming into range of Deuteronomy's main radar array,' she announced. 'I've plotted a course to take us into the landing zone with minimal engine activity. The computer's logged to show us up as an unmanned automatic cargo lander.'

'Righto.'

'But we'll have to go quietly. That means lights out and no whistling. We need to keep detectable noise to an absolute minimum.'

Smith frowned. 'I don't like it, Carveth, all this creeping around. It's like we're playing their game. We're Imperial citizens, for heaven's sake: we ought to be able to walk right up to them and say, "Listen here, Johnny Godpants, I happen to be civilised and I'm coming through", not creeping around like a bunch of Wheezing Willies.'

'Point taken. But until we get the supralux fixed we're strictly in derring-don't territory. We need this, Captain.'

'I know. But it bothers me.'

'Well, we need to do this quietly. Once we're down on the planet we should be fine. But until we can make contact with Andy's friends in the resistance, we have to go in with as little fuss as possible.'

'What about the radio?'

'I'm not sure. I thought we'd radio them once we're in the atmosphere. It'll give the police less chance to get the signal before we get the ship underground, and there should be plenty of background radio noise to confuse anyone.'

'Good plan. But how do you mean, underground?'

'Callistan is a wasteland. All indigenous life is extinct and there's hardly any atmosphere at all. All there is above ground is bunkers. The wallies who run Callistan have wasted it.'

'Wasted it?'

'Environmental meltdown. Rhianna told me about it. It's on the Friends of The Various Earths website, apparently.'

The radio crackled into life. A fanfare blasted out across the control room. Carveth fumbled for the switches. 'It's automated,' she whispered. 'We're just picking it up.'

'On the hour, every hour, hourly!' the radio cried. 'This is Eden Space News – True and Accurate! Today – British Foreign Secretary meets with bearded man. We ask: Is this evidence of Satanism? How could it not be?'

Smith stared at Carveth. 'What's this?'

'Must be their version of the news,' she replied.

'Can't be. Nobody shouts on the real news.'

The radio bellowed on. 'The bearded "man" met with foreign secretary Lucy "Fur" Wilkins, ostensibly to discuss trade at a conference near the Baltic Sea. Baltic Sea – or Here-Sea? You decide. Damn right, it's heresy! Good decision! For more stories on this story, stay tuned to me, Edward Cauldron, sending unbelievers straight to hell on the Edward Cauldron Truth Show! And now for a message from our new friends in the Ghast Empire.'

Smith reached up and flicked the radio off. 'Foreign propaganda,' he said. 'A mere mouthpiece for the state.'

Carveth shrugged. 'On the plus side, they are re-running Space Confederates.'

The city of Deuteronomy was almost invisible from the air, as if it had escaped the Last Judgement by burrowing into the ground. On the surface, only squat bunkers broke the useless earth, linked by land-trains like fortresses on wheels. Beneath ground level, the citizens eked out their lives.

Satellites studded the sky: some relayed orders from the

rulers of the Democratic Republic, on their more luxurious worlds, while others broadcast propaganda to any other chunk of space that would listen. Rival human empires switched off; aliens puzzled over the messages from the New Eden for a little while and switched off too. But most of the satellites were for gathering information, not for sending it out.

Carveth's approach was clever, mainly because someone else had planned it. The *John Pym* drew closer in an arc, avoiding the long-range surveillance drones at the edge of Callistan's orbit, slipping past the barrage of police stations that hovered over the main settlements. They were aiming not for any of Deuteronomy's major space-ports, but for the shipworks on the edge of the city, the industrial area that the authorities treated with too much contempt to study closely. Here thousands of nobodies lived, welding and repairing ships in endless shifts, all of them too poor and badly-organised to be worth policing with anything more than the occasional riot squad.

As a result, nobody bothered the *John Pym*. No-one cared that it was not an automated ship at all, or that its crew had spent the past day and a half failing to pay for the TV channels they had received. The only drone that checked them recorded nothing more than the fact that the vessel was unarmed. Their descent was quiet and untroubled, until at last a voice came across the radio and said, 'Dude, this is Neil.'

All was dark and quiet in the *John Pym*. Carveth had fetched the covers from her bed, laid them across her lap and was now sleeping in the pilot's chair, the door closed.

Suruk, a stranger to innuendo, had retired to his room to polish his favourite bone. Smith decided it would be a good moment to make friends with Rhianna.

Quite how was another matter. He could not ask Carveth for advice, as that would be embarrassing, and he could not ask Suruk, because he was asexual and would inevitably suggest ripping off Carveth's head and presenting it to Rhianna, who was after all a vegetarian and would not be very impressed. It was difficult.

Rhianna made him feel crass and ignorant, in the way that the Hillaries back home did not. 'What ho!' a random Hillary would shout, slapping dirt off her jodhpurs, and Smith would only have to reply 'Quite!' or 'Bloody good, that!' to draw her attention from the Labradors to himself. Rhianna came from a more sophisticated world, where trading with aliens was not supposed to involve exchanging shiny bottle tops for priceless cultural artefacts and, despite coming from Australia, AC/DC did not qualify as World Music. After lengthy deliberation, he decided to cook some food for her.

They ate by the light of an emergency hand-warmer, the closest thing to a candle on board the darkened ship. 'I really appreciate this,' Rhianna said, before Smith brought the food to the table. She smelt strongly of Patchouli oil, which meant that she might not be able to taste what he had made so easily. That could only be a good thing. 'It's very kind of you. What are these pink floating things?'

'Ah,' said Smith, 'Special recipe. All completely without meat. You see, what you've got floating there is synthetic

synthetic ham. We usually get given synthetic ham to eat, which contains ham extract and we spacefarers shortened to Sham. But this is synthetic Sham, which doesn't even contain any synthetic ham and which the company used to call Sham Light but don't any more because we shortened it to Shite. It's not really shite, actually,' he added, feeling that this explanation had ended on a weak note. 'Well, it's not got any meat in it, anyway.'

'It looks very... cubic,' Rhianna said. Smith put some of the stuff into bowls, reflecting on the rather runny sauce and the oddly furtive way that the pieces of Sham Light broke the surface before ducking out of sight again. He passed one of the bowls to Rhianna. She tried it. 'Mmn!' she said. 'It tastes... cubic, too!'

Smith frowned. 'I tell you what, let's have some music, shall we?'

He crossed to the cassette player at the rear of the room, and selected one. 'You might not have heard this before,' he said, activating the machine. 'It's by Mozart, a historical British chap.'

'Mozart, British? Wasn't he from Vienna?'

Smith frowned. 'I don't think so. He was English, Mozart.'

Rhianna grinned. 'You mean Wolfgang Amadeus Mozart?'

'That's the one. English to the core. Take "Piano Concerto 21", for instance. Or "The Requiem". He wouldn't have given them English names if he wasn't from England.'

Rhianna put her hand across her mouth and gave a

small snorting laugh. 'How about "Eine Kleine Nacht Musik"?'

'Well, he had to give it a German title. It was written for a German, you see. For Elise.'

'You really are quite a man,' Rhianna said. 'So much for the brown questions.'

'I'm better on Elgar, to be honest.'

Smith sat back down and looked at the meal he had made. With the sophisticated music playing around the room, he felt as if he were being piped to the table by an honour guard in preparation for eating a bag of chips. His meal lay sadly on his plate. He put a dollop on his spoon and raised it lipward. It sat there insolently, like a small animal that had made a dirty, sit-down protest on his spoon. 'Mm,' he said, opening wide. 'Looks nice – flughk! Oh Christ, that's disgusting!' He reached out and dragged her bowl towards him. 'You are *not* eating any more of that.'

Rhianna nodded. 'Well, now you mention it, it is kind of funny-tasting.'

Miserably, he said, 'It's foul, isn't it?'

'Not foul as such, no... foulesque, perhaps.'

'I'm very sorry,' Smith said. He shook his head. 'All this is rather difficult, I'm afraid.'

She stood up, ready to take the bowls away. 'Oh, don't worry about it. I can't cook to save my life. I appreciate the effort, though.'

'I don't mean that. I mean having a woman on board.' He pinched the brow of his nose, suddenly surprised to find himself in this territory. So much for seduction, and tact: like a drunken man leaving a waterfront bar and strolling gaily off the pier, he suddenly found himself in difficult, uncharted territory. Time to thrash his way to the surface and escape. 'I mean to say, there's Carveth of course, but she's not really a woman.'

'She is a simulant.'

'I was going to say "harridan", but yes. Which leaves, well, you.'

She sat down. Rhianna put her elbows on the table and leaned on them. It made her look very earnest, and gave her face a serious beauty. She said, 'Is it bad luck, having me on board?'

'Only for you,' said Smith.

She laughed. 'Oh, it's not too bad. Sure, the cuisine could be better, and the beds are kind of funny, and I get a bit nervous sometimes with Suruk and all those skulls he collects, but there's loads of ways it could be worse, like...' she thought about it, 'loads.'

'I suppose so,' Smith said, unconvinced.

She sighed. 'Look. I think I know what this is.'

'You do?'

'Sure. I'm a woman, you're pretty much a man, it's—'

Carveth walked in. 'Alright all. Good news is we're on the final phase to touch down, bad news is where we're touching down. I've got through to Andy's contact on the surface, who's called Neil, and he's sorting stuff out. I couldn't understand half of what he was saying, but we seem to be alright.'

'That sounds like a pretty comprehensive "maybe",' said Smith. 'Carveth, could you go out and come back in five minutes, please?'

'Um, not really. You see, there's a bit more. This Neil man thinks I'm the captain.'

'What? Why?'

'I don't know. He just sort of got the wrong idea. I think it was me telling him that I was that did it.' She sighed. 'I thought it might take the heat off us a bit.' Exasperated, she twirled her hands. 'It just seemed like a good idea. Except it wasn't, and now I regret it.'

Smith grimaced. 'Just stick us down, Carveth.'

'Right. I'll see you in a minute,' Smith said to Rhianna, and he got up and followed Carveth to the cockpit. She dropped into the pilot's seat and he stood behind her, watching as the ship sank into Callistan's ruined atmosphere.

'You're a bloody idiot, pretending to be the captain,' said Smith. 'I mean, whoever heard of a woman called Isambard?'

Carveth said, 'You do realise I gave them a false name, don't you? A girl's name?'

'Well, that's slightly better, I suppose.'

The radio crackled. 'Captain Daisy Chainsaw? Is that you?'

'Or arguably worse,' said Smith.

'Ah, yes, yes indeed, that's me,' Carveth said. For some reason she had deepened her voice, as if the previous exchange had confused her into thinking that she was indeed a man. 'We're just on our way down now.'

A young man's face was on the screen. He had a pointed chin and wore sunglasses with slanted lenses that made him look like a previous century's idea of an alien.

'Okay, that's cool. How come you're flying it with controls? Isn't there a neural port?'

'Sometimes it's easier to do things by yourself. Space is full of incompetents.' She turned and whispered, 'That was in character, Boss.'

'Way true,' said the face on the screen. 'These days, half of the old reality's just a bulletin board for burnt-out squat-jockeys, you know? So, when're you cowboys due to jack in here, huh?'

Carveth glanced at Smith, who shrugged. She turned back to the screen. "Um, both?"

In the cockpit of a small, fast craft, Dreckitt studied his instructions. His android brain memorised the face of the woman called Polly Carveth. He fed her picture into the onboard computers and they showed him how she would look with different hair, glasses and a false moustache, from behind. Dreckitt committed a thousand different disguises to memory and waxed his long brown coat.

Polly Carveth seemed like an ideal target. She should be a simple opponent: small and isolated, a civilian masquerading as crew on this British ship, the *John Pym*. From the look of her, she would have no fighting ability and not much resourcefulness. An easy kill.

Those were the best sort. Among the non-cognoscenti, it was often thought that bounty killers took a certain pleasure in their work, that they appreciated the artistry and skill that went into a difficult job. Dreckitt, of course, took no real pleasure in anything (although he got a certain grim satisfaction out of eating cold Chinese food under a flickering neon sign), but had he been capable of *joi de vivre*, he would have found it elsewhere. He would far rather have had a weakling as a target than a dangerous foe. Some nights he dreamed of being paid to hunt down a particularly ferocious kitten, and awoke suspecting that he was in the wrong line of work.

Bounty killers were a bad, solitary bunch, and Dreckitt had always preferred to work alone. They were brutal, amoral and fond of doing things like wearing powerful rocket packs, which made them dangerous people to fight alongside – or, more specifically, beneath. The only people Dreckitt had met who were any worse were space pirates, who although less coldly sadistic were annoyingly prone to burst into song.

Only one thing bothered Dreckitt, existential angst aside. Carveth had no history. Six months ago, she simply disappeared off the records. There was no date of birth, no record of employment, no next of kin – nothing, in fact, to prove that she was older than half a year.

That smelt of android to Dreckitt, and he was not going to kill one of his own. That lawyer had frightened him.

He lit a cigarette. I could get it wrong, he thought. I could mistake a human being for a simulant. I need to be absolutely sure with this one.

That meant that he would have to get close, insinuate himself with her to make sure, use the Hoyt Axton test before moving in for the kill. This was going to take charm as well as firepower. He decided to brush his teeth with toothpaste instead of whisky today.

*

Smith left Carveth to talk with their new friend. If she wanted to be captain, she could deal with all of the captain stuff, which seemed to include communicating with a man who spoke a language of his own invention, badly.

Annoyingly, but predictably, Rhianna had retreated to her room. Smith thought about going to see her and decided that there was no point, as he would only cock things up further. Somehow he needed to start a conversation with her without opening his big stupid mouth. The best bet would be semaphore, he decided bitterly.

Suruk was in the hold, standing still, eyes closed. Smith had never worked out quite what he did at these times, whether he was meditating, thinking, or simply resting his brain for later use. Whatever it was, he needed to persuade Suruk to remain out of sight until they had finished their negotiations. If anything was guaranteed to spoil a delicate black-market deal, it was a frog-faced savage with a skull fixation.

As he entered, the alien turned, his tiny eyes opening to squint at Smith.

'We're setting down in about half an hour,' Smith said.

Suruk made his croaking sound. 'Excellent. I shall fetch my weapons.'

'Um, no. I'd rather you stayed on board.'

'On board? You do not wish me to leave the ship?'

'Well, yes. Actually, could you just sit in one of the storage lockers?'

'I shall not.'

'Well, could you at least stay out of sight? I mean, it's not as if there'd be anything to do here. There're no shops, murder is illegal – I just think you'd get bored.'

Suruk scowled behind his tusks. 'You would rather I remained in the ship?'

'Yes.'

'Huh. Some holiday this is turning into.'

'You could have plenty of fun here. You could, oh, hunt rats or something.'

'Very well.'

'Brilliant. I appreciate this, Suruk. It's just that the people here are not very open-minded and may get offended by you being here.'

'All the more reason to open their minds up, with an axe.'

'I agree – but not this time, eh?'

'Huh. Very well. I shall not lower the tone. You can do that for yourself,' he added, turning away and crossing his arms.

'Don't be like that,' said Smith. 'It's just for now. I promise when we've got the engine back we'll go and find somewhere primeval for you. Alright?'

'Primeval *and* brutal?'

'Absolutely. I promise. Now, could you help me sort the guns out, please?'

# 8

# Cyber-gangsters in Martian Death Pact!

Below the *John Pym*, a great iris-lock sat flush with the earth, as if some vast camera were hidden below the rock. As the ship descended, the lock slid open with a harsh scraping noise they could pick out even over the howling wind. The *Pym* sank down into the earth, into a massive tunnel of shining metal, and the iris closed above it.

Suddenly the permanent storm was gone. The ship's engines thrummed, echoing in the tunnel. There were pilot lights on the tunnel walls, rising in the windscreen as they went down.

'This doesn't look good,' Carveth said.

'The big rifle's under my bed,' Smith replied. 'I've put the Maxim cannon in a cargo box, in the hold. If there's trouble, get back to the ship and we can arm up there.'

'Right.'

'Offer these people the guns Andy gave us. If they seem interested, invite them into the hold to have a look at the merchandise. Then at least we'll be able to talk to them on home ground.'

'I'm not sure I *can* talk to them,' Carveth said.

The radio crackled. 'Ho, dudes!' Neil exclaimed. 'You're straight in the pipeline, five by five!'

Carveth grimaced. 'You see what I mean? Could be Swahili for all I know.'

The ship landed, the legs folding slightly to take its weight. Smith felt the cabin sway a little, compensated by hydraulics, and he saw the place that held the ship: a great round hall walled with stainless steel. Little people moved about in tough working clothes or long coats: technicians, probably. Almost nobody's eyes were visible: all wore dark glasses. It looked like the foyer of a spy convention.

Smith said, 'You know what to do?'

'Yes, I do,' Carveth replied. She had a service revolver strapped to her hip. 'I feel nervous, though.'

'It's not easy, being the captain,' Smith replied. 'It takes skill and talent.'

'I wish you'd told me earlier. I wish they'd told you, for that matter.'

'We'll be watching you. Keep on the side, where the camera can follow you.' Smith wore the Civiliser he had taken from Corveau in a holster under his arm. 'I'll be ready.'

Carveth stood up and Smith took the pilot's seat. 'Just in case we have to make a quick escape, this button makes us go up,' she said. 'You'll know when we reach the top.'

'The bumping sensation will be a clue, I expect.'

'As will the subsequent plummeting and screaming,' she added, and she smiled grimly as she walked to the airlock. 'Let's go.'

She pressed the button and the door unlocked. The door opened on a joyless, silvery world.

*

Smith spent the next half-hour watching the monitors in
the cockpit. Rhianna made tea. Smith was on his fourth
cup when Carveth returned. Three people followed. They
wore long coats and sunglasses.

Smith leaned in to the intercom. 'Heads up, chaps,
foreigners on the way. Looks like a delegation from the
nerd homeworld.'

Rhianna wandered into the control room. 'They look
absurd,' she said, peering at the monitor. 'What's Polly
making that signal for?'

'Ah. She's telling me I've got the outside speakers on.
They look like very clever nerds, though,' he added,
loudly, and he flipped the switch. 'Balls.'

The doorbell made an ugly screeching sound. 'Best let
her in,' Rhianna said.

'Right. To your places, everyone! Remember, the
charade must be kept up at all times!'

'You don't have to shout,' Rhianna said, and she wandered back into the hold.

Smith opened the door. 'Hello Carveth. Bring back
some chaps, did you?'

'That's Captain Chainsaw to you! Step back from the
door!'

Carveth strode inside, followed by her visitors. 'Some of
the incompetents you get on board, eh?' she announced.
'If it wasn't for my captaining this ship would just drop
out of space.'

'It wouldn't drop,' the woman behind her said. 'It
would drift. There's no gravity in space.' She peered
around, unimpressed. Her black lenses made her look like
a gigantic locust, with lipstick. 'And it's captaincy.'

A youngish, spotty man followed her. 'Ho,' he said, noticing Smith.

'This is Neil,' Carveth explained. 'This is Trinny, and the man at the back is Morris.'

Morris, a tall black man with a bald head, looked around very slowly and declared, 'Your... ship. It has a certain aura, a sensibility... an odour.'

'That'll be him,' Carveth said, cocking a thumb at Smith. 'Right then, who wants to buy some lovely guns?'

She strode towards the hold. 'Tea for me, fizzy soft drink for the delegates,' she called back at Smith, and he turned and headed for the galley. 'On the double!' she added.

Smith made the tea and took it into the hold along with a bottle of some filthy brown cola stuff he found in the bottom of a cupboard. The three visitors stood around the table in the centre of the hold, on which Rhianna and Smith had laid the guns they had taken from Corveau's men. Carveth and Rhianna stood a little way back, to allow the rebels to examine the merchandise. Suruk was nowhere to be seen, which meant that he was probably creeping up on them all.

'Ah, there you are,' Carveth said. 'Here's the drinks, gentlemen. Put them down there, Isambard.'

'Isambard?' Neil glanced up. 'That's your name?'

'Well, not really,' Smith replied, remembering that he was a wanted criminal. 'It's Isambard... Jones. Sort of a *nom de plume*, except that I don't write anything.'

'*Nom de guerre*,' Trinny said.

'Right. But not my real name. Which isn't Isambard either. That's just made up.'

'Isambard. I like it. Good handle you've got there,' Neil said.

'Thanks. I grew it myself.'

'I meant your name, not your moustache. You know, your handle. What you use when you jack in.'

Smith's eyes narrowed. 'Are you getting funny with me?'

'Let's move on,' Trinny said. She stood with her hands on hips, feet apart, like a superhero waiting for adulation. Under her shiny coat she wore tight shiny things, as if hit by bin liners in a wind tunnel. 'This is what you're selling, then.'

'Yes,' said Carveth.

'I see. They could be better. But they're not licensed, not tracked. They could be of use to us. The street finds uses for things.'

'Yet all is traceable in the era of the *zaibatsu*,' Morris said cryptically. 'All things become elements in a whole... fragments in ice.'

'Riiiight,' said Carveth. 'Super. Are you lot going to buy these guns or what?'

The three exchanged a glance. It was clear that their sunglasses completely prevented them reading one another's expressions. 'We need to confer,' Trinny said, and they took out mobile phones.

'Why don't we leave you to do so?' Smith said. 'We'll have our tea outside.'

'Who are these idiots?' Smith whispered as soon as they were in the corridor.

'They're not that bad,' Carveth replied.

'They're complete arseheads. And why do they talk like that?'

'The regime tightly controls all information on technology,' Rhianna said. 'Apparently it's virtually impossible to get hold of any literature written after 1989.'

'Awesome to the max!' Neil exclaimed in the hold. 'Mondo narly!'

'I see,' said Smith. 'Couldn't we have found anybody else?'

Carveth shrugged. 'What do you want? These people are anti-government, for one thing. For another, the only other person Andy said was looking for unmarked guns is called Doctor Apocalypse and runs a lobster-enlargement programme from a secret island base.'

'Fair enough, then. And calm down, Carveth; stop ordering everyone about. Just because you're captain doesn't entitle you to behave like an idiot.'

They returned to the hold.

'– and I got eight on a d.12, and totally passed my saving throw,' Neil was saying. 'Whoa – it's them again.'

'We have come to a conclusion,' Trinny announced, folding her shiny arms around her shiny cleavage with a loud squeak of PVC. 'We think yes. We'll give you six thousand plus information.'

'We wanted seven,' Carveth said. 'How good's the information?'

'Good is... subjective,' Morris said. 'In a culture of data, information is not just money... but blood.'

'Anyone else want to try?' Carveth said.

'Nobody comes here unless they have to,' Trinny replied. 'You're not here to trade – you're here because you need to be. A trader would send a drone, not wetware. You need something, otherwise you would use the True Reality, not the flesh. And what you need is probably information.'

'Um,' Carveth said.

'So, what do you need to know? Our knowledge is the best in the metaverse. Knowledge is our only true weapon.'

'And guns,' Neil said. 'Loads of guns.'

'We need computer parts for a ship,' Smith said. 'Equipment to power a supralux drive.'

'Supralux, huh? Figures, if you want to get out of here,' Trinny replied. She glanced at Morris, struggled to peer through his lenses, and gave up. 'If it's black market equipment you want, there's one person you need to talk to. Well, when I say person, I mean thing.'

'Thing?' Carveth said.

'He's reliable enough,' she said. 'I just wouldn't trust him too far.'

'Well, let's see the cash, before you turn us over to Johnny Alien,' said Smith.

'Pipe down, crew!' Carveth barked. 'Who gives the orders here? It's me, by the way. Now, can we see the money, before you turn us over to Johnny Alien?'

Trinny pulled a wad of creased notes out of her coat and tossed it onto the table. 'Six thousand two hundred. That's more than these weapons are worth. I'll call up Lupin and Spandex and have them collect the guns.'

'So where is this person who can get us the parts?' Smith said. He would have let Carveth take control, but she was preoccupied counting and smelling the cash.

'He... exists... elsewhere,' Morris said. 'In a place... different to this.'

It occurred to Smith that Morris might not be wise so much as a bit special.

'We can take you to him,' Neil said. 'His name is Ordo.'

It was not easy to land legally on Deuteronomy. Dreckitt's spacecraft was small, badly-lit and soon very smoky, and he left much of the driving to the autopilot while he sat about in his coat and cleaned the enormous pistol he used for killing humans. Once he was in orbit around Deuteronomy, he submitted his Warrant of Operation to the authorities and waited for a response. The security services of the Republic of Eden were notoriously complex.

The agency responsible for monitoring space traffic was the Department of Internal Liberty and Democracy Operations, which towards its upper end entered the Agency for Securing Security. The Agency for Securing Security was in turn connected to GROIN, the Government of the Republic's Operational Intelligence Network. The whole arrangement was somewhat incestuous.

It took a day before Dreckitt's warrant was processed. He was sitting slumped in his chair, smoking a cigarette and raising a glass of cheap whisky to his lips, when the terminal began to beep. Startled, he opened his mouth, dropped his cigarette into his drink, and burned his eyebrows off. He had been granted clearance.

In theory, the agencies of the Republic were supposed to monitor the influx of spies, terrorists and other subversives, then reduce their numbers by arresting them. In practice, the agencies increased the number of spies and so on by arresting large numbers of unusual-looking people and beating them until they confessed to being such. After this beating, the suspects, who if not unusual-looking before certainly were now, would be removed to Camp Joyful in the neutral wasteland area just outside Republic territory, and might on occasion be allowed to return in order to be publicly executed. Unsurprisingly, each suspect only received this privilege once.

The Devrin corporation was powerful enough to bypass most of the Republic's security controls. Nobody bothered Dreckitt as his ship dropped into one of Deuteronomy's seedier loading ports. Nobody demanded details of his mission: it was enough that the company had sent him. From then on he was left to his own devices.

He pressed his finest pinstriped suit. He wore a white handkerchief in the top pocket and his best socks with clocks on them. He slid the Assassinator into his shoulder holster and put on the tie that nobody had ever tried to strangle him with. Dreckitt brushed down his hat and placed it carefully on top of his well-combed hair. He was reasonably presentable and he didn't care who knew it.

Time to make a killing.

'So then,' said Isambard Smith, 'tell me about this Ordo person.'

'Shush!' Neil hissed. 'Keep it down, dude!'

They were walking through a colossal hall, one of Deuteronomy's massive, vaultlike caverns. It seemed to be a gigantic shopping centre as far as Smith could tell. Little groups of teenagers – many of them dressed like Neil and his friends – loitered around benches, while herds of bored citizens ambled past. Uniformed guards strode up and down, shock-sticks and machine guns in their belts and caps pulled down low, the visors hiding their eyes.

'Sorry,' Smith said. 'Didn't realise it wasn't safe.'

'It is never safe,' Morris observed from the rear of the group. 'The... very notion of "safety" is... unfeasible in our age.'

'Righto.'

'They're always watching,' Neil said. 'This way.'

It was an ugly place, Smith thought, all gleaming metal and soulless, wipe-clean surfaces. Where was the wrought iron and polished brass, the cogs and mock-gothic arches of the Empire? Deuteronomy was aggressively pleasant, as if built by people fanatically devoted to blandness. He glanced at what looked like a big carpet store, and was surprised to find that it was a church. Had Smith been a deity, he would never have gone inside. Unless he needed a carpet.

They stepped onto an escalator and rose fifty feet to the next floor. Amid the crowds of shoppers in their jolly, pastel clothes, they were a sombre, skinny little group. Neil pressed a button on the wall and a service door slid open. They stepped into a tiny lift, their coats squeaking as they pressed together.

Smith thought: if they try anything on me, they're at least close enough to hit. Fend them off with the left and draw with the right. The lift started to descend.

'We will need to wear filter-masks,' Trinny remarked. 'Ordo's metabolism is unlike ours.'

The three of them took out black, gilled masks and sealed them over their mouths. Neil passed Smith a mask of his own. It looked like the kind of thing recommended for DIY.

Smith put it on. 'He's a Marty, is he, this Ordo?'

'He is no mere human,' Neil said. 'He's an amazing dude. He's a master of black science. He's like a dude who schemes with both hands. Except they're tentacles.'

'Marty, then?'

'Ordo is one of the city's most important black-marketeers,' Morris explained, in a rare burst of coherent speech. 'He is vital to our mission, but he is concerned only with himself. Even his conversion to Edenism was false. We wear these masks because he lacks the immune system of a normal human being.'

'So he's a Martian, then?'

'Yes, he's a god-damn Martian,' Trinny said, and she made a huffing noise. They finished their journey in silence.

The lift doors slid open and Neil stepped out. Smith followed him, casual but wary. 'This way?' he said, nodding down the corridor.

'This way,' Neil replied, and he led the group.

This must be some kind of service corridor, Smith thought: the sides were rough concrete, the pipes exposed. Smith could feel the closeness of his new friends. They were well-positioned to attack him with their fists, but a little too close for gunplay. Duck low, he thought, barge them aside and turn round with a gun drawn. The

210

Civiliser lurked under his arm, pressed against his side.

Neil pointed at the doors at the end of the tunnel. 'Here,' he said. He leaned in to a crude-looking intercom bolted to the doorframe. 'It's us.'

A muted hooting came from the plastic speaker, like wind catching on a Swannee whistle. 'Okay,' Neil said, and he stepped back and looked up at a video camera installed above the doors.

The hooting began again. 'Aw, c'mon,' Neil said. 'I can't do that. I'm... y'know, with people. It's embarrassing.'

'Your Clanger chap sounds a bit demanding,' Smith observed. Trinny turned to face him, her sunglasses hiding what he suspected would have been a withering stare.

Neil continued to remonstrate with the whistle. A particularly vigorous burst of hooting parped out from the speaker, and sulkily Neil pulled his mask down, looked into the lens and took his sunglasses off. 'Not fair,' he said, blinking.

An iris-recognition system beeped. The speaker crackled and fell silent.

'Looks like we're in,' Trinny said. The doors scraped apart, and they stepped inside.

They walked into a room-sized airlock, a corridor overgrown with wires and junk, like the hideout of some gigantic magpie. Trestle tables stood against the walls, piled high with manuals, tools, circuitry and half-dismantled components. Several of the ceiling panels had been opened up for no apparent purpose other than to use the wiring as bunting. A vaguely meaty smell hung in the air, like old pizza.

'Batchelor, is he?' said Smith.

'We wait here,' Morris said grimly. Fans spun in the ceiling, and the air suddenly acquired a detergent tang.

Neil leaned in close. 'Remember, dude, keep your mask on.'

The doors at the end of the corridor slid apart. Neil nodded to Smith and as a group they walked into a single large chamber. This place had been an apartment once: traces of the partitions still remained. Clusters of screens filled the corners. A red potplant had climbed up one of the walls. Slowly, the being in the centre of the room turned around – or rather, the machinery that supported it did.

It looked like a fat octopus on stilts. The bulk of the thing, at once bloated and sagging, overhung a delicate arrangement of joined metal limbs, like a walking gallows. There were clumps of slender tentacles at the front of the thing, just below its eyes and beak. As Smith watched, disgusted, it put out a ropy limb and lifted a tool from its metal waist and held it in front of its mouth. Speakers on the waist crackled into life.

The voice that came out of the translator was rich and deep. 'No-one would have believed, in the middle of the twenty-sixth century, that my affairs would have been of sufficient significance to be watched from across the void of space. And yet, here is a visitor. I am Ordo. Welcome, sir. Feel free to put on some gloves and shake my approximation of a hand.'

'I'm well, thank you,' Smith said coldly. 'I'm here to do business.'

'A harsh attitude, sir,' Ordo replied. 'I welcome the

British. I find you a pleasant, cultured, flammable race. Still, perhaps we can find some common ground to talk about, maybe?'

Ordo's eyes were reflective lenses. Smith looked around the room. Had it not been full of women, nerds, aliens and half-baked mystics, all of them foreign, he might have been unnerved.

'Well, let's get down to business,' he said. 'I need a plotting unit for a Sheffield light freighter, and I gather you can help me.'

Half an hour later the four humans left Ordo's lair. They walked silently down the corridor and Neil pressed the button to call the lift.

'Dude,' said Neil, 'this is where we split, like two console jocks riding the same hack.' Before Smith could work out if this was vulgar he added, 'Thanks for the deal. I hope it comes through alright for you.'

'Thank you,' said Smith. 'And good luck overthrowing the government.'

'Well, we've got some really important stuff to do, back in the True Reality,' Neil said. 'Maybe we'll meet again, either in the world of flesh, or the digital reality. If ever you happen to jack into the matrix, I'm a level forty-two wizard in *Galaxy of Battlecraft*.'

'Goodbye,' Trinny said.

'Bye. And bye to you too,' Smith added, as Morris started to speak. 'You don't need to say any more. I never liked long goodbyes. Best of luck, all.'

He stepped into the lift and the doors slid closed. The cyberpunks did their equivalent of waving, and the lift carried him out of their sight.

The shopping centre was full of slow-moving fat people. Above them, a huge TV screen was showing some girls dancing in very little. It didn't do a lot for Smith, especially since they were dancing round a huge crucifix.

A guard watched the screen, tapping his shock-stick against his leg in time with the music. He hardly noticed Smith as the captain walked past.

Hearing a sudden sparking noise, Smith glanced over his shoulder and was rewarded with an unusual sight. One of the dancers had begun to shake her backside in an odd, spasmic manner, which had prompted the guard to tap his leg harder and harder, until his shock-stick went off. He was currently lurching about like a newborn wildebeeste, a zombie on ice. Smith stood there a moment, feeling that there was some important meaning in the scene, but also aware that he was far too much of a heathen to work it out.

He returned to the ship.


'Reckon y'all best mosey back to your homeworld,' the television said. 'There ain't nothin' here 'cept me and Clyde – and Clyde's mighty quick with a positronic disintegrator.'

Suruk pressed his yellow eye to the view-slit and opened the front door.

'What's going on?' said Isambard Smith as he closed the door behind him.

'Much has changed. A woman and man wish to spawn, but the cowardice of the man delays their unwholesome rubbings. Meanwhile, slaying is done on a desert world, for the sake of meagre coins. Life is cheap.'

'Meaning that you've all sat watching *Space Confederates* for the last two hours, while I've been risking my hide dealing with the lowest beings known to man: treacherous aliens and computer scientists.'

The door to Carveth's room opened and she skipped out. 'Hello there!' she said merrily, and she hurried past him. She was wearing her blue dress.

'Why the Alice in Blunderland get-up?' Smith said, following her into the sitting room. 'You've not been chasing trouser while I've been away, have you?'

Rhianna was sitting in front of a screen on which space-craft were dogfighting. Smith had a feeling that the screen had been connected to something rather important in the past. She beckoned them in. 'There's a good part coming up.'

Carveth dropped into a chair. 'Right,' Smith said, pulling up a seat. 'I've got some good news, everyone. I've managed to find a new plotting computer. Bad news is that it's currently in the possession of a Marty.'

'What's a Marty?' Rhianna said.

'What you'd call an Aresian,' Carveth said. 'Galactic nomads, originally from Daluria. They used to have a base on Mars. It's long gone now. Last used in the late Victorian era.'

'Martians? You mean, Martian martians?'

'The sort from Mars? Yes, that sort.'

'Well, I never knew that. I thought it was just fiction.'

'Government cover-up,' Smith explained. 'Of course, H.G. Wells exaggerated terribly, but they landed all right. The thing is, they're incredibly vulnerable to disease and they dropped dead as soon as they came into contact with

Surrey. One of them got as far as Egham before he keeled over, but then, nobody likes Egham very much.'

'Yeah,' said Carveth. 'Jeff Wayne tried to blow the lid off it back in the twentieth century, but he weakened his case by doing it through rock opera. That's always a mistake. It was centuries before the truth was acknowledged. Still, it's surprisingly easy to hide alien stuff. Eh, Rhianna?'

'I really wouldn't know.' Rhianna frowned. 'But if it wasn't mankind that drove them from Mars, who did?'

Carveth looked shocked to hear such a basic question. 'Durr. The spiders, of course. Everyone knows that.'

Smith sensed bickering and woman stuff on the horizon. 'The being in question tells me that he can have the part ready by nine this evening, local time. Once I've collected it, we need merely wire up the ship and go.'

'The wiring's not difficult,' Carveth said. 'It's just a matter of clipping it in place. You could do that in orbit.'

'Good thing too. The sooner we're away from this awful place the better. Midlight may have criminals, but at least they're human. If I'm going to deal with a black marketeer, I'd much rather deal with one that doesn't have hundreds of tentacles.'

'And presumably many offspring,' Suruk said.

'*Tentacles*, Suruk.'

'I see.' Lounging by the door, Suruk had taken a little file from his belt and was carefully sharpening his tusks. Smith glanced away and realised that he still did not know why Carveth was wearing her dress. 'Why *are* you dressed like that, anyway?'

'Like this?' She smiled. 'Ah, I have a date.'

'You can't have a date, Carveth. That's absurd. We've been on this wretched planet about three hours. Even you don't work that fast.'

'That'll be my android super-senses.'

'Or your complete lack of taste. The people here are either police thugs or pastel-coloured blimps. I'd be very disappointed if you'd chosen the latter. And very disgusted with the former.'

'It's not either. He's a commercial traveller, like us. He's from somewhere called Carver's Rock. It's kosher, I promise: he's got entry permission and everything.'

'He *does* work fast,' Rhianna said.

Surprised to hear her making innuendo, Smith glanced at Rhianna and she winked. Unbidden, his mouth became an imbecilic grin.

'Well, alright,' Smith said. 'but make sure you're back by eleven. Because we're moving then.'

'Really?'

'Absolutely. I mean it: as soon as I've got that part we are leaving. Besides, if we miss out on this opportunity we'll be shopping with Doctor Apocalypse and his mutant lobsters. Now, if nobody minds, I'm going to my room to have a nap.'

Smith slept for two hours. Someone knocked at the door.

'Yes?'

'It's me, Rhianna.'

He opened up.

She was dressed as if about to appear in a play crudely satirising herself: she wore a floor-length skirt with some half-formed swirly pattern, an undersized and

217

non-matching T-shirt and a huge cardigan that looked as if it had been knitted by ogres out of rope. It was unable to cover both shoulders at once. She had done something with her hair, or failed to do it, so that it had formed ratty dreadlocks. Her usual plastic sandals had been replaced with a grubbier pair. From the looks of her, she had dressed at random and would smell of fresh sweat.

God, what a woman, Smith thought.

'Captain Smith?' she said.

'Yes, indeed,' he replied.

'It's probably time you ought to set off.'

He glanced at his watch. 'Ah, yes. Best get going.'

'And Isambard?'

'Yes?'

'Don't mess up.'

'I won't,' he said proudly.

'I just want to be away from here. This is a bad place. It's . . . soulless. Fascist oppressors have turned it into a patch of acne on the soul of Gaia. So don't screw up. I really mean it.'

'It's very sweet of you to say that, Rhianna.'

'I mean it: don't. I may be a pacifist, but I'll be so angry if you mess this up. You don't want me getting non-violent on your ass.'

'Thanks,' said Smith.

'For all that's wrong with you, you're brave,' Rhianna said, and she stood on tiptoe and quickly kissed him on the cheek. She stood there looking at him, blinking back a tear caused by getting the end of his moustache in her eye.

'Cheers, girlie,' he replied. Feeling very tall and broad suddenly, he stepped past her to the door. At the door he turned and gave her a perky salute. 'See you later,' he said. 'Don't wait up.'

Dreckitt scraped a match against the wall, did it again and realised on the third try that these were safety matches and the wall was chrome-plated. 'Two bit joint,' he said. He was tired, and full of no dinner and less whisky.

Then she came into view, and the strip-light-lit night changed.

She had a small round face with a nose, mouth, some eyes and trouble written all over it. She wore a dark blue dress with a white part down the front that Dreckitt was too masculine to know the word for.

He tossed his cigarette into a bin. She was a blonde. He'd always known she'd be a blonde.

He waved, and she grinned and waved back.

'Hello,' she said.

'Hey, Daisy,' he replied. 'Glad to see you again. Nice dress.'

'Really? Thanks. I got it free from a woman on a planet full of rednecks,' she added, immediately regretting that she had.

'It's interesting,' Dreckitt managed. 'You want to get a drink?'

'Oh yes.'

'From what I know, this is the liberal area of the city. We don't have to be married to go into a bar.'

'Wow. It should be a pretty fun night.'

'I hope so,' Dreckitt said, and he managed not to sigh, as he tended to do when he said those words. An auto-mated buggy-train rolled up beside them and they stepped inside. 'So,' said Dreckitt, 'Chainsaw. That's an unusual surname.'

'Actually, it's heraldic,' Carveth replied, and the cart whisked them away.

Smith pulled the facemask on again and prodded the doorbell, humming to himself. Above him, the video camera swung around, then down, then up a bit, as if surprised that he was so tall.

'Hello,' he said. 'It's me.'

The deep, sonorous voice came crackling from the speaker like an announcer on an old record. 'So it is.'

'Can I come in?'

'Yes.'

The doors slid apart and Smith walked into the chaos of the connecting passage. 'One moment,' the speaker said. 'I'll just suck your filthy human germs out of the air. Thank you for waiting.'

Smith stood in the corridor, listening to the front doors close behind him, wondering if Doctor Apocalypse might actually have been a safer bet. Idly, he picked up a device lying on the floor and turned it about in his hands, wondering what it did. Judging from the pipework, it seemed to be a fuel injector for a hovering vehicle, but judging from Smith's knowledge of technology, it might also have been a Pez dispenser.

'Get your dirty microbes off my stuff!' Ordo barked.

Smith set the machine down. He had not realised that he was being watched. 'Sorry.' Good thing I didn't check my gun, he thought. Might have put a damper on the atmosphere.

The doors slid apart. He looked into the main chamber, with its screens, machinery and exposed wire, and Ordo lurched into view. He was still a shock to see, like a trifle in a plastic bag balanced on an expensive lemon squeezer. As he hooted softly into the microphone he held in front of his beak, the machine translated.

'So, the engineer returns. I trust you have enjoyed your time on Callistan – or under it, more appropriately?'

Smith said, 'It's bearable. Although I find it a little, um, oppressive at times.'

'Well said. Not only is this world ruled by a vicious junta, but it is nearly impossible to get a good takeaway after ten p.m. Still, a being with the right connections can acquire anything – am I not right?'

'You're right.'

'Music to my tympanic membrane. Now then: it was a plotting computer you required, yes?'

'That's right.' Too many questions, Smith thought. Too much beating about the bush.

The alien turned and pulled something out of one of the heaps of machinery. It looked like a child's toy, Smith thought, the sort of thing you could buy in Brampton's Colonial Emporium for £19.99 Adjusted Sterling. Only when Ordo held it up did he see that the back had been torn off and handfuls of extra wiring thrust, seemingly at random, into the hole. He did not feel entirely convinced.

'This is suitable. You should be able to install it as easily as playing a game. I trust you use an ion driver in the engine room?'

'Don't think so. I'm not really much of a man for golf.'

'It will be fine. Now, pass me the money and we shall part.'

Smith took out a wad of notes and placed it on a patch of spare desk. Ordo produced a pair of tongs, picked up the notes and dropped them in a plastic bag. 'I shall have to launder the cash,' he explained. 'To wash out the bacteria.'

Lazily, with an odd grace, Ordo reached out a tentacle towards the plotting computer. 'Take it. It's yours.'

'Cheers. Thanks for your help.'

The tripod took a step away from him. 'A pleasure.'

Smith turned and reached for the door. Behind him, something moved, and Ordo said, '*Ulla tulla*, Smith?'

Smith turned. Ordo's tentacles were wrapped around a device somewhere between a rifle and a box kite. The pyramid-shaped tip of the weapon, the part pointed straight at Smith, glowed red.

'A heat ray,' the Aresian explained. 'Although I should imagine you are aware of that.'

'Would you like the plotting computer back, then?' said Smith.

'Alas, no. Much as I hate to betray the confidence of my customers, rumours of a considerable reward have been circulating in the underworld. Which I intend to claim. The authorities have been notified.'

'You rotten little traitor!' Smith exclaimed. 'You'd trade me in to those zealots after I did good business with you?'

'Indeed I would.'

'You bastard! I'll pull off your beak and use you as a space hopper!'

'You shall not.' Ordo made an expansive gesture with

his tentacles and the glowing barrel pointed upwards. 'You see, my mind is immeasurably greater than your own. I have studied humans as a scientist studies bacteria under a microscope. You have been outwitted, human, and – *ullooo!*'

Smith leaped on him. It was a brief, vicious struggle. Ordo snapped at his throat with his beak, struggling to haul Smith closer to deliver a death-bite – but in one sudden move Smith whipped the pistol from his pocket and shoved it where the alien's chin would have been had it not out-evolved the need for one.

Smith stood up and kicked the heat-ray aside. 'You were saying, Marty?'

The wrong way up, Ordo's walking machine jutted into the air like a small, crashed satellite. He hooted with fury. 'Curse you and your big legs!' the translator said. 'I shall drink your blood!'

'Got my doubts about that.' He stepped back to the door, plotting computer in hand. 'I've only got one thing to say to you, Martian. A—'

'What?' Ordo demanded, rising.

'A—'

'No!'

'Choo!' Smith pulled down his facemask and sneezed loudly.

'Not the microbes!' the alien cried, and Smith closed the door behind him.

That taught you, you double-crossing alien foreigner, Smith thought as he marched away. You were lucky I didn't beat you to death with your own third leg. He smiled grimly. Then he remembered that he had left his money in there. And that Ordo had notified the authorities. And that Carveth was somewhere in the city, with some man.

This looked bad.

'This looks good,' Dreckitt said, pointing into a bar.

Carveth squinted into the dark. 'Mmn,' she said, mustering enthusiasm like a sergeant shoving recruits into line. 'Smoky!'

They entered. Inside, a number of people dressed like Neil and Trinny sat at tables, smoking and talking intently about art or computers. It seemed to be a serious faux pas among the cyberpunk underground to remove one's sunglasses, and every so often the hum of conversation was broken by cursing as somebody walked into the furniture. The ceiling fan was low and the lighting dim, and it occurred to Carveth that a tall man in a hat could have a lot of problems here.

Looking slightly ill at ease, Dreckitt pulled a chair back and Carveth sat in it. As he leaned over for the wine list, she saw the bulge of something big under his shoulder, where a holster would be.

'So, is that a gun under your arm, or just an unusual mutation that's happy to see me?'

Dreckitt looked surprised. 'Uh? Oh, this? Yeah, um, that's a gun, actually.'

'Can I have a go?'

'I'd rather you didn't, lady.'

'Go on. Please, please?'

Well, thought Dreckitt, I'll slip the safety catch on. I've always got the knife in my sock. It'll help get her trust. She won't know how to switch the safety off.

'Sure,' he said, and he passed it to her.

Carveth turned the Assassinator over in her small hands and marvelled at it. It was not quite as big as a howitzer, she noticed. Lights blinked along its length, possibly to stop low-flying aircraft crashing into the barrel when it was drawn.

'Quite a piece,' Dreckitt said.

Carveth pointed it at him across the table and flicked the safety off. 'So, matey, what's the big idea?'

Dreckitt swallowed hard. The barrel of his own gun looked big enough to live in. 'I'm an android bounty killer and I've come here on a mission to murder you,' he said.

'Just kidding!' Carveth put the safety back on and placed the gun on the tabletop.

'You know what?' Dreckitt said sourly. 'Me too.'

'Hey,' said Carveth, 'both of us!'

'So,' said a voice at the side of them, 'Ready to order?'

Dreckitt holstered the gun and turned to the waitress. Her grin remained, but the confidence was gone, as if behind it her face was planning a very different expression for later use. 'Burger,' he said. 'And some whisky.'

'That's a two-pound burger with bacon and cheese. Fries come with a choice of our own special tomato sauce, French-style with mayonnaise or blessed by the Religious Police to reduce cholesterol in the life after this.'

'Special sauce.'

'And your wife?'

'Same here,' Carveth said. 'Nothing on the chips, though. I'll just borrow some of his. You don't mind giving me a squirt of your special sauce, do you?' she asked, immediately making a mental note never to say anything like that again.

The waitress moved away. Dreckitt looked across the table at his date and target. He wondered what had driven her to dress up like that. That didn't seem like the sort of thing a simulant would do. But it was not enough. He recalled the last batch of assassinations, the lawyers and accountants who could almost have been cold, inhumane machines like him, and shuddered. This time round, he needed to be sure. He activated his detection software.

He leaned across the table and looked into her eyes. 'Daisy, can I ask you something?'

She leaned closer and smiled. ''Course you can, Rick.'

'You have a puppy – a cute puppy – but you flush him down the toilet. Why did you do that, Daisy?'

'A puppy?'

Dreckitt's eyes bored into her. His voice was quick and hard. 'A cute fluffy puppy with floppy ears. He loved you but you flushed him down the toilet. He's spinning round and round, his big eyes pleading with you as he sinks. He's saying, "Mummy, why am I sinking?" Why did you flush him down the toilet?'

'Guess he just pissed me off or something,' Carveth said. 'I dunno. Why'd you ask?'

'Just wondered,' Dreckitt said, and he leaned back.

Carveth felt that the spark wasn't quite there.

Dreckitt's mind raced, computating as he reached for his whisky. The emotional response to his crafty questioning suggested that she was an android. That wasn't the kind of thing a meatbag would have said. Biological humans were unnecessarily sentimental about animals, family members and the like. Perhaps she was a synthetic after all – or just an unexpectedly rational human being. He needed to know more, to slip another test into the conversation.

Dreckitt elbowed his fork onto the floor. 'Whoops,' he said.

He swung down under the table and picked up the fork. He glanced left, then right, then slipped a small magnet out of his coat and held it close to Carveth's legs.

She wasn't made of metal. Some older androids had mechanical implants to make them more durable. Of course, that was no guarantee: the newer variants, like himself, were almost entirely biological. Either she was indeed a human, or an android sufficiently advanced to do a very good impersonation of a human who was not very advanced at all.

Uncertain, Dreckitt turned to sit up, and came face to face with Carveth.

When Dreckitt had disappeared under the table, she had assumed that their date was going rather well, so she looked down to check. She was less pleased to find him investigating her lower body with a magnet. She looked at the magnet. 'I'm not wearing a chastity belt,' she said. 'Though it's nice of you to try and pick it open.'

They sat back up and the waitress brought them drinks. On the radio, 'The Safety Dance' ended and another song began.

'Ah, Men Without Hats,' Dreckitt said, 'where are you now? You know,' he added, 'that reminds me of something.'

'Oh yes. What's that then?'

'Someone gives you a baby-skin handbag and pair of shoes. What do you do?'

'Um,' said Carveth.

'Pure baby-skin. Are you repulsed by the gift? What's your emotional response?'

'Do the bag and shoes match?'

'How should I know?' Dreckitt said.

'Well, you asked.'

'It's a hypothetical question.'

'You mean you're not really giving anything away free?'

'No. The bag and shoes don't match, by the way.'

'Oh.' Carveth went back to her drink. 'That's terrible!' she exclaimed. 'I reject the bag and I say how bad it is to make things out of babies!'

'You're an android,' Dreckitt said.

'No I'm not.'

'Yes you are.'

'Am not.'

'All the evidence points to it,' he said.

'Am not. Not not not. If I was an android, I'd be making a much better job of arguing my way out of this. I'd use logic and stuff. Explain that.'

'You're a renegade android that's violated its programming and is on the run from its designated duty,' he replied. 'Who knows what sort of systemic malfunctions the violation of your primary rationale has caused?'

'That's what *you* say,' she said, and she stared huffily at the wall.

'Polly?' he said. 'Miss Carveth?'

'What now?'

'Got you!'

'Oh, tits!' she said, wishing she'd kept hold of the gun. This was just typical. The date had been going fine and now he'd turned out to be an android bounty killer. Bloody men!

'I knew you weren't a real human being,' Dreckitt said, leaning back in his seat. 'Several things gave it away. Firstly, you seem to be dressed as Alice in Wonderland. Secondly, using my special training, I seamlessly inserted questions into our conversation that would betray the kind of emotional response a biological human would give, thus revealing you to be synthetic. And thirdly, you're obviously not the real Daisy Chainsaw because I own their first album.'

'Good, isn't it?'

'Yeah, not bad. But let's get back to the whole bounty-killing thing.'

'Oh, yes. Perhaps we can work something out. Do you accept sexual favours?'

'I'm not going to kill you, Polly.'

She blinked. 'Would you accept them anyway?'

Dreckitt gave a brief snort of amusement and said, 'Polly, let me tell you something. I'm an android too. And not a good one. Truth is, I'm nothing but a two-bit grifter with a cheap suit and a big piece – that's a gun. I've got nothing to offer the world except a hard-luck story and a hand-cannon – which is also a gun, so don't get any ideas. I've not got much to thank my creators for – no friends, no family. But I am glad I'm not saddled with an over-active sex drive and a lemming's instinct for danger. I'm through with killing my own kind. Finished.'

'You didn't answer my question.'

'You can go, Polly. I can't say you've got much of a chance, kid, and it cuts me up to tell you that.'

At the far end of the bar, some sort of commotion was going on. A group of police was attempting to enter, their armour catching the bad light of the bar. A waiter was remonstrating with them, waving his hands. The police looked at one another, their visors blank. They made Carveth think of androids more primitive than herself, automata.

Dreckitt reached into his coat. 'Trouble,' he said.

Suddenly the waiter folded and dropped out of sight: he'd been punched in the gut. A baton whirled and hit something out of view that Carveth knew would be his head.

Dreckitt stood up. 'There's a back door,' he said, nodding towards the rear of the bar. 'Go, Polly.'

The raiders, more like stormtroopers than what she thought of as police, were busy irritating people at their tables: tipping drinks on the floor, knocking plates down, pulling customers out of booths and shoving them against the wall. Carveth got up.

'Wait,' Dreckitt said.

She looked at him.

'A pair of androids like us don't add up to a whole load of bits in this galaxy,' Dreckitt said. 'But I reckon you deserve to get out of here more than me. They screwed me over on this, and now I reckon I might just screw them back. Come here, sister,' he said, and he grabbed her and held her close. 'Gimme some interface.'

He kissed her fiercely then let her go. Dreckitt drew the Assassinator. 'Run, Polly!' he said, and he lifted the huge pistol in both hands. 'Run!' Then: 'Hey, you!' he called, and as Carveth ran for the rear door, she heard the gun-fight begin.

Half a mile from the *John Pym*, Smith drew the Civiliser and held it in the folds of his coat. The security forces of the Republic of Eden would be armed, but so was he.

Fifty yards away, he heard sounds. A mercenary soldier stood in the corridor that led to the ship, his back to Smith. He wore army gear, customised to a level that would have had him court-martialled back home, with sunglasses and driving gloves.

This would take some skill. Smith turned the Civiliser around in his hand.

The man was listening to something on his headset. Smith bashed him with the butt of the gun, and for a disappointing, confusing moment, the man just stood there and said 'Huh? What're you doing?'

'Knocking you senseless, my good man,' Smith said, and hit him again, and the man went down.

His gun was much bigger than Smith's. It looked like an air-powered dart-gun, probably loaded with tranquillisers. Useful for riot control, although without the loud banging sound Smith would have expected Gilead to enjoy. He decided to stick to the Civiliser.

Smith stashed the plotting computer by the side of a battered vending machine. Taking a pen from his pocket, he scribbled a few M'Lak characters onto the plastic. They would look like graffiti to an untrained eye.

He drew his gun, crept to the edge of the corridor and peered around.

In the shadow of the spaceship an odd scene was being played out. A dozen armed men stood in a ring around Rhianna and Gilead, who were arguing bitterly.

'... and you come here in your stupid little fascist hat and start oppressing people with your jumped-up mercenaries, with no moral right or authority—'

'I bear the Word of the Lord!' Gilead yelled, while Rhianna continued to rage at him. He looked stupid, huge and vastly arrogant, as usual, and he had twelve armed men on his side. On the other hand, at least he wasn't trying to cop off with Rhianna again.

'– No appreciation of the rights of other people, just your narrow-minded militaristic diktat forcing people to conform to your oppressive stereotyped—'

Blimey, thought Smith, struggling to keep up with the torrent of left-wing invective, perhaps he was better off on his own. If Rhianna kicked off like that about being detained by enemy soldiers, what would she be like when the time came for her to do his ironing?

'– ruined this planet and all the other ones your tinpot junta owns. Your dictatorial regime spits in the face of Gaia and denies the natural truths that have turned your so-called Eden into a wasteland. You have no love for Mother Earth—'

'I have heard enough!' Gilead cried. 'Take this pagan Jezebel away!'

'Not so fast, Gilead.' Smith stepped out into view, and Gilead's men turned around, covering him. The huge barrel of the Civiliser pointed straight at Gilead's head. A dozen guns pointed at Isambard Smith.

Gilead looked no more surprised than usual. 'Well,

well. Captain Spiffy. I've already got your friend and now I've got you too.'

'Let the woman go, Gilead. She's part of my crew, and you've no right to detain her here.'

Gilead snorted with contempt. 'What'll you do, arrest us? Me and all of my men?'

Smith said, 'No, your men can go free. But I'm taking you in, Gilead. Don't make me use force.'

'Force? Hah! You know nothing of force. I shall wipe you away! You shall be scattered and cast asunder to gnash your teeth on stony ground!'

Smith said, 'You shout a lot for a God-botherer, Gilead. Haven't you ever heard that the meek shall inherit the Earth?'

'I *am* the god-damned meek!' Gilead bellowed. 'Take him down!'

Something hit Smith in the side. Rhianna screamed. Gilead drew a truncheon and bashed her over the head with it. Smith fired: the shell hit Gilead in the chest and threw him onto his back as half a dozen darts appeared in Smith's flank. Gilead was shouting something.

Smith stepped forward and cocked the hammer. It was as easy as juggling rhinos. He tried to lift the gun, and found that the air had turned to porridge.

'I'm... going to... settle your hash, you... complete... arse... wipe,' he said, with great difficulty. His record seemed to be playing at the wrong speed. He looked down: the darts protruding from his leg reminded him of bunting. 'Balls, you've drugged me,' he added, and like a felled tree toppled over onto his side. The last thing he thought as he hit the floor was, 'Bollocks, that's a solid-looking floor.'

They caught Carveth easily. She was trying to trick an ammo-dispenser into accepting Adjusted Sterling and had resorted to thumping the machine to get her way. Two policemen concluded that she was some kind of transvestite dwarf, itself a capital crime in the Republic of Eden. They were surprised when she turned out to be a woman, but they took her in anyway.

She was led into a little room where some armed heavies prodded her into a seat. On the opposite side of the desk sat a big, hard-eyed man with his arm in a sling. He had a blandly handsome visage without defects or personality, the Dairy Milk chocolate of the facial world.

'My name is John Gilead,' he said, 'Captain in His Wrathful Lordship God the Merciless Annhilator's space fleet. I have captured your friends: Rhianna Mitchell, a communist agitator and subversive, and Isambard Smith, an imbecile. My men are currently searching the nest of fornication you call your ship.'

'I've never heard of either of them,' Carveth said. 'Naff off and let me go!'

One of the guards jabbed her with his gun. 'Watch your mouth, little lady.'

'You can stick it too. *Sum civis Britannicus*, tit-face!'

The man jabbed her again, hard. 'Hey! Do the words *head*, *your*, *blow* and *off* mean anything to you?'

'A good night in?'

'Leave it!' Gilead said. 'I know how to get results. The

bar you drank at was bugged. We know who you really are. You're Polly Carveth, a renegade android.'

'No I'm not!'

'Because you are company property, I'm prepared to hand you back to the people who created you instead of having you killed out of hand.'

'In which case I am her, actually. I was just lying back then.'

'Good. Then we are agreed. Tomorrow Mr Devrin gets you back.'

Carveth thought about it for a moment. The idea of returning to the Devrin corporation made her feel unwell. Didn't this mad bigot understand exactly what that would entail? There had to be some other option, surely.

'Look,' Carveth said, leaning forward, 'can we just talk about this? You're a moral, God-fearing sort of man, right? Pro-morality, anti-fun, that kind of thing? You realise what you'll be sending me back to, don't you? Sex. That's what I was made for. Tons of it: steamy, non-marital, dirty sex. You can't condone that, can you? That's why you have to let me go, to escape all that sin and get back on the path of righteousness or something.'

Gilead rubbed his chin with his left hand. 'Hmm. You've got a point there. If I hand you back to the Devrin corporation, you'll merely lapse into depravity. You're right, I can't do that.' He shrugged. 'Drug this heathen. Lock her in their ship and launch it into the sun!'

'Well,' Carveth said as the dart-gun fired, 'I suppose it was worth a try.'

# 9

# Cultists Filched My Trousers

Smith came round without his trousers on. His head still hurt from the sedatives and his first instinct was to congratulate himself on a good night's drinking. He looked around to see if any girls were involved and saw only Captain Gilead standing on the far side of the cell.

'Damn!' said Smith.

'Well, looky here,' Gilead said. 'How the mighty's belt has fallen. Welcome to my ship, Captain Smith.'

'Gilead, you worm! Go to hell! But give me my trousers first!'

'Oh no.' Gilead grinned, showing his improbably even teeth. 'You're going nowhere. Well, you are going somewhere, once you've told us a few things about your crew. Somewhere rather special, where you'll learn some piety. We're going to bring you closer to the Lord.'

'I won't have to go to church, will I?'

'Oh no.'

'Phew.'

'We're going to crucify you.'

'Ah. Not phew at all, then. I mean, that's hardly brotherly love, is it?'

'You're not my brother,' Gilead replied. 'You're a Heathenite. And a fool.'

'Oh really? Well how about you, the maddest loony in Loonyland? And how can I be a fool if I've outwitted you and your little helper Corveau, who was also a fool? If I'm a fool and I outfooled your foolish minion, who was the bigger fool for appointing him: the fool who killed him or the fool who made that fool his fool?' Smith's voice had been rising through this sentence and now he stopped and blinked, a little surprised to find that he was no longer talking. 'Eh? Got you there, haven't I?'

'What the hell are you talking about?'

'You're a prat. Besides, keeping me here is pointless. I'd sooner smear my testicles with cheese and entrust them to a gang of hungry mice than squeal on my crew.'

'Humn,' Gilead said. He turned to the intercom. 'Control, do we have any hungry mice on board?'

'They're using them down the corridor,' a voice replied. Gilead shrugged and turned back to Smith.

'I was telling you that you're stupid,' Smith said, 'You look stupid, you act stupidly, you come from a stupid regime and you follow a load of stupid beliefs. So leave my crew out of it and bugger off.'

'I don't understand,' Gilead said. 'Why do you have any respect for those losers?'

'They're not losers,' Smith replied. 'Well, I've never actually seen them lose at anything. They're my crew. I rather like them.'

'Well, I wouldn't bother. They're probably dead by now,' Gilead said, some of his confidence returning.

Smith studied him coldly. 'You know, Gilead, I've met

people like you before – generally after I've paid a showman. You're not as smart as you think. You'll slip up, just like everyone else who tries to mess with the British Empire. They all get it wrong somehow – forget some detail, make some tiny error, invade Russia – and then it's all downhill from there.'

'I doubt it. It's you who makes the mistakes. Hell, you're so stupid even if I told you the truth you'd be too dumb to understand.'

'Why don't you try me?'

'Alright. The reason we want Rhianna Mitchell is that she is an angel.'

'Well, that's too bad. Kind sentiments, but I can assure you she's good as taken. It's the moustache, you see.'

'I don't refer to fornication. I mean an Angel of the Lord.'

Smith had no drink to splutter into, and no trousers to splutter his drink on, but he tried anyway. 'What? What? Are you mad? Well, yes, obviously, but *really*, man, *really*.'

'I knew you wouldn't understand, being an unbeliever.'

'That's bloody ridiculous! She's not an angel – she's more like an art teacher, if anything. She works in a health food shop, for Heaven's sake – more burning weed than burning bush, I can tell you. I mean, religious interpretations differ, but I can't remember Gabriel having a toke between annunciations, can you?'

'We shall see. Soon we will be beyond Republic space, and then only God will ever know what happens to you – and God's on my side. Once I've finished with you, the Ghasts will use their technology to draw Rhianna

Mitchell's spirit from her pagan body, whether or not her corrupted will resists. And then – then the Republic of Eden and the Ghast Empire will be invincible, with the Angel of the Lord marching on before!'

'What utter bollocks. It's us who'll win. We humans will save Earth from the Ghasts, just you wait.'

'Huh. You see, Smith, you're making a basic mistake. You assume that I don't *want* the Ghasts to conquer planet Earth. But that's where you're wrong.'

'But why, man? Why sell your people down the river like that?'

'Not my people!' Gilead cried, and suddenly he was enraged. '*Your* people: unbelievers, blasphemers, unarmed fools bleating about civil rights and democracy! That pansy crap is over! These are the End Times, Smith. The apocalypse is coming and it is coming in the form of the Ghasts. It is my sacred duty to hasten that day of weighing-out, and the powers of Rhianna Mitchell shall aid me in my divine quest. And then, when fire and destruction envelops the sinful Earth, the righteous shall ascend, and eternal life and a whole host of angelic handmaidens shall be mine.'

'Oh dear,' said Isambard Smith, and a cold certainly swept over him. 'I'm going to have to settle your hash, aren't I?'

Carveth awoke to the sound of whooping. Somewhere behind her head, people were hooting and yelling, celebrating. There was an angry, triumphant note to their voices. They didn't sound like friends.

She opened her eyes a crack. The ceiling was very

bright. She must be looking straight up at the bulb. It must have quite a wattage, she thought. Then she noticed that she was sitting upright and looking into the rapidly growing sun, and she became rather more concerned.

She was tied to the chair. Crap. She squirmed around, silently, and discovered that she could not escape. Well, she thought, that's just great. You go out on a date, your date turns out to be a robot assassin with baggage and then, just when you think it can't get any worse, religious fanatics shoot you into the sun. I want to go home.

Boots rang on the metal floor. She froze.

'Alright, let's move. We've done good, but it's time to go.'

'But we've not looked properly, Boss.' This voice reminded her of a violent, outsize idiot and probably belonged to one, the sort of dim-witted thug who would chew a bit of straw inside his space helmet.

'We've looked.'

'But there might be guns, Boss. We could keep 'em.'

'Take the guns for ourselves, you mean? Yeah, maybe. Alright. Me and Zeb'll check the rooms and the hold. You look in here. But we've got orders to be out in five, alright?'

'Yep!'

One set of steps faded away down the corridor. Carveth heard someone stomp around behind her, then slowly became aware that somebody was leaning over her shoulder.

'Hey, I can see down her dress! I can see her dirty pillows, Boss! That you, Boss?'

'Not exactly,' Suruk the Slayer said, and there was a

sharp, messy crash as he took the man by the throat and threw him scalp-first into the ceiling.

Carveth opened her eyes. Never had the tusked, piranha-toothed nightmare of Suruk's face looked so welcome. 'Hey there!' she said.

'Good day,' he replied. 'Enemies are on board the craft. Would you care to join me in slaughtering them?'

'Cut me free, would you?'

'Of course.' She heard his knife hiss through the rope, the cords fell away from her and she sat forward and rubbed her wrists. 'What's going on?'

'Smith and the shaman woman are gone. Our enemies explore our vessel, despoiling it with their quest for loot. They have programmed a course that will take us into the sun. Soon they will call a shuttle from their own ship to collect them. We must slay them.'

'This whole sun thing bothers me,' Carveth said. She glanced at the instruments. 'That's a big sun alright. Where're the guns?'

'Stored in the hold. The enemy have the keys to the box, but they do not realise that it contains our weapons. We will have to ambush them and retrieve the key. In the meantime, I have acquired this cudgel.'

He pulled a rather familiar-looking item from his belt: a foot-long piece of black rubber, rounded at one end.

'That's mine!' Carveth said.

'Indeed. I did not realise that you were skilled in hand to hand. It is an excellent club, and if I flick this switch in its base, it massages my palm and imitates the voice of the bee.'

'Can I have that back, please? That's the closest thing

241

I've got to family. Look,' Carveth added, 'I'm just slowing you down, right? Why don't you go on ahead and get some killing in, eh? I'll just stay here, and, um, do useful stuff.'

'Humn. Your remaining hidden may be of use to me, cowardly one. Go into the captain's room and see if there is a firearm. He may have concealed a weapon there.'

'Alright.' Carveth doubted that Smith was sufficiently organised to do this, but the idea of a gun was a good one. Preferably a really big gun that could be operated from a long way off.

'I, meanwhile, shall slay my enemies. Good hunting.'

'You too. Be careful.'

'Fear not. I am renowned for my cunning in war. It has been said that I put the 'savvy' into 'mindless savagery'. And arguably the 'canny' into 'cannibalism', but that might be stretching the point.'

With that, Suruk bounded into the corridor, almost silent on the lino. Carveth counted to five and crept to the door.

She glanced into the passage. The room doors were all open and she could see into the hold. A soldier in scrappy, converted armour stood with his back to her, a rifle in his hands. Suruk was nowhere to be seen.

She sneaked out and ducked straight into Smith's quarters. Sighing with relief at not yet being shot, Carveth closed the door behind her and began to search the room. The wardrobe yielded nothing except a lot of tweed. She pulled the bed apart. Under the pillow she found a neatly-folded pair of wynceyette pyjamas. She knelt down and searched underneath the bed, and found only a picture of the Queen and a well-thumbed Laura Ashley womenswear catalogue.

From the hold came a shout. 'An alien! Kill the green-skin!' someone yelled – and then silence.

Carveth took a deep breath and returned to the corridor. There was a sudden loud bang, like a door slamming, and she leaped back into Smith's room and stood there panting until Suruk called from the hold, 'You may emerge. They are defeated!'

He was waiting at the door to the hold. One of the mercenaries lay in the corner, his neck broken. The other seemed to have trodden on something volatile, which had thrown him against the wall with fatal force.

'This fool panicked and stepped into a trap that he had made himself,' Suruk said.

Carveth nodded. 'Hoist with his own retard,' she said. 'Is that all of them?'

'Indeed. We are all ready to fly. I found the plotting machine you needed hidden near the ship. It must have been Smith that placed it there.'

'Thank God for that. Saddle up then, Suruk. We're going home.'

She turned to the doorway, meaning to reset the navigational computer. As she reached the door the alien said, 'Home?'

'Yep. Let's get out of here.'

'But Isambard Smith is still a prisoner. Do you not have a plan for what we should do next?'

'Sure. I've got two plans: cut and run. Come on, let's go.'

'We go nowhere. We rescue our comrade.'

'Bollocks to that! We're off home.'

'Wrong,' Suruk said, and suddenly Carveth was not so happy to have him on her side. His jaws attempted a smile. 'I intend to enjoy my holiday. So far, it has been disappointingly without incident. Yet perhaps I shall start to remedy this by shedding blood. Either you can prepare to fight our foes, or you can experience me forcing the contents of the cutlery drawer up your snivelling behind. Turn the ship around and show the enemy our mettle, or I shall turn *you* around and show you mine.'

As he approached, making a weird croaking noise, Carveth realised that she was in a quandary. She did not know which she would rather face: death at the hands of Gilead and his brutal mercenaries, or death by rectal spoon insertion. It was a close call.

The door slid open. 'Attention, scum!' barked a voice, and 462 marched into the room. 'Silence!' he cried, despite the conversation having come to an end.

He looked like an ant in a trenchcoat. Despite the similarities to a locust and stick insect in the body, and despite the approximation of a face at the end of his bulbous head, it was as an ant that Smith would remember him: a gigantic red ant propped on its hind legs, draped in a long coat and decorated with a load of meaningless insignia – no doubt prizes for being best in show at a shouting contest or something of the sort.

462's small eyes roved the room. 'So,' he said. 'The mighty Captain Smith. We meet again, except for the first time.'

'I've no idea,' Smith replied coolly. 'You chaps all look the same.'

'Silence! It is fitting tribute to your crushing stupidity that for you, Earthlander, the war is over before it has even begun. Soon we shall commence our plans, and then planet Earth shall lie open to us for the taking.'

'I have my doubts, alien. If you think the Earth's a pushover, you've clearly never been to Woking.'

'Hah! Neither you nor your puny planet is in any condition to resist the might of the Ghast Empire. Humankind will be destroyed and my service to my species will be rewarded!'

'What will they do, promote you to 461?'

'How dare you seek to mock me! It will in fact be 460. 461 died in a bizarre saluting accident. But I digress. You are doomed. Evolution has raised us far beyond your feeble species.'

'Now that's just a theory,' Gilead put in.

'If I might just get a word in edgeways, inferior human scum,' 462 said crossly, 'you are doomed. Our fleet will scatter the nations of mankind, descend on Planet Earth and destroy its useless liberty. The populations of Earth shall be put to work for our ends, and we, the Ghasts, shall crush mankind under an iron fist!'

Smith looked at Gilead. 'I hope you're listening to all this,' he said.

'So, your efforts to oppose us are worthless,' said the Ghast commander. 'With the secrets we learn from your captured breeding-partner, we shall sweep the galaxy clean of inefficiency. Now, I have business elsewhere.'

462 turned to go. As he reached the door, Smith said, 'Wait.'

The Ghast turned, attempting a smile. 'Ah, so you wish to beg for clemency, do you?'

'I just wanted to say something.' Smith fixed the Ghast's hard eyes with his own. 'Now listen closely, alien. You may be about to conquer the galaxy, but at least I've not got a great big arse.'

462 paused and looked over his shoulder at the large red thing, shaped like a wasp's nest, that protruded from the back of his trenchcoat. 'That is not an arse. That is my stercorium.'

'No doubt. I'm sure it is… fatarse.'

'Ignorant human! This organ is essential to my digestive system, far more efficient than yours, and is used to produce nutrients that give me the strength to conquer lesser specii like your own!'

'Sorry, could you repeat that? I couldn't hear past your great big red arse.'

The Ghast commander snarled. 'Hah! Laugh while you still can, puny Earthman. But I promise, there will be no mercy for you, Captain Smith. You will be crushed – utterly!'

'You're going to sit on me, then? With your big arse?'

462 gave a yelp of rage. He whipped around, his antennae quivering. 'You have mocked my backside for the last time! You, guard! Fetch the cage!'

'Stop it!' cried Carveth. She was the wrong way up, dress over her head, arms flapping. Suruk held one of her ankles and was shaking her up and down. On the plus side, he had not injured her with spoons, but on the minus side, she was sure that her breakfast was about to get acquainted with her dangling hair. 'Let go of me and put me down!'

'As you wish,' Suruk said.

Carveth landed on her head and said, 'I meant the other way around.'

The alien sighed. 'You sadden me. Has mankind become so decadent that its pilots are not willing to charge into a savage gunfight they will almost certainly lose anymore?'

Carveth rubbed her head and said, 'No way. There's two of us, Suruk! There must be a hundred of them. How are we to deal with that?'

'Three. You forget Gan Uteki.'

'Who's that?'

He turned and reached for a spear by the door. 'Gan Uteki, weapon of the ancestors, blade of the spirit world.'

'Well, thank heaven for that,' Carveth replied. She climbed to her feet. 'I was wondering when the Stick Cavalry would arrive. Absolutely no and no again.' She moved towards the door: surprisingly, he stepped out of the way. Feeling bad and angry with everything, including herself, Carveth stomped down the corridor towards the beer fridge.

Why couldn't this have happened to someone else? Carveth thought, taking out a can and opening it up. Why did life have to expect heroics from someone who wasn't a hero? You didn't expect the man who cleaned the toilets to conduct operas, so why should you expect a daring rescue mission from someone who was much happier cowering under a rug? She slammed the fridge door.

A picture was stuck to the door. Carveth had not noticed it before. It showed four stick-people in a row, two of them women. One of the men had tusks and was holding up an axe. Suruk's work, she thought. There were labels on the people: 'I myself', 'Izmbard Smith', 'Riana' and 'little fat cowad woman', along with helpful labels like 'bludd' and 'sevid hed'. Written above Smith were the words 'My best frend ever'.

Carveth took the picture and held it in her hands, furious at the guilt it made her feel. For a moment she felt like ripping the damned thing to bits and flushing it down the waste disposal unit. What a shameless piece of manipulation, what a crude attempt to affect her feelings! 'Little fat cowad woman' stared out from the picture in her hands, smiling and waving.

'Fat?' she said, staring at the picture. 'Fat! I'm not fat! I'll show you, you cheeky bastard!'

She turned and stomped back to the cockpit, dropped straight into the seat and turned the spaceship round. She set a course for the *Fist of Righteousness*, full speed.

It was at that point that she realised that 'my best frend' might have referred not to Smith but to the axe Suruk was waving over Smith's head, but by then it was way too late, for the M'Lak's smiling head leaned around the cockpit door.

'We have changed course,' Suruk said.

'Change of plan,' Carveth said, trying to sound confident. 'You know I said we were going to cut and run? Well, we've done the running part. Get your knives.'

*

The guards brought a cage into the room. Hardened killers themselves, they quailed when they saw what moved inside: a mass of matted fur, seemingly without limbs or head, squeaking and battering the bars.

'Only a few minutes before we leave Republic of Eden space,' said 462. 'And then, then we shall see who looks amusing.' The cage rattled as its occupant thumped against the bars. 462 smirked. 'Tell me, Smith, have you ever seen a hungry trobble leap through the air?'

Carveth met Suruk in the cargo hold. Suruk was covered in weapons, blades strapped to his thighs, chest and hips, pushed into his boots and the bracers he wore on his arms. In his hands was his spear. Less explicably, he was wearing a top hat.

'We are ready?' he said as she approached.

Carveth nodded. 'I'm all juiced up,' she said. She had just washed a handful of Peptos down with navy rum: she felt sharp and deadly. She wore the Maxim cannon on a harness over her dress. It felt incredibly heavy and cumbersome, as if she had put on a building site. The gun was in its folded position, the barrel jutting up from her back like a chimney.

'Fourteen minutes till we dock,' she said. 'I got the docking codes off a card one of the mercenaries had. We're due to link straight up.' She licked her lips. 'Then, I guess the fighting starts.'

'Yes.'

She walked across the hold. Suruk stood there, flexing his fingers calmly, and it occurred to her that she really didn't understand the first thing about him. He was inscrutable to her, and she doubted that even the finest minds of Earth would be able to scrute him properly. 'Suruk,' she said, 'does anything frighten you?'

The alien frowned. 'That I might never do battle with worthy enemies,' he said. 'Clowns. Some dairy produce frightens me, as well.'

'Those aren't things that worry me particularly,' she said. 'I'm frightened of dying, Suruk.'

'That's quite understandable.'

'It is?'

'Of course it is: you are a wretched coward. Normally, I would rather feed my breeding tubes into a printing press than even look at you. However, these are strange times, and I shall fight beside you today. So be it. You are war-kin now and, no matter what happens, there is a part of you that will always remain close to me. Admittedly, it may well be your skull on my mantelpiece, but the point is made.'

'Cheers,' she said.

Suruk raised his spear. 'Not long, I think, until we meet our destiny. Now, I must obey the traditions of my people. It is time for me to sing the death-song of my ancestors. As you are kindred, I shall translate it for you.'

He threw back his head, opened his mandibles and, in a mighty voice, he sang:

> *Today we raise our weapons high,*
> *Today we prepare for death.*
> *We might be slain; alternatively we might not.*
> *Lie-la-lie, la-lie-lala-lie,*
> *Lie–la-lie, la-lie-lala-lie,*
> *Lalalala lie.*

'That's it?' said Carveth. 'That was rubbish. It didn't rhyme and I reckon you stole part of it. And if you're going to die, you could at least listen to something good first.' She grinned. 'I know! You want to hear real music, get this!'

She disappeared back into the ship. Suruk frowned.

Something came over the interior P.A. system, a low, flat twang, a sound from far away and deep down. Suruk shuddered and adjusted his hat.

A slow, rattling drum crackled through the hold. From the bottom of a well there crept a woman's voice, a lost, hungry ghost. Suruk ran one of his thumbs along the razor edge of Gan Uteki, the sacred spear. Hunting music, indeed.

Carveth stepped through the door, the Maxim cannon levelled and ready to shoot. Her blonde hair was held back by a radio headset. She straightened her blue dress and wiped a bit of foam from the corner of her mouth.

'Jefferson Airplane,' she said. 'I thought we needed a rising sound. Let's go.'

A soldier barged into the room. 'Sir?'

462 whipped around, and for a moment Smith thought he was actually going to attack the man. 'Who is this moron?' he barked at Gilead.

Captain Gilead turned to the man. 'What's going on?'

'Sir, problem, sir. Docking codes from the incoming shuttle are wrong.'

'How do you mean, *wrong*?'

'Sir, they're not right, sir. They're for the wrong ship. Our ship. It's the *John Pym* coming in to dock, not our

TOBY FROST

ship.'

'The *John Pym*? *His* ship? Could it be our people on board?'

The mercenary shook his head. 'I don't think so. We received a message, sir. It doesn't sound like our men, sir.'

From the other side of the room, Isambard Smith spoke. 'You fellows are in a good deal of trouble,' he said, 'but I can help you. If you surrender now, I'll make sure you get a fair trial before they string you up.'

'Shut up,' Gilead said. 'I want to hear this message. Put it on the speakers.'

The soldier paled. 'Sir, I don't think that it's quite—'

'Put it on!'

They listened.

'Hello arseheads! Still bothering God? Right, listen carefully. I've got a fast ship about to dock with you and a crew of angry people, and I've come here to bring succour to the injured and injury to the suckers. Bring the Cap to the airlock and let him go, and we won't do you over. Because if you don't I'm warning you; I've got a degree in kicking arse and I'd have a doctorate in not giving a damn if I'd bothered to attend the ceremony. So open up, alright?'

'Well,' said Smith, 'you heard. My elite soldiers await the moment to strike. You've had a fair innings, Gilead, but it's time to head back to the pavilion before you get your bails knocked off. Give me my trousers and we can call it quits.'

Gilead leaped up, his eyes gleaming. 'A draw? Screw that! Not while I have the Angel of the Lord in my custody, and not while your yellow-bellied, black-hearted, white-trash, pinko-liberal crew takes my name in vain! You!' he

252

cried, jabbing a finger at the mercenary, 'Watch this man. And you,' he added, turning to 462, 'come with me. I'll show you how we deal with unbelievers round here!'

'It seems we will meet later, Captain Smith,' said 462. 'Until then, goodbye.' His face managed a smirk. 'Remember the cage, Smith. They can bounce straight through a man's head.'

With a swish of leather and a twitching of antennae, he was gone. The door slammed. Smith looked at the mercenary.

'I can see your underpants,' the mercenary said. 'That's funny.'


In the airlock, the walls rang with whooping and the clatter of loading magazines. Men clenched fists and put their sunglasses on, checked stubble and stuffed copies of *Merc Life* into their back pockets.

Grace Slick's voice rang out across the hold of the *John Pym* like a jilted, malevolent ghost. 'White Rabbit' was reaching its peak.

Carveth upended a bottle of Peptos and crunched eight times the recommended dose. 'Any moment now,' she said.

Something massive struck the side of the ship. The clang rang through the hold as if they stood in some gigantic bell.

A voice came over the PA system. 'This is the *Fist of Righteousness*. We are outside your airlock. You will open up and surrender immediately or we will tear open your airlock and mess you up so bad even Satan won't recognise you!'

'Like bollocks we will,' Carveth said. 'Surrender at once!'

'Don't give me that!' said the PA system. Carveth glanced at Suruk. He stood beside the airlock doors, spear in hand, one finger poised over the manual override switch. Carveth reached out and turned off the light. Darkness in the *Pym*. Half a dozen flares were attached to the airlock, the flare units taped to the frame, the pins that would activate them soldered to the doors.

'You've had enough time,' the voice cried over the loud-speakers. 'That's it, we're coming in.'

Carveth pulled the cannon into her hands. She narrowed her eyes and said, 'Do it!'

Suruk hit the switch. At the first sign of the Pym's doors opening, the mercenaries opened their own airlock, the pins came free and the flares hissed into sudden, blinding life. Someone yelled, 'Trap!' Silhouettes threw hands over their eyes. Carveth pulled the trigger.

She let the motion sensors on the gun do their work and it swung and bucked in her hands. The round counter spun as it spat half a magazine into the airlock and she braced her legs and hoped it would be over soon.

'Wait!' Suruk growled, and she stopped, panting, the air full of smoke. The flares sputtered around the door, at once evil and festive, the entrance to some sinister funfair.

Suruk stepped into the airlock, treading carefully. His boots squeaked a little on the tiles. He stepped out of view.

There was one shot, the whipping sound of a blade cutting the air and Carveth heard something heavy hit the floor. Suruk looked back around the edge of the airlock. 'This will be unpleasant,' he said.

'Lots of enemies?'

'Hideous décor. Follow me.'

The décor was indeed hideous, although getting the bloody hell out of here pressed more deeply on Carveth's mind. She trotted behind Suruk, glancing over her shoulder so often that she might as well have spun round like a top, well aware that it was only the Peptos that were keeping her jittery finger on the trigger. She thought about a lot of things as they hurried down the corridors of the ship: dying, getting killed, getting shot, death and even being murdered crossed her mind. She was afraid.

A sound behind her and she whipped around, hit the trigger and in a roar of bullets a man clutched himself and fell, dead. A second mercenary ducked back into cover, reaching for something attached to his vest, and Suruk leaped in after him. A man screamed and fell silent, and the M'Lak returned, whistling between his teeth.

'I have rigged a grenade behind a pressure door,' he announced. 'Very soon it will explode. Fires will distract our enemies.'

'Good,' said Carveth. 'Are we nearly there yet?'

'Nearly where?'

'Well, wherever they're holding the captain.' She peered at him. 'This is a rescue mission, right? We're going to rescue the captain. What the hell did you think we were doing, getting an ice cream?'

'Ah,' said Suruk, 'Good point. Do you think the captain would mind if I got a little extra slaying in on the way?'

\*

'What do you mean a fire?' Gilead barked into the intercom.

'Big orange thing, quite warm, setting the ship alight?' the intercom replied.

'Send a team down to deal with it. Dammit, what the hell is going on down there?'

On the other side of the bridge, 462 was leaning against a bulkhead, listening. He sighed and stood up and walked over. 'Your men seem to have been repulsed,' he said, peering at the camera screens. 'You should give the orders to repel the boarders or die fighting. Your crew are weak.' 462 tutted and wagged his antennae at Gilead. 'I am not impressed, ally. Not impressed at all.'

As they turned the corner, half a dozen soldiers sprang out at them and suddenly gunfire raged down the corridor. Carveth threw herself into an alcove on one side of the passage, Suruk on the other. She saw him lean out and hurl a knife, and a huge moustachioed man like an enormous P.E. teacher staggered into view and fell, the weapon jutting from his neck. Carveth pushed the barrel of the maxim cannon around the corner and fired off a few rounds, then ducked back as the mercenaries replied.

Why me, she thought, and why here? She looked around her alcove for anything that might help but found only a poster that said, 'Your civil rights have been suspended pending Armageddon'. I wish I was at home, she thought. Everyone was shooting at her: even Suruk, who was supposed to be on her side, was waving his arms about and pointing at her feet.

What's wrong with my feet? Carveth thought as a fresh

burst of gunfire rang down the hall, and she looked down and saw a small cylinder next to them. She picked it up. 'Is this yours?' she yelled across the corridor.

Suruk, by means of cowering, indicated that it was not his. She wondered what it might be. It was difficult to think straight, what with all the noise. Some sort of tinned food, perhaps? Maybe it was cola. She looked at the side, caught a glimpse of some writing, and thought for a split second that it might be Grenadine.

She screamed and hurled it back down the corridor and it exploded, killing three soldiers who were advancing towards them. Taking advantage of the situation, Carveth shouted 'Like that, do you?' and ran out, Suruk striding alongside her.

The last mercenary took one look at the pair of them – a furious woman in a blue dress, covered in guns, and a maniac alien in a top hat – and ran.

'Look!' Carveth said. She pointed to a sign on the wall. There were little arrows on the sign, pointing to various parts of the ship. Under 'cinema' and 'brig' was 'discussion chambers'.

They hurried down the corridor. There were glass port-holes in the wall: one of them led into an ante-room full of lockers. As she peered through, she caught a glimpse of something brown hanging up within – Smith's coat. 'Here!' she cried.

Voices rang from further up the corridor – lots of them. Gilead's men had sent for reinforcements.

Suruk glanced down at her. 'Go,' he said. 'Fetch the captain.'

The voices were getting closer. Carveth caught a glimpse

of a man in a gas mask at the far end of the corridor, making a fist and whirling it in some kind of code. 'What about you?' she said.

Suruk's awful face opened in a kind of smile. 'I intend to enjoy my holiday – at bloody last.'

Carveth said, 'I'll be back soon.' She reached out, one hand on the trigger still, and threw open the door.

A small man in a long black coat was smoking a cigarette. As the door opened he threw open the coat and reached for his gun – and she shot him.

Carveth hurried across the ante-room and searched the man in black. He had a keycard on his belt, and she pushed it into the door and saw the light above the lock flash green. Behind her, the first sounds of battle began. Gan Uteki, sacred spear of Suruk's tribe, was having a jolly time.

She opened the cell door and rushed in. Smith was in the middle of the room in his boots and no trousers, squatting over a soldier who lay full length on the floor. 'Don't mind me,' Carveth said.

'Carveth!' Smith stood up. 'Thank God!'

'It's me alright,' she said. 'We're here to rescue you. We thought—' Smith turned round and her mouth fell open. She said, 'Oh my God. Are you inflamed or something?'

Smith frowned. 'What?' He followed her eyes and looked down at himself. 'Oh, you mean my underpants? Sorry about that. They stole my trousers to break my will.'

'It doesn't look broken from here. You're a bloody Martian war machine. Do you make Spice with that thing?'

'Listen, Gilead's probably quite annoyed right now. He'll

probably send some heavies down. I saw a lot of dubious sorts hanging round upstairs. We ought to leave now.'

'No shit, Shergar – I mean Sherlock. Let's go.'

'I need a gun,' said Smith.

'Got it here.' Carveth spun round awkwardly, feeling rather like a packhorse under the weight of the cannon. Smith rooted about and lifted out the rifle. He buckled the Civiliser around his hips and put on his long coat. 'Let's go,' he said. 'Suruk needs our help.'

As they reached the door, Suruk gave a bellow of glee and threw a knife at someone far down the corridor. The two humans rushed to his side.

'Back to the ship, men!' cried Isambard Smith.

A man rushed into the corridor and Carveth whipped around and gunned him down. 'Ha!' she cried. 'This isn't so bad,' she said, patting the barrel of the Maxim cannon, 'I could get used to having one of these sticking out in front of me.'

'Penis envy, no doubt,' Smith observed, scanning the corridor for more enemies.

'Humans are strange,' Suruk said. 'Why would anyone envy a penis?'

Suddenly new shapes ran into the corridor: trenchcoats flapping around them, big heads wobbling on spindly necks, pincer-claws rising above their shoulders like broken wings.

'Ghasts!' Carveth called.

Smith lifted the rifle, took aim down the scope and fired. The nearest Ghast flew over in a whirl of leather, its legs kicking once before lying still. 'Let's move,' the captain said, and they ran.

# 10

# Pursuit

They ran into the *John Pym* and slammed the airlock shut. Behind them, something was exploding in the *Fist of Righteousness*, far away. Did we do that? Carveth wondered. Smith was in the cockpit before her as, with a great lurch, the *Pym* pulled free of the stricken warship. Carveth stumbled and fell onto her back, and remained there until Suruk undid the catches on the gun harness as he stepped over her on the way to his room.

She found some beers in the galley and brought them to the cockpit. The main engines fired, and in a moment they were putting thousands of kilometres between themselves and Gilead's ship.

'We did it!' Carveth cried. 'We rescued you!'

'Indeed you did. Thank you, Carveth. You're a good sort.' Smith stood up and motioned to the control seat. 'The helm is yours, pilot.'

'Thanks, Boss.' It was good to be back in the driving seat, she thought: less good was the fact that Smith was still in his boots, jacket and underpants and his groin was now at the level of her head, an issue about which she had decidedly negative feelings. 'Good to be back,' she said. 'That gun was heavy.'

'You were wise to take it,' Smith said, opening his can and taking a deep swig. 'If you're facing desperate men like that, you don't want to go in half-cocked.'

'Frankly,' Carveth said, 'you're not going to have that problem. Would you mind putting your trousers on, sir?'

'Trousers it is,' Smith declared. 'In the meantime, set a course – for adventure!'

'Any particular direction?' Carveth said. She felt that after the success of the rescue mission, things had got back to normal distressingly quickly.

'Hmm.' Smith put his hands on his hips and frowned thoughtfully. 'Well, they've still got Rhianna – I don't know why, but she matters a lot to them. Not only is she a woman in distress, but getting her back would throw a spanner into the Ghasts' evil works. I suggest that we pull back and wait. I think they'll transfer her to the Ghast ship. Then we follow the Ghasts, keeping back so as to avoid their scanners. Then, when they're least expecting it, we can attack and rescue Rhianna.'

Carveth nodded. It would be pointless to try to explain how frightening this plan sounded. 'Will do, Boss.'

'Make it so, Carveth.'

'I just said I would.'

'Well, keep making it.'

Smith strode down to his room, found a pair of suitable trousers and put them on. Returning to the cockpit, he noticed that the door to Rhianna's room was open. He paused with his hand on the door handle, glanced around and slipped inside.

It smelt of students, as usual. There were some books on the table, about meditation and things like that. Smith picked one up at random: a retrospective of Japanese cartoon art entitled *Look Back in Manga*. Baffling stuff. He smoothed down his moustache and put the book back.

Smith stopped before the dresser, thinking. Why did the Ghasts what Rhianna so much? What was the reason for her powers? He decided that for the good of the Empire and mankind he would search the room for clues, starting with Rhianna's knickers drawer. He closed the cabin door and began his quest.

Smith perused the contents of the drawer, awed by the notion that such small items could do the job. At the back was a red tin box with a label stuck to the top. Perhaps it would contain something that might help. He pulled it out and prized off the lid. Mmm, biscuits.

Carveth was reattaching Gerald's water bottle to the cage when Smith returned to the cockpit. 'Hey there,' he said. 'Find anything?'

'Plenty,' Carveth said. 'I've scanned the surrounding area. They're moving deep into no-man's-land, into territory none of the Great Powers have claimed, human or alien.'

'Strange. I'd have thought they would want to take her to their leader. Go on.'

'Well, whatever it is they're planning, they must be planning to do it quietly. Which means, judging from their course, they're heading here.' She pointed to a small, grey planet on the edge of the screen. 'Drogon. Ooh, are those biscuits?'

'Yes. Here you go. What's this Drogon place like?'

'Thanks. Well, from what I gather, it's horrible. The

*Lonely Planets* guide says that Drogon has a "vibrant local youth culture founded on milk-based intoxicants", but if it's where I'm thinking of, it's the crappest planet in the galaxy. Other worlds are more violent, depopulated or unsuited to human life, but Drogon is the closest thing to an Arndale Centre that has ever occurred naturally. It could be a tough job. Are these raisins in my biscuit? I don't really like raisins.' She took a bite and said, 'Erm . . . Where did you find these, Captain? I'm not sure we should be eating them.'

'They were in Rhianna's room. I wouldn't look so worried, Carveth. If she hadn't made them for interstellar travel it wouldn't say 'Space Cakes' on the lid.'

The long, sleek form of the *Systematic Destruction* slid out of the darkness and swung towards Drogon. At first it was visible only as a shadow, an absence of stars, but as it passed the *John Pym* the weak rays of Drogon's sun caught the craft and gave it a silhouette. Light crept around the edges of the Ghast ship like dawn. Lasers and missile batteries took shape on its hull; spiky Ghast lettering appeared on the prow as if branded there by the sun. And at the very front, the painted head of a Ghastish animal, antennae raised and wolfish jaws open, as if howling into space.

Carveth tracked the enemy ship on the radar. The Peptos had worn off and she was cold enough to have put a blanket over her knees. As she watched the *Systematic Destruction* slide by, she shuddered. Her small hands plotted its trajectory and she tried not to think about anything other than programming the computer: things like

Rick Dreckitt, now almost certainly dead, or their on-coming showdown with the Ghasts. Even space itself seemed like an enemy now, frigid and unwelcoming, the last place for an android who wanted little more than a cheap drink and a date. I'm getting the fear, she realised.

Smith lay on his bed, feeling unusual. He was drowsy and felt strangely content. He shifted position and smiled, thinking of Rhianna. Then he remembered that she was captive, and his smile disappeared. Not to worry. He'd get her back soon, and then, well, maybe they could go on a picnic together or something.

A picture lay across his lap. It had been in Rhianna's room. It showed a tallish, wire-haired woman who looked as if she should be saying wise things to the medieval peasantry. Several cats were attached to her. She looked like a sterner, more gaunt version of Rhianna: the family resemblance was obvious. But the other half of the picture, where the father should have been, was obscured by smoke. Mist swirled at the woman's side, as if she had conjured it. Hold on, Rhianna, Smith thought, I'm coming to rescue you. Whatever you really are.

In his room, Suruk was arranging his possessions. He'd had a good time on the *Fist of Righteousness*, and had been able to bring back a couple of souvenirs. Suruk's ancestors were pleased with him: they had enjoyed the fight, he knew. If you thought that was fun, just wait until we reach Drogon, he told them. Don't touch that dial, ancient ones.

It was raining on Drogon. In Vorlig, its capital and only city, the few citizens looked up at the sky and shrugged.

Once, before the Russo-Anglo-Sino-Peruvian border war, Drogon had been a colony of the Collected Russian Federation, but tectonic instability had made it unsuitable for full-scale colonisation. Now, only a few citizens remained in the grey, dilapidated housing blocks, drinking cheap liquor, laundering illegal data and emptying their bladders in its many broken lifts.

A small man wheeled a trolley full of boxes past a rusted statue of a dancing boy and girl. The girl had lost all the fingers but one on her upraised hand; the boy's head had been long stolen and was now part of an illicit whisky still. As the small man reached a block of deserted flats he noticed a group of lads in an underpass. They called after him but he hurried on, head down.

The youths wandered down the underpass, drugged-up and bored, looking for someone to rob. They emerged into Drogon's overcast daylight, onto a patch of wasteland where a factory had once stood. Glass crunched under their heavy boots.

Two figures stood on the far side of the wasteland. One was a man in his thirties, in a long brown coat and a red jacket that they did not recognise. Beside him stood an alien, a tall, greenish-grey stick of a being, with elaborate mandibles and little yellow eyes. The gang leader nodded, and they pulled their hats down low.

Suruk watched the gang approach. 'Trouble,' he said.

Smith shook his head. 'Nonsense. Whenever did you hear of a chap in a bowler hat being trouble? I say, you there!' he called. 'Have you seen an alien spacecraft, perchance?'

There was a pause. The gang looked at one another. Their leader took his walking stick in both hands. 'Let's get 'em!' he yelled. 'Cronk his smogbox, men!'

Returning to the ship, Smith joined the others around the dining room table and studied a map that Carveth had printed out. 'That was informative,' said Smith, tucking into a Sham sandwich. 'Thanks for the help back there, Suruk.'

Suruk shrugged. 'Have a hat,' he said, dropping a bowler onto Carveth's head. 'The human braves told me some interesting things, before their heads came off. Behold the map.'

Spread across the table was a large-scale printout of the area. Various bits of cutlery had been used to represent civic buildings. Smith put his sandwich down and leaned over it.

'The pepper pot on the map indicates the likely landing-point of the Ghast spacecraft. The teabag represents our current location,' he added, pointing. 'As you can see, the area is built-up but has largely fallen down.

'The Ghast ship is large, and likely to contain many enemy, perhaps over two hundred drone-soldiers. We – represented by the salt cellar – need to move east in order to approach the ship. Carveth, broom,' said Smith, and Carveth wearily pushed the salt cellar across the table with the ship's broom. When Smith had said that they would be using a complex computer to illustrate a plan of the area, she hadn't realised that this would entail the ship's android shoving condiments around with a wooden pole.

'We need to surprise the enemy in order to gain the upper hand, since they considerably outnumber us. As a result, I will go out and assess the area and try to get an idea of enemy troop movements. I'll skirt the locale and approach from the flank to reconnoitre. Broom please.'

Carveth pushed the salt cellar in a wide arc so as to creep up on the pepper pot and reflected that the role of women in warfare had not made great strides over the last few centuries.

'So,' Smith said, 'shortly I will head out to the east and survey area with the aim of getting past their sentries unseen. Any questions?'

'What about this shuttle to the west?' Carveth said.

'That's not a shuttle,' Smith explained. 'That's my sandwich.'


A broken, battered landscape. The shopfronts were dark, the writing on the glass unimportant. Rubble lay in the street, clumps of grass jutting out from between the paving stones like shocked hair. On the walls there were scraps of posters, some advertising, other giving warnings from a government that collapsed years before the buildings did. Entropy and rot: Drogon was dying, and taking its time.

Suddenly, the ruins stirred. Pebbles turned and rolled and something inhuman rushed out from a gateway in a swish of leather, hurdling one of the fallen blocks. It scurried forward, helmet bobbing, and stopped in the shadow of a burnt-out car.

The reddish body straightened, and one of the trillion soldiers of the Ghast Empire stood up. It was scrawny and

TOBY FROST

hard, the legs powerful and hooved for kicking downed enemies, the mantis-arms tipped with stabbing claws. There were three long-tailed bio-grenades in its belt and a disruptor in its hands.

One day, it thought, all of mankind's worlds would look like this. One day, Earth would be a ruin like this place. The last soldier would be dead, the last island pacified, the final baby rendered into a nutritious babyshake. It grinned and took a step forward.

Straight into the sights of the rifle. Crouched behind a wall, Isambard Smith lined up the crosshairs with its chest.

'Cheery bye, Gertie,' he said, and fired.

'That went well,' Smith declared a little while later. He stood in the dining room with Carveth, stirring the teapot. Since his return from surveying the area, there were two new markers on the table: a boot, representing the Ghast ship, and its lace, laid out to show the perimeter of a large building.

'They're all holed up in there,' Smith explained, pointing to the bootlace. 'It's a municipal sports centre, disused of course. It's where they've taken Rhianna, and where most of them will be, guarding her. That's where we need to be.'

Carveth frowned and watched him pour out two cups of tea. 'I don't get it. Why take her there – or to this rotten planet at all? Why don't they just whip her back to their homeworld? They're stuck out on this rotten peehole of a place when they could be in the middle of their own empire. It doesn't make sense to me.'

'Who knows?' said Smith, passing her a cup. 'They're aliens; who knows how they think? They may want to do their dirty work where nobody would think to look, somewhere unimportant. Or maybe they're afraid that what they've got planned may go wrong and they want to keep it away from their top brass. Whatever it is, it's evil science, and we have to put a stop to it. Now, the grounds of the sports centre are well-guarded. The first stage will be getting past their sentries.' He leaned around the door-frame and called into the hold, 'Suruk. are you finished yet?'

'Nearly done!'

'Of course,' said Smith, 'that's not the only difficulty.'

Carveth said, 'You're telling me. There's three of us and two hundred of them.'

'Which means we need a way in, a way of immobilising them. Effectively, a way of getting the sentries to drop their guard and let us in.'

'Sounds like we're stuffed,' she said.

'I've thought of a way around that, but I'll need your help.'

'Not liking this plan,' she said, shaking her head.

'Don't worry. There's no need for them to attack you, none at all. In fact, you'll be a far less obvious target than either Suruk or I would be.'

She sighed. 'Well, this idea of yours might have some sort of merit…'

Smith walked to the door. 'Come this way,' he said. 'I'll show you what I've got in mind.'

She followed him into the hold, and the first thing that struck her was the large red object dangling from the roof. It looked like an enormous shrimp, minus its insides, and it seemed to have been rubbed with jam.

The second thing that struck her was that Suruk was drying some large piece of material on the workbench, and using her hairdryer to do it.

'Yuck!' she said. 'What the hell is that?'

'Our enemy,' Smith explained, gazing up at the thing that dangled from the roof. 'That is a partly-skinned Ghast Shock Adjutant, which I bagged while I was outside. You see, the Ghast doesn't think quite the same as we do: his brain is less advanced than that of an Englishman, or indeed a woman. Thousands of years of mindless obedience have left him with a corroded mind, reduced reasoning capacity and almost no discernable backbone. What little brain he has is attuned to recognise simple shapes, insignia, things like that.'

'How does that help us, Boss?'

'Well it means that if it smells right, and looks vaguely right, the chances are that he'll think it's a Ghast. And if it's shouting at him and wearing a bigger coat, he'll probably salute it.'

A wave of realisation swept over Carveth, like nausea. This plan had a strong whiff of cockup about it. With dread she said, 'You're turning it into a pantomime horse, aren't you?'

'Yes.'

Suruk turned from the workbench and held up the result of his efforts. It was a long coat, with a Ghast's head sewn into the lining. With its helmet still on, it lolled crazily. The two pincer-arms stuck out the back, held in place by a clever framework of industrial wire, sticky-backed plastic and string.

'The coat can be draped over the wearer's shoulders,' Smith explained. 'The head would sit on the user's head, like a sort of big hat with teeth in.'

Carveth shook her head. 'It's totally unconvincing. You couldn't make a worse disguise if you put a stick up your bum and claimed to be a toffee apple. It doesn't look anything like a live Ghast, and what's more, you'll be far too tall with that thing on your head. You're about the same height as one of them as it is: you'd be a head too tall if you wore it. You'd have to use someone much... oh no. No, no. You must be kidding. I won't do it. I won't—'

Divisional Shock Adjutant 84309/G approached the sentries with an odd, shuffling gait, head rocking back and forward as if to an unheard beat. To Isambard Smith, who was crouched in the rubble watching through the ship's binoculars, it looked as if the Shock Adjutant had consumed several bottles of wine.

Two sentries stood in front of the gate to the sports centre. They held their disruptors across their chests and stared straight ahead.

'This is insane,' the Shock Adjutant whispered from its chest.

'Shut up and get on with it,' Smith said into the radio. 'Keep looking in the phrasebook and make sure the translator's on. If it gets nasty, pull rank on them.'

The sentries stamped their feet as Carveth approached. Peering out of the front of the Adjutant's coat, she was spared the sight of its lolling head flopping forward and fixing the nearest sentry with an idiotic, unfocussed gaze.

There was a short pause.

'Um, hello,' said Carveth.

'Sir!' the sentry barked. 'Show your identification!'

The translator was working, but the vocabulary was not. Within the coat, Carveth rifled through her notes and said the first thing she saw.

'Silence! You will all be shot!'

The sentries drew themselves up and were very quiet indeed. Inside the coat, Carveth tried not to whimper with relief.

'Traitors will be stamped out ruthlessly!' she continued, warming to her theme. 'Earth must be destroyed!'

'Yes!' the sentry said. 'Of course, sir, but we need to see your pap-'

'Hands up, Earthman! These prisoners are of no further use to us! Quick, quick!'

The sentries exchanged a glance. 'We shall fetch a superior officer to make this decision,' said one. 'You must wait here.'

They turned, opened the gate a fraction, slipped through and it slammed in Carveth's hidden face.

'Well, that went well,' she said into the radio. 'Now they've gone to get a bigger gun.'

'Stay there,' Smith replied. 'They're going to let you in.'

'Not so much "let" as "do",' Carveth said, and the gate opened behind her.

Another, smaller Ghast stepped out. How many of the damn things were there, she wondered? They seemed to have so many medals, symbols of rank and general purpose sinister-looking junk attached to them that it was hard to tell who was in charge until they started to shout.

The new arrival took off his cap and ran a hand through his antennae. 'So!' he said, 'You are late returning, Divisional Shock Adjutant 84309/G. Your uniform is uneven. This is intolerable! Stand to attention!'

Carveth tried, acutely aware of the wobbling of the large head she wore as a hat.

'This is a disgrace!' the officer yelled. 'Explain yourself, 84309/G!'

Apologetically, she said, 'Destroy all humans? Quick, danger?'

'Enough!' the officer stepped forward, drew back its arm and backhanded the wobbling head around the face.

'How dare you answer back a superior?' the officer barked. 'I am a—' One of the sentries nudged it and pointed to the head. About to embark on a furious lecture, the officer peered at the target of its abuse and realised that 84309's head was now the wrong way round.

The officer looked at its hands, both puzzled and impressed by its own strength. 'Whoops,' it said, and took a step back.

Carveth slid a hand onto her gun. In the shelter of the abandoned brewery, Smith watched through the binoculars and said, 'Arse.'

'You did that,' said the officer to the sentries. 'I outrank you, and I saw you doing that. It's all your fault his head has done that.'

'Nobody move!' Carveth yelled, and in a frantic, leathery spasm she drew her pistol and shrugged the greatcoat onto the floor. The service revolver trembled in her hand. 'Nobody move! Stick 'em up! All of 'em!'

They stared at her.

'Well?' she demanded. 'Do it!'

'You said 'Nobody move',' the Ghast officer said, 'but you also want us to raise our hands. We do not understand. These orders are contradictory.'

'I so want to obey my orders, but I can't!' the left sentry said miserably. 'I feel worthless and unhappy! What should I do?'

'I don't know, do I?' Carveth replied. 'Look: put your hands up and then stay still. Good. Now, open the doors.'

The three Ghasts exchanged a hopeless look. 'But—'

'Move, put your hands down and then open the sodding doors! God, it's no wonder you need a glorious leader to tell you what to do. If it wasn't for Number One none of you thickos would ever wipe his own spiracle, let alone conquer the galaxy.' She turned to the wasteland. 'Captain, I'm having problems here!'

Smith and Suruk emerged from the rubble and joined her. 'It didn't quite go as planned,' she said. 'They sussed me when my false head came off. Then they all turned out to be wallies.'

'Not to worry. Let's get ready and go in.'

Suruk had brought the Maxim cannon, and once again Carveth strapped it on. Smith took the slimy, pulsating guns from the three Ghasts and threw them away as Suruk tied the aliens up.

Smith loaded his rifle. He put the Civiliser into his shoulder holster and opened the blade of his penknife.

Suruk helped Carveth into the Maxim cannon. She

cleared the mechanism and slapped an ammo drum into place, watching the round counter spin up to 999. Smith took a large metal cylinder out of his rucksack and strapped it to his back. What, she wondered, was that?

Smith looked down at the three Ghasts. Suruk had bound them with plastic bin ties and now they lay in a neat row on the pavement, pressed together like politically extreme sardines. Smith bent down and took the officer's identity pass from his coat pocket.

'Now,' he told them, 'you are all captives of the British Space Empire. I am a man of my word, and I can guarantee that so long as you remain civil and don't try to invade anywhere, the worst you can expect from us is an educational film about voting. But I warn you, gentlemen' – and he scowled over his moustache at them – 'should any of you try it on, you will be in very, very serious trouble indeed. For there is an innocent woman inside that you have taken hostage, and we look very dimly upon that. I tell you, I am a man of steel, and I don't take kindly to interfering—'

'Boss,' said Carveth, 'let's just get the doors open.'

'Right,' Smith replied. 'Let's go, shall we?'

She swallowed and looked him in the eye. 'Why not?'

Suruk chuckled.

Smith ran the officer's identity pass through the lock and pushed the doors apart.

Into the gap stepped the biggest Ghast Smith had ever seen: comfortably six feet six, darker in colour than its comrades, the praetorian looked down at them and drooled.

'Move and I shoot you,' Smith said. 'Take us to your leader.'

'No!' said the praetorian. Its voice was a low, evil growl.

'We have an officer here,' Smith suggested. 'We wish to exchange him for our friend.'

'Officers are replaceable. There is no reason why you should speak with our commander.'

'Well,' said Smith, 'how's this for a reason, then?' He shrugged, and the silver cylinder slid into his arms. 'I've got a thermonuclear detonator.'

# 11

# Gertie Takes a Pasting

It had been a night of hard and determined celebration. Despite the crippling of his ship, Captain Gilead felt that he was on the cusp of a great victory. While the Ghasts paced back and forth and listened to a speech by Number One, Gilead and his men opened some beers and enjoyed a screening of *Helicopters Blowing Up Sheds*, Gilead's favourite film. Eventually, having drunk himself silly and yelled himself hoarse, he passed out during the second reel of *100 Wackiest Executions*. Now he blinked and watched Isambard Smith and his heretic crew approach, like hangovers made flesh.

They walked in a row, armed to the teeth, between rows of Ghast troopers and confused, beer-addled mercenaries. Heads turned, comments were whispered and guns were drawn as Smith, Suruk and Carveth strolled into the middle of the enemy camp.

A little group of soldiers looked up from their breakfast and fell silent. Someone turned a radio off. Nobody tried to stop them.

Gilead winced. Sometime during the night his eyes seemed to have been taken over by a chameleon, and the three newcomers moved back and forward in his vision like little men with hammers on an old Austrian clock. They still looked like idiots, he thought, but they were not hung over. Gilead picked up his jacket, on which a pigeon had deposited solids while he was drunk, and clambered into it as they drew near.

The praetorian led them to a long table outside the sports centre. Here, surrounded by minions and loose Drogonian women of startling ugliness, Gilead and his closest comrades had passed out.

A man lurched in front of Smith. 'Hey!' It was Gilead's second-in-command. He blinked a couple of times, as if unsure of how he'd ended up in a uniform with a gun in his hand, and said, 'You! What the hell do you want?'

'They want the angel,' a voice slurred behind him. Captain Gilead stepped out, looking very low. His jacket was open and stained, his shirt a rumpled mess. A ceremonial sword dangled from his belt like a broken tail. He turned his head ponderously and fixed his gaze in the area around the praetorian. 'Why aren't these disbelievers dead?'

The praetorian regarded him with as much disgust as its face could manage. 'They are armed with a nuclear weapon,' it said, pointing to the silver cylinder Smith carried on his back.

Gilead took a step closer and squinted. 'That's not a bomb, you dumb bastard,' he said. 'That's an old beer keg with a yellow sticker on the side.'

'Not so, Gilead,' Smith called. 'It's an important reactor-part of our ship. We have dismantled it and rigged it to explode at the slightest touch.'

'Then why's it got a tap on the side, huh?'

'That's how the atoms get out,' Smith said, thinking quickly. 'It's an atom tap.'

Gilead threw back his head and laughed, and immediately regretted doing so. 'You make me laugh!' he said, grimacing. He strolled over, shaking his head. 'You're pathetic. You come in here with a beer keg and the only person you fool is this stupid ant-man here.'

The praetorian hissed. 'You will have respect for us!'

'Ah, go polish your thorax. You're such a two-bit operation it's wonderful, Smith. But you're outgunned this time. Take a look around you. You see all this?' he demanded, taking in his men with a great sweep of the arm. 'See those boxes over there? That gun under the netting? The heavy disruptor on that tripod? You know what that is? Military force. Not your little arsenal but *force*: real, serious, hot, holy, sexy military force. I could use that walkie-talkie there and call up an orbital missile that'd wipe you off the planet and take a picture of your face as it flies up your nose. I could take you out just like that. I've got half a mind to do so, too.'

'Still looking for the other half, eh?' Smith fixed him with cold, calm eyes. 'You're contemptible, Gilead. You're so stupid you probably think "erudite" is a type of glue.'

'I like you,' Gilead said. 'But I don't like you half as much as I hate your ungodly guts. I've been waiting for this moment: you and I face to face, man to pansy unbeliever. Your precious bomb is nothing more than a beer keg. You've got nothing left, Smith, no cards to play, and all I've got to do now is to choose how best to send you all to hell.'

279

'You're forgetting something,' Smith said. 'It's a forty-five Markham and Briggs Civiliser, and it's pointed right at your gut. I was hoping you'd come closer to gloat. It makes you an easier target. Make one move, you mad fanatic, and I'll martyr you all over the back wall.'

Gilead paused. His eyes met Smith's for a long moment and, very slowly, he looked down. The gun jutted from Smith's hip, the long barrel pointed straight at Captain Gilead's chest.

'You were too busy ranting to see me draw it,' Smith said.

'That's not fair,' Gilead replied. 'That's not fair!' he yelled. 'You can't do that! I'm the one with the guns here!'

'We want Rhianna,' said Isambard Smith.

'And you could throw some beer in too,' Carveth said. 'But none of that tasteless rubbish. Good stuff only.'

Something broke in Captain Gilead then. He looked at Smith, the man he'd dismissed as a weakling that he could bully and sweep aside, and knew that these people, with their broken spaceship and their shabby empire, were the rock against which he would bash himself to death.

'I hate you!' Gilead screamed. 'I hate you! I hate all of you people, with your make-do attitude and your not shouting all the time! Look at you, with your stupid moustache and your stiff upper lip. You make me sick, you atheist agnostic heathen!'

Suruk said quietly, '*Urug mashai nar sergret, Mazuran.*'

Smith glanced at the tripod-mounted heavy disruptor and nodded. '*Jaizeh, Suruk. Urenesh*, old friend.'

'Good luck to you too.'

'You accursed, hell-spawned, democracy-loving

bastards! And look at this, this so-called woman of yours, wearing trousers in public. Woman? Whore of Babylon, more like! If you were one of my wives, I'd have you stoned to death!'

Carveth shrugged. 'Stoned as in rocks, right?'

'Of course rocks!'

'Nah, I don't fancy that much.'

'And you're fat!'

'You're dead,' she said.

'Fatter than all my wives laid end to end! And then this thing, this disgusting mockery of the sacred human form!'

'Hello,' Suruk said.

'This thing should be shining shoes, not walking around like a man! You call this frog-monkey-thing a *friend*? It's bright green! It ought to be a *slave*!'

Suruk laughed, a reliable indication that violence was near. Carveth was surprised to find that she was too angry to be afraid. Son of a bitch called me fat, she thought. And some other stuff. But mainly fat.

'Damn you,' Gilead yelled, 'damn you all, you hell-bound blasphemers! You wrecked my ship and beat my men! But not any more, because now I'm going to cut off your stupid heads!'

He drew his ceremonial sword and waved it in the air like a dervish.

'Finished,' said Smith.

'Oh, I'm just starting,' Gilead replied.

'That wasn't meant to be a question,' Smith said.

The shot hit Gilead smack in the chest and threw him thirty feet. He kicked once and lay still.

They stood there in the silence that followed, in the eye

of the storm. Carveth glanced around the crowd, waiting to spot the fool who made the first move. The Ghast Empire froze. The Church of God the Annihilator stared back at her, enraged but afraid. A slight breeze stirred the sacred banners. She looked down at Gilead, lying in the dust.

'What a cult,' she said.

The praetorian jerked up its gun and the safety catch clicked off and Smith whipped around and blasted it in the side, looked down the barrel of his pistol and shot it twice again.

Suddenly, in the crowd, mayhem.

As one they grabbed, cocked, loaded and drew a hundred guns. A great wave of movement ran through the men and Ghasts, and they surged forward as the first shots burst out. Carveth braced herself and the Maxim cannon yawed around and cut down the first rank of mercenaries. Above the rattle of her gun, she was yelling.

A Ghast trooper ran to the heavy disruptor on the table and started it up. Suruk roared, threw his spear and the trooper dropped across the controls. He bounded after his spear and into the middle of the Ghasts, a long knife rising and falling in either hand.

Smith emptied the Civiliser into one of Gilead's fanatics, felt the hammer click on an empty chamber, tossed it aside and pulled the rifle into his hands. Gilead's ranting had made him furious: this was no longer about bagging a couple of Gerties for the mantelpiece, but something darker, more fundamental. This was decency against madness, people who'd never gone looking for trouble against zealots and tyrants. He fired without aiming, knocking a Ghast to the ground. A disruptor beam shot past his head and he cranked the handguard and fired again. 'Come and get it!'

'Mazuran! Here!'

He whirled and saw Suruk at the centre of a scrum of Ghasts and men. Too close to use their guns, they had drawn knives and shock-sticks, and were faring badly. Smith ducked down and ran low, Carveth's wild firing accidentally providing him with cover. He brained a Ghast with his rifle butt and reached the M'Lak's side.

'Aha,' said Smith, and he shoved a dead Ghast out the way and grabbed the controls of the heavy disruptor. 'Here we go—'

'*Ak!*' half a dozen Ghasts yelled as Smith aimed the disruptor and vapourised them. He swung it left and right, reaping a great swathe across the yard, turning brick to dust and cultists and Ghasts to smoke. 'Who wants the Empire?' he cried. 'Come and get it, you little buggers! You think you can bully me?'

Carveth was out of bullets – the Maxim cannon clicked where it should have roared and suddenly she felt much smaller. She tore at the straps and the gun dropped away. Drawing her service revolver, she ran towards the others.

Suruk was fighting a pack of men and Ghasts, beating them back as they tried to reach the table-mounted gun. The heavy disruptor thrummed as it threw out pulses of energy. Smith hit a box of homing grenades and it exploded, throwing one of Gilead's men into the air as he tried to type their co-ordinates into a guided rocket.

'Who wants it?' the captain shouted. 'Who wants to

empty my pockets now? Oh, you want my dinner money, do you? I'll take the whole class on! Not so big now, are we, Curtis Minor!'

Carveth saw the way out: doors behind the flailing mass that was Suruk and half a dozen others. 'Cover me!' she yelled, more a plea than a command, and she took out a screwdriver and shoved it into the side of the control panel. Her fingers tore off the front of the panel and yanked wires apart. Running out of hands, she leaned in and ripped out the green wire with her teeth. Something hit the door above her head – a disruptor bolt, followed closely by a severed arm.

The heavy disruptor ran out of power. The remaining soldiers charged them.

Carveth shoved two wires together and the doors burst apart. She leaped into the space between them and Suruk sprang into the dark after her. The doors hissed in their grooves and, as they started to close, Suruk grabbed the nearest one and pulled it back. 'Now, Mazuran!'

'And that's for my tuck money!' Smith roared. His rifle cracked out. He leaped through the doorway, coat flapping behind him, and Suruk let go and the door slammed closed. Something thumped against the other side, but to no avail. The three of them stood in the dark of the sports centre, dust swirling around them, panting.

Smith's hands were shaking. 'Damn you, 3B,' he said.

From the floor, Carveth said, 'You have issues about your schooling, don't you?'

'Yes,' said Smith. 'And you know, if I hadn't repressed them all these years, I'd never have found the furious anger needed to drive off that horde of lunatics out there.

And that, men, is why I'm proud to be British. Now, come on,' he added. 'We must rescue Rhianna!'

Meanwhile, in what had once been the badminton courts, the Ghasts were rigging up their camera equipment. With the help of a couple of Gilead's mercenaries, they had connected their long-range telecasters and were ready to broadcast to glorious Number One.

462 tapped his microphone. 'One-two, one-two,' he said, and stopped when one of his subordinates started marching. Ghast scientists bustled past and the lead technician came over and brushed some red dust on his face and antennae.

'It is just for looks,' the technician explained. 'It is terrible when you have an important speech to make and you just do not look the part.'

462 adjusted his trenchcoat. 'Does my stercorium look big in this?'

'No bigger than mine!' the technician said. 'You look marvellous. And ever so evil.'

462 strode in front of the nearest camera. To his left, on a stretcher-bed, lay Rhianna, comatose. The brain-scanning helm had been placed on her head, and behind it loomed the huge machinery of the scanner with its twin Tesla coils.

A worried-looking functionary jogged up. 'Glorious Commander!' it barked.

'What is it?' said 462.

'There is trouble outside! Space Captain Smith has arrived!'

He shrugged. 'Have Gilead's men deal with him. They

are all disposable. Nothing must interrupt my moment of glory. Roll cameras!'

The technician gave him a nod. 462 looked into the lens.

'All hail glorious Number One! This is Medium Attack-Ship Captain 462, reporting from the planet of Drogon, a wretched outpost of contemptible human space! Here, our iron will has enabled us to destroy our opposition and score a mighty triumph for our Empire! Before you, All Knowing Leader, we have the captured woman from whom we shall construct the ultimate bioweapon. Today, we shall take one step closer to our goal of conquering the galaxy! Behold, as our technology harnesses the power of her mind!'

He turned to the scientist operating the scanner. 'You, minion! Turn the dials up to… four!'

The leisure centre had the same look as everything occupied by Ghasts. Despite being there for about five hours, they had covered it in banners and propaganda posters, announcing that the swimming pool and judo mats had been annexed for the good of the Greater Ghast Empire. Smith cocked the rifle and ran deeper into the complex, aware that the survivors of the fight outside would soon find another way in.

'This looks like it!' Carveth said, pointing to an enormous poster blocking the way to the badminton courts. The poster showed a small, pompous Ghast waving its fists and glowering into the middle distance. Both its antennae were slicked over to one side of its head.

'That's Number One,' said Smith. 'Their god.'

The sound of breaking glass came from behind.

'Mine,' Suruk said, looking over his shoulder. 'Go.'

Smith turned to Suruk and met his friend's villainous eyes. 'Good luck, Suruk. Is there anything I can do?'

'I have a sharp spear and an empty mantlepiece,' the alien said. 'I need no more than that. Now go.'

'This way!' Carveth cried, and Smith rushed up the stairs after her to the viewing gallery.

Smith booted the door open and charged through, saw the stretcher and the machinery behind it, lifted the rifle and yelled, 'You there! Stop that at once!'

Ghasts spun around. Smith fixed the sights on 462's bulbous skull. 'None of you move, or I'll bag your leader!'

The Ghasts froze. Electricity crackled between the conduction pillars. Above Rhianna's head the air had become a little hazy, like smoke.

Smith surveyed the scene with horrified awe. 'What the devil are they doing down there?'

'How should I know?' Carveth said from his side. 'I'm only a spaceship pilot.'

'Stop that nonsense!' Smith called down. 'Release that woman right now, or by God I'll put a bullet in your Tesla coils!'

462 attempted a winning smile. He took a step towards the viewing gallery. 'Of course, Captain Smith. But before you unleash righteous mayhem, perhaps you would like to know what we are doing here, yes? I think so. For that is what unites us, Smith, much as we may fear to admit it.' Still smiling, he stepped out into the open. Smith kept 462's head in the crosshairs. 'You and I are both on the

same quest, you see: the quest for knowledge. You too have stared up at the stars and thought, *What secrets does the galaxy hold, and how can I beat them out of it?* Does it not pique your scientific curiosity to know that you are standing in the room where history will be made? That you, Isambard Smith, are about to witness the greatest experiment your world will ever know?'

'No, not really,' said Smith.

'Oh well. Kill him,' he said.

Smith fired and the technicians scattered. The bullet hit 462 in the helmet, ricocheted into the ceiling, hit a joist, shot down, struck the control panel and spun the dial to eleven.

Above Rhianna the cloud grew and grew. As it billowed out Smith cried, 'Oh my God, no! I've cooked her head!'

462 laughed triumphantly, despite cowering on the floor in the shadow of the stretcher. 'Fools! Victory is mine! Look!'

Something was forming in the smoke. Awed, Ghasts and men stared at the column as it twisted and condensed into the shape of a human being wreathed in mist. It turned to look over the room, and in its serene, smoke-swathed face Smith caught an echo of Rhianna, the girl he had fallen for and might even have loved had she been a bit cleaner.

The spectre shook its dreadlocks and looked around.

462 broke the silence. 'Ahahaha! Can you not see? The perfect weapon!'

'The Angel of the Apocalypse!' cried one of Gilead's men.

'It's Casper!' Carveth gasped.

'We have separated her Vorl soul from her puny human body!' the Ghast commander cried, leaping up and shaking fists and claws in triumph. 'Without humanity to limit her, she will serve the ruthless logic of the Ghast Empire! The Vorl will be ours, and with their strength we shall annex the Earth!'

'Annex this!' Smith replied. His rifle cracked out and 462 fell clutching his eye.

'Fight to the last! Anyone surrendering will be shot!' the Ghast shouted. 'You will never defeat me!' he added, and he ran from the room.

Something crashed through the doors behind them and a huge, lumbering thing bounded down the gallery, hissing and drooling. Panic flooded Carveth's senses: the revolver in her hand seemed to flick up of its own accord, and in a moment she had pumped four shots into the praetorian's chest. Behind it, she saw dark shapes gathering on the staircase: Ghasts, mustering for an attack.

She glanced around. In the main hall, the spirit-thing was taking on a different appearance – it seemed to be stretching into something leaner, more gaunt, altogether more grim. Slowly it reached out towards them with a wisp of a skeletal hand.

'I think we might be in the soup,' Smith said. 'Looks like it's ghost or Ghasts. Any ideas?'

'How about we cower and squeal?'

He nodded. 'For once, you may have a point.' He turned to the nebulous creature floating opposite them and said, 'I say, you! I am a citizen of the Brit—'

The Ghasts charged up the stairs.

Things went rather distant for Polly Carveth then. Part

of her watched Captain Smith get knocked to the ground by a wave of force that threw her down beside him. Another part of her realised that this wispy thing must be a Vorl. But the majority of her was watching the heads of a dozen Ghast soldiers explode like popcorn.

The camera lenses cracked. The control panel of the Tesla machine burst into sparks, frying several Ghast technicians. The first soldier rushed onto the gallery, clambered over the dead praetorian and popped. The second soldier said, '*Ak?*' and burst. And suddenly a crackling bolt of energy ran through the sports hall, overturning the ping-pong tables and singeing the posters about verruca health, and it was all Carveth could do to crouch down and keep her bladder under control.

And then it was over. The room was full of dead Ghasts and the smell of ozone. A scrap of paper floated down from the ceiling. It said, *Will patrons kindly refrain from*, but it didn't get any further because the rest of it was burnt and covered in alien blood. Carveth stood up, ears ringing, numb.

'Well, that's told them!' said the Vorl, surveying the carnage and putting its insubstantial hands on its hips. It floated outside the gallery, its head gaining bulk as it changed back from a skull to a human face.

'Hand, Carveth?' said Isambard Smith. Carveth put out a hand and helped pull him up. He brushed his tunic down and said, 'Thanks. Right then. You, ghost fellow – what the devil do you mean by hiding inside Rhianna like that? I demand an explanation.'

'You saw what I just did,' the Vorl replied. 'You should fear me, Captain Smith.'

Smith took a step towards it. 'I refuse to be intimidated by a talking fart!'

At his side Carveth whispered, 'It just rescued us. It is Rhianna.'

'Oh, I see,' said Smith. 'Right. Well, thank you, Rhianna's ghost or whatever you are. Very decent of you to help out like that.'

'I am indeed Rhianna, but only a part of her,' the Vorl said. 'The Ghast machinery separated the two parts of her being. In doing so, they unleashed me. But I am incomplete, and I must return.'

Smith whistled softly. 'So Rhianna was half-Vorl! Golly. And to think I fancied her!' he added in what he thought was an undertone. 'But... how is that possible?'

'Rhianna's parents were hippies,' the swirling thing explained. 'They travelled the cosmos, seeking new experiences and enlightenment. One night, they visited the Vorl homeworld. Her mother and my father met up over a few joints and... well, you know.'

'Of course. I saw a picture. God, she must have been high as a kite.'

'I don't think either party was very proud come sunrise,' said the Vorl. 'Now, would you mind deactivating that machine, please?'

'Goodness knows how we'll break it to her,' Carveth said as they picked their way down the stairs, past the fallen Ghasts. ' "Terribly sorry, but not only are you half-woman, half-alien deity, but your mum got knocked up by Will'o the Wisp." For that matter, *shall* we tell her at all?

What happens if she gets pissed off on the way home and zaps us all?'

In the middle of the sports hall, Smith turned down the dials and pulled out the wires. 'Thank you,' said the Vorl, and as they watched, it diminished, sinking down into Rhianna, sucked back into her sleeping body.

She stirred in her sleep. She was still beautiful, Smith thought, although this was not quite the way he'd envisaged her waking up beside him. He reached out and gently put his hand on her brow.

Rhianna's eyes flicked open. 'Get your hands off me! Ugh! I'm covered in electrodes!' She sat bolt upright and looked down at herself. 'What the hell have you done with my bra, you fascists?'

'Oh my God,' Smith said, averting his eyes.

'Oh, it's you,' Rhianna said, calming down. 'Sorry. Hi, guys. Um, could someone find my top, please?'

Carveth put Rhianna's clothes on the bed and she got dressed under the sheets. 'So, er, what happened? I remember a dream... about smothering, I think... or maybe hovering... and then – well, then I was here.'

'The Ghasts were experimenting on you,' Carveth said. 'We raided them and rescued you. Were it not for the captain here and his incredible and frequent acts of death-defying bravery, you'd be dead.' *You owe me big*, she mouthed at Smith.

'Well, yes,' said Smith. 'There was a certain amount of heroic derring-do, now you mention it – and a fair few alien invaders got their comeuppance.'

'Wow,' said Rhianna. 'Of course, I wouldn't usually

condone anything involving vi – Oh, screw it. Knowing you did that really turns me on.'

'Good-oh,' said Captain Smith. 'Now, let's go back to the ship and have some tiffin.'

Suruk was waiting at the ship. 'I got locked out,' he said. 'These will look great on the mantelpiece,' he added, indicating two large carrier bags. 'It's been quite a day. So, did the Vorl appear and kill everyone with lightning?'

'*What*?' said Carveth.

'The Vorl. Did one of them turn up and use psychic powers and lightning to save the day?'

Smith gave Suruk a hard stare. 'You knew? All this time, and you knew that's what would happen?'

Suruk shrugged. 'Of course. It's an old legend of ours.'

'So why the hell didn't you let on? It could have saved us some bother, you know, if we'd known what we were up against.'

'Oh, come on,' Suruk said, 'I do not wander about telling silly stories all the time. I would look like some sort of benighted idiot. Now, who has the keys? I cannot wait to get the stove on and start cleaning up these skulls.'

# 12

# Back in the Empire

The *John Pym* touched down at Midlight central terminus on Kane's World six Greenwich Standard days later. Under a vaulted, scrollworked ceiling, they waved good-bye to Rhianna and watched her wander into the crowds, oddly conspicuous amid the sober, busy citizens of the Empire.

'I rather liked her,' Smith said, more to himself than anyone else. 'But I never knew what to do.'

'I know,' Carveth said. 'Never mind, Boss. Other fish in the sea.'

'Maybe we'll see her again,' said Smith, but he didn't sound convinced.

A few days later, much to Carveth's disappointment, they received no medals in front of any cheering crowd. What they had done was to stay secret. In place of the proud march between ranks of the Empire's finest soldiery, Mr Khan faxed them some luncheon vouchers and they went out for a curry instead.

It was a strange end to the job, Carveth thought, but not a bad one: drinking several pints of imported lager, laughing at Smith's uncanny impersonation of Florence Nightingale and watching Suruk ladle frightening amounts of Prawn Madras into his mouthparts. Everything was going well and Carveth was drunk enough to be humming along to the piped sitar music when a tall, gaunt man stopped at the end of the table.

'Isambard Smith?'

Smith looked up. 'Yes, that's me.'

The newcomer was about fifty, with a tired, battered face that looked much less healthy than the mess of black hair on top of it. He had a pencil moustache and deep-set eyes that were by turns kindly, hard and wise.

'I need to talk to you. I'm a friend of your employer, Hereward Khan. Here.'

He passed Smith an envelope in one large, bony hand. Smith tore it open and studied the contents.

'Well, you clearly know Mr Khan,' he said. 'Can I ask your name?'

The newcomer looked awkward. 'Well, I can't really tell you that. It's secret. Suffice it to say that when you were sent on this mission on behalf of certain unnamed people, I was one of them. May I?'

'Go ahead,' said Smith, and the man sat down.

'Before I say anything else, I must remember to give you this.' He reached into his jacket and took out a second envelope. 'Here,' he said, and he passed it to Carveth. 'For your good work.'

She held it up to the light, saw no cheque-shaped silhouette inside and opened it anyway. A passport and a driving licence fell out.

'What's this?' she said.

The visitor's lined face twitched into a smile. 'Have a look.'

She opened the passport. 'It's me,' she said.

The man crossed his long legs. 'That's right. It's you. You're an Imperial citizen now, Miss Carveth. The appropriate papers have been filed and there's nothing to prove that you're anything other than a fully-functional simulant who has spent the last three years working for a boring haulage firm.'

'You mean they can't come after me?'

'Absolutely. The corrupt plutocracy of the Devrin Corporation will have no more fun at your expense. You can assert your citizenship anywhere and rely on our battleships to back it up.'

'Wow,' she said. 'Thanks!' She glanced through the documents. 'Says here I'm the visual equivalent of twenty-eight. Whoa, I'd better find a man before I'm too old.'

'You'll all be rewarded financially,' said the visitor. 'You've set back the Ghast plans for galactic domination at least three weeks, if not more.' He leaned forward and said, 'But I'm afraid I've got a favour to ask of you. I want your help.'

'Need someone's head cut off?' Suruk growled.

'Not exactly. But there's need for a fast civilian ship these days. You see, a great conflict is coming, and it will not be politicians who save the galaxy. Mankind needs common men like yourselves – ordinary, bog-standard, unimpressive, slightly dull men who will defend it from the scourge of Ghastism. The common people of the Empire will not stand for tyranny!' he cried, and his eyes seemed to catch fire. 'No! The Imperial people will rise, and Ghastist blood will run wherever tyrants dare threaten our way of life! The alien dream of an enslaved

Earth will be over, and the golden light of Democracy shall shine like a beacon across space! We shall tear down their citadels and planetscape their worlds into the likeness of sacred Albion!'

He hit the table with his fist, sending Carveth's pint rocking like a broken chess-piece. The room was silent. The sitar music started twiddling in the background.

'You see my point,' the agent said.

'Absolutely,' Smith said, nodding quickly. Here was a man even more determined and fanatical than himself. He could now understand why girls tended to shrink away from him when he started talking about cricket.

'My cover is that I work as a journalist,' said the visitor. 'I'll contact you when the Empire has need of your services. In the meantime, should you have any problems, ask for me.'

He took out a pen and wrote a letter on a napkin, followed by a number. He pushed it across the table to Smith. 'That's my codename,' he explained. 'It means "Master Spy".'

'W', said Smith.

'Other way up.'

'Oh, right.'

'Well,' said W, 'I'd love to sit here and chat all day, but I'm not some sort of useless Nancy and I've got to get on. If I need you, I'll let you know: and if you need me, let me know that I ought to let you know.'

'What about Rhianna?' said Smith. 'What will happen to her?'

'You're worried about her?'

'Well, yes. She was a good friend to all of us.' Smith had

had an unsettling mental image of the security service putting Rhianna in a packing crate and wheeling her off to a warehouse full of other packing crates, and leaving her there.

'Absolutely,' Carveth said, reaching for the poppadoms. 'I'm worried sick. It's put me right off my food.'

'Well,' said W, 'I can't tell you much. Suffice to say that her help against the Ghasts will be invaluable. She'll be quite safe, and you have my word that she will come to no harm.'

'Good,' said Smith, 'that's a relief. But will I ever see her again?'

W stood up and shook his head. 'I hate to say it, but I very much doubt you will.'

'Bugger,' said Isambard Smith.

462 was picked up by a Ghast supply ship several days later and taken to Selenia, homeworld of the Ghasts. His wounds were severe, and in normal circumstances he would simply have been shot and rendered into nutritious soup. The fact that he woke in a bed frightened him because the only reason to keep a failed minion alive was so he could be tortured to death at some more convenient moment.

On the third day he was able to get up and assess his injuries. Smith's bullet had removed one of his eyes and, unaccustomed to putting their colleagues back together again, the Ghast doctors had been untidy when fitting its replacement. 462 stood in front of a full-length mirror and, had he possessed tear-ducts, he would have wept. 'Look at me!' he hissed, 'Look at me! How am I supposed to look like an officer of my rank with facial scars and a metal lens instead of one eye?' He pulled on his trenchcoat and, feeling sorry for himself, walked out to meet his superiors.

An unmarked hovercar took him to another unmarked hovercar, which took him to a vast building that jutted out of the city centre like a gigantic black fridge. Half a dozen praetorians escorted him through a hall big enough to produce its own atmosphere. A sign on the wall read: *Party Rally here later – Rain Expected.*

The praetorian on the door saw his scarred face and stepped aside. The door slid back and he was led into the presence of Number Two.

Number Two was small and ferret-like. He had cameras instead of eyes: rumour had it that these relayed everything he saw to Number One and were only turned off when he had a bath – which almost never happened. He was fanatically loyal and smelled bad. At present he was stamping a huge pile of paper.

'Greetings,' he lisped. His voice was thin and high.

'Strength in conquest, glorious Number Two!' 462 yelled, struggling to keep the fear from his voice. 'May I sit down?'

Number Two stamped half a dozen sheets of paper. 462 looked around the room, which was decorated like a teenager's bedroom. Pictures of Number One were everywhere: on the walls, the desk, even, worryingly, on the ceiling above the pull-down bed.

'No,' said Number Two. 'Make yourself useful – sign a few of these death warrants.'

'Yes, glorious Two! With my own signature?'

'Of course not. You are disposable. Sign it as me.'

'As a number, or in letters, sir?'

'Your choice. Knock yourself out.' Two pushed a wad of paper across the desk, and the biopen wriggled after it. 'Now, you are probably wondering why you are not dead yet, yes?'

The mention of his death made 462 so nervous that he accidentally signed one of the warrants as Three.

'You continue to exist because you are the only surviving member of our species to have seen the Vorl. I wish it was I who had witnessed this sight but, sadly, the fates were against me. Your experience makes you useful. You now exist for one purpose only: to locate the Vorl again and bring it to us for experimentation.'

'Is that not... erm... two purposes?'

'Who is Number Two here? Now, go. A ship and a suitable number of personnel will be placed at your disposal. Feel free to use them as you will, provided you do exactly as I say. Understand?'

'Yes, glorious Two!' 462 was delighted. Not only was he not going to be made into dinner but he was being sent out to wreak revenge! A fast ship, a powerful weapons system and more minions than you could shake a failed minion at – who could ask for more than that?

'Good. Proceed to your ship and await orders. We shall capture the Vorl and Earth shall be ours! Hahaha!'

And Isambard Smith shall be mine as well, thought 462. Then we will see who the clever, deadly, efficient one of us really is. Ten to one it is still me.

'Yes!' he cried. 'Hahaha!'

*

John Bradley Gilead was woken by his medical team. He blinked, felt the soft pillow around his head and saw the doctor lean in over him.

'Where am I?' he asked.

'In hospital.'

Hospital, yes. Gilead remembered what had happened now: he'd been about to cut the head from that unbeliever Isambard Smith, when the man had pulled a gun and shot him. Ah, yes.

'I can't feel anything,' he said. 'How badly did he injure me?'

'Badly, actually,' the doctor replied. 'It was serious, I'm afraid. We had to amputate.'

'Amputate? What the hell did you amputate?'

'Your body. On the bright side, we've given you free cosmetic surgery. Your chin looks great now.'

Gilead took it quite well. After he had stopped screaming, he said, 'You mean that's all I am? Just a severed head?'

'Oh no,' the doctor replied, a little surprised. 'Goodness no. We salvaged your bladder, too.'

'That's it? That's all I am, a bag of piss with a head on top?'

'How things change,' a hard voice said from the other side of the bed. Gilead glanced around and a one-eyed, trench-coated thing leaned over and studied him. Before, 462's face had looked like a twisted caricature of a man's. Now, he was a monocled, scarred, parody of a twisted caricature. Judging by the state of his face, he'd tried to French kiss a combine harvester.

'Welcome back, Gilead,' said 462. 'We have work to

do, I believe.' He took a step closer. 'Isambard Smith lives.'

'God damn him!'

'Indeed. The half-alien – or, as you would put it, half-deity – Rhianna Mitchell is in British space. You and I are going to get her back.'

'And that heathen Smith?'

'Of course. We shall deal with Captain Smith.'

'Hah! He'll wail and gnash his teeth, once I've handed them back to him! Why, when I get my hands on him, his life won't be worth living!' He frowned. 'I will get some hands, won't I?'

The Ghast attempted a smile. 'Oh yes. You'll get everything you need. I have been ordered by mighty Number Two to provide us with the equipment to hunt him down.'

Gilead smiled. 'Well, that's something. Alright, 462, let's go! We're going to party and all I need is some body to go with!'

Under an orange sky, Midlight clanked and smoked. Steam blasted into the air from the vents of several dozen landed spacecraft, spread out across the docking area. Towers loomed over the great shipyard and enormous cranes rolled back and forth like siege engines on cata-pillar tracks, their sides dotted with lights. Every so often, a flurry of sparks would leap into the air in a glowing arc as new armour was welded to a ship in preparation for the war to come.

They were already calling it the Ghast War, although it hadn't started yet. The empires of Earth were arming themselves: in the galactic West, the M'Lak tribes were preparing to renew their feud against the vicious Yull.

Around the *John Pym* sat mighty drop-shuttles, each capable of making planetfall with a full battalion inside. The *Pym* looked like the runt of the litter.

In the cockpit, Polly Carveth was on the phone. '*I* don't know,' she said, 'you're the bloody expert. Lasers or something, missiles, maybe. How about missiles with lasers on? What do you mean we can't have any? Well, what about one of those guns with all the barrels that spins around? Right, whatever you say. Thanks a bunch.'

She put the phone down, got up and wandered into the living room. 'Fleet Command is being an arse. No space-ship weapons for the likes of us,' she said.

Smith stood by the door. Suruk was holding a large wooden shield up against the wall. On it was the stuffed head of one of 462's praetorians. 'That's a shame,' said Isambard Smith. 'I suppose they need them more else-where. Up a bit. That's it.'

Suruk banged a nail into the wall and they stood back and admired the praetorian's head.

'Looking good,' Carveth said. 'He's nicely stuffed.'

'He was nicely stuffed the moment he raised a hand against the Empire,' Smith replied, and he laughed.

Chuckling, they left Suruk to admire the trophy. Smith stepped into his room and Carveth stood by the door, waiting for him. 'We'll be cleared for takeoff in forty minutes,' she said.

Smith sat down on the bed and sighed. 'Then we can get back into space and crack on with another adventure, I suppose,' he said, a little sadly.

Carveth nodded. 'What's up, Boss? You don't look too happy.'

The captain shrugged. 'Oh, you know. It's not that I'm not pleased to have stopped our sworn enemies creating a bioweapon of incredible power… it's just that, well, you know, I had these feelings for Rhianna but I never really got the chance to, well, to—'

'Get her drunk and show her your guild navigator?'

'That's a very crude way of putting it, Carveth. What I felt for Rhianna was noble and pure and far above such base considerations – but yes.'

'You see,' Carveth said, 'it wasn't meant to be with you and Rhianna.' She sighed and sat down beside him. 'I'm sorry,' she said gently. 'But you're a fleet officer, and she's made out of gas. Some things just aren't meant to be. Take me for instance—'

'I think you're being a bit harsh on yourself there.'

'I've not finished. Take me for instance and that Rick Dreckitt. Okay, he was dead tasty, but he was a homicidal bounty killer and I was on his hit-list. That's no basis for a proper relationship. We'd have been incompatible. And I'm afraid it's the same with Rhianna and you.'

'Maybe,' said Smith. 'But at the time it just seemed so right, you know?'

'I know. But some things aren't meant to last. Listen,' Carveth said, and she shifted position and broke wind noisily. 'Now, take what I just did. It was satisfying when I did it, and in its own way it was special and beautiful, but its moment has passed, and now it's gone.'

'It hasn't gone, actually,' Smith said.

'No, you're right,' she said, sniffing and getting up. 'That's horrible. I'm off.'

'Carveth, please tell me that there was a purpose to this beyond coming in here and farting on my bed.'

'Of course. I was just showing you that, you know, things mean stuff and – oh look, there's somebody at the door.'

The doorbell made its butchered-cattle noise and Carveth looked into the corridor. 'Well, guess who?' she said, and she grinned and hurried to the airlock to let their visitor in.

'*Namaste*, Polly,' said a voice.

Smith seized a can of deodorant and began a frantic dance around the room, blasting the edges of the room in a bid to make it smell less like a decaying vegetable. 'Hey there,' said a voice from the doorway and he froze on one leg, the can in his hand.

Rhianna looked no less beautiful and dishevelled than before. She wore a new top, Smith suspected, although all her clothes looked scruffy and smelt of joss. She slipped her shoes off at the door and came in.

'Hello there,' Smith said with awful jollity, the deodorant still in his hand. 'Just doing my exercises, with this can.' He pumped the air a few times with it and tossed the thing on the bed, feeling feeble. 'How're you?'

'Oh, not too bad. I'm okay.'

'Good. Good, super. Glad to hear it.'

'And you?'

'Fine, fine. So, um, how's tricks?'

She shrugged. 'Better for you saving my life. I've got to see some people from the Colonial Security Service: they

305

want me to stay here a while and help them. I get to wear a colander on my head. It's for the war effort, you see.'

'Oh, right. Well, we've got to be off, I'm afraid. We're needed back on New London and we've got to go soon. Schedules to keep and all that, you know.' He laughed nervously. Seeing that he was not going to see her for a very long time after this, he did not know why he did.

'Forty minutes,' Rhianna said.

'You know?'

'Yes. I hurried here when I found out. You see, I never got to say thank you for rescuing me, Captain Smith – at least, not properly.' She tapped the door with her heel and it swung shut.

'Oh?' said Smith.

'Oh,' Rhianna said and she approached, smiling. She sat down next to him, rather closer than was normal for a chat in Woking.

'You see,' she said, and he could feel her breath, 'I never quite got to do what I wanted, either. But I thought, maybe now we've got a little while before you've got to go, we could get to know one another properly.'

'Get to know each other?' said Smith.

'I thought we could – you know – get friendly,' and she took off her scarf, leaned back and sighed. Her eyes met his. 'Don't you want to be friendly with me, Isambard? After all we've been through together?'

'Well, yes, actually,' he said. 'Let's be friendly. I'll put the kettle on, shall I?'

# Acknowledgments

My thanks go to my friends and family for their help, encouragement and assistance, without which this novel would never have been written. I'd also like to thank the members of Verulam Writers' Circle and the Goat-people of St Albans for their comments and suggestions, without which it would be a lot less likely to be read. The British Space Empire salutes you all.

# About the Author

Toby Frost studied law and was called to the Bar in 2001. Since then, he has worked as a private tutor, a court clerk and a legal advisor, amongst other things. He has also produced film reviews for the book *The DVD Stack* and articles for *Solander* magazine. *Space Captain Smith* is his first novel.

Smith and his crew blast off again! Join them on their next adventure...

*Isambard Smith and the God Emperor of Didcot*
by Toby Frost

Tea... a beverage brewed from the fermented dried leaves of the shrub *Camellia sinensis* and imbibed by all the great civilisations in the galaxy's history; a source of refreshment, stimulation and, above all else, of moral fibre – without which the British Space Empire must surely crumble to leave Earth at the mercy of its enemies. Sixty per cent of the Empire's tea is grown on one world – Urn, principal planet of the Didcot system. If Earth is to keep fighting, the tea must flow.

When a crazed cult leader overthrows the government of Urn, Isambard Smith and his vaguely competent crew find themselves saddled with new allies: a legion of tea-obsessed nomads, an overly-civilised alien horde and a commando unit so elite that it only has five members. Only together can they defeat the self-proclaimed God Emperor of Didcot and confront the true power behind the coup: the sinister legions of the Ghast Empire and Smith's old enemy, Commander 462.

ISBN 978-1-905802-24-1

£7.99

Launched by Myrmidon Books in Autumn 2008